THE NEGLECTED ONES

C. L. SALASKI

LOURDES HOUSE

This is a work of fiction. Names, characters, places, events, and incidents are either products of the author's imagination or are used fictitiously.

Cover photo by Swen Zinecker

www.swensartwork.com

Dedicated to my mother,
Martha Jane Salaski

Roses love sunshine,
Violets love dew,
Angels in Heaven,
Know I love you.

"Speak up for those who cannot speak for themselves; ensure justice for those being crushed."

—Proverbs 31:8

CHAPTER 1

David Reid would never forgive himself. Never. He had made one wrong move, and now his mother was in that awful place.

Huge waves tumbled furiously before crashing into the jagged rocks at the base of the cliff. The wind was vicious that night, so angry it tried to tear everything apart. The tall, slender young pines at the top of the bluff bent over, clinging to the earth, trying their hardest to avoid being uprooted.

Frightened birds, skirting the gale-force winds, settled on the sturdy branches of the ancient white pines, their talons closing tightly upon contact, their tiny bodies swaying on the creaking perches. A path led away from the edge of the cliff and wound its way toward a massive structure. On both sides of the trail were large, stately trees, some with trunks the size of barrels. These were the one-hundred-year-old red oaks that surrounded Haven, a nineteenth-century Neo-Gothic-style building.

At that moment Haven's green-capped towers, turrets, and pointed windows were nearly obliterated by the relentless blast of sideways rain. Most of the windows were dark. Only a few spots of amber light appeared here and there. One of those lights came from a small lamp inside the room of an elderly woman who was cowering in her bed.

Zelda Reid could not remember where she was. Or how she had gotten there.

"Mary," she called out. "Mary, help me!"

The howling wind rushed past her window. Rain pelted the glass. It was night, but she could still see the blurry images of trees in the distance, noble sentries rooted to the ground, their black limbs trembling as they fought the strong gusts of wind. Flashes of lightning lit up her face, the spears of flickering light leaping about the room. Then thunder exploded overhead, shaking the room so violently Zelda felt her bed lurch. She grabbed the faded blue bedspread and yanked it up to her chin. Her teeth chattered as she shivered with fear.

"Please God," she whispered. "I want to go home." A tear rolled down her pale cheek. She groped around for the call button, found it, and clicked the red button several times. "Where is that aide?" she groaned. "Help me. I have to pee!"

Staring at the gnarled, withered hand holding the call button, she found it hard to believe it was hers. In the dim light, she inspected the bulging blue veins snaking their way up the back of the hand like interstate freeways on a road map.

A tapping noise at the window caught her attention. Dark, spindly branches were striking the rain-splattered glass. The branches looked like long, crooked fingers.

Zelda pulled the bedspread up to her eyes. She noticed the shadow of the twisted branches dancing on the wall across from her bed. As she watched the delicate, lacy patterns move back and forth, another shadowy form merged with the sinuous branches. The strange new shape glided up and over the edge of a framed painting. The frame quivered, then slid down the wall and crashed to the floor.

Zelda gasped. And then frowned as she felt warm urine gush into her pants.

The frightening shape increased in size and then vanished, leaving behind an icy chill that frosted the window panes.

"Mary," Zelda called out, a cloud of cold air floating up from her lips. "Help me, Mary. Help!"

A dark figure appeared in the doorway.

Zelda heard a click, and blinding light filled the room. The temperature returned to normal as if the light bulbs had the power to warm up the room like the rays of a hot summer sun.

Taylor Hanson, a pretty but slovenly nurse's aide, charged over to the bed. "What's wrong now?"

"I had to pee."

"Had to? Don't tell me you pissed your pants again."

"I couldn't help it. You kept me waiting for an hour."

Taylor seized Zelda by the arms and jerked her up into a sitting position.

"Ow—you're hurting my arms!"

"This is the third outburst you've had tonight. I'm sick of your shit."

The aide scowled at Zelda and shoved her back onto the mattress to check her briefs.

"I've got eighteen other residents I have to take care of," she said, brushing away a strand of straggly blonde hair from her forehead. "I can only be in one place at a time."

Taylor ripped open the tabs on Zelda's disposable underwear and inspected the padded lining.

"Your diaper's sopping wet."

Zelda looked up at the ceiling, eyes brimming with tears, hands shaking. She had never been so humiliated.

"Your sheets are wet too. Who's the moron who forgot to put a bed pad on your—"

"I don't wear diapers."

"What?"

"I said I don't wear diapers."

"Really?" Taylor held up the wet briefs and pointed to them. "What do you call this?"

"Disposable underpants," Zelda said with a sob.

"Bullshit. It's a diaper."

"No, it's not," Zelda cried out. "Babies wear diapers. I'm not a baby."

"Keep your voice down."

"I don't wear diapers!" Zelda screamed.

Taylor grabbed Zelda's arms and shook her. "I am so sick of you I could puke!"

Like a scolded child, Zelda began to wail hysterically.

Rain pounded the studio's skylight. Thunder rumbled overhead, interrupting the classical music of "Barcarolle" by Roberto Occhipinti.

David Reid scrunched up his eyes as he studied the large oil painting on his easel. After a moment, he knew what his final step should be. He dipped a well-worn bristle brush into a mound of cadmium yellow paint and mixed it into a pile of cadmium red. Adding a little burnt sienna, he transformed the mixture into a bright, luscious gold—a color that looked stunning on the dark, shiny patina of his decades-old palette.

Like a dashing pirate, David held out his loaded brush as if it were a sword and made his move—several quick, confident dashes of gold to a patch of fallen leaves. He stepped back to survey the painting. Now sunlit, the leaves sparkled.

He smiled at the result.

This man loved to paint. Lived to paint. And this painting reflected that devotion. It was a masterpiece.

Satisfied that the work was finished, David wiped his hands with a paper towel and walked over to the sink to wash up. He felt elated. He had just completed the best piece he had ever done. But unfortunately, the buyers weren't there. Wall Street traders had sent the entire global economy into a tailspin and crippled the markets for high-ticket items like fine art. But David had faith. Faith that the buyers would soon be back. So until then, he decided he would keep painting.

The running water felt nice and warm as he lathered up with a green bar of artist's soap, the refreshing scent of mint and lanolin filling the air. He noticed a scratch on the side of the stainless-steel sink. He tried to rub it out with his thumb, but it was no use. It was now a part of the sink.

While he was drying his hands, he spotted a small puddle on the floor. He looked up and saw water leaking from the skylight's framing.

"Oh, not again," he said, staring at the skylight with weary eyes. He was exhausted and didn't want to deal with the problem. He opened a closet door, pulled out a gray plastic bucket, and placed it beneath the site of the leak. As he watched water droplets fall and splatter against the bottom of the bucket, the gentle sound of a harp caught his attention.

He crossed over to his tabouret and picked up his iPhone. The caller was Haven. He tapped the green accept button and raised the phone to his ear. "This is David Reid." He listened for a moment and then said, "Sure. I can hold."

Turning to face a picture on the wall, he studied it while he waited. It was a magnificent painting with a sky so incredibly beautiful it put all other skies to shame. Storm clouds seemed to drip from the upper atmosphere to the horizon, clouds that were dark gray and creamy white with streaks of violet and pink running through them. And then the sky itself: dark blue overhead and a lighter blue near the horizon. A desert was in the foreground, with a path leading to a dusky blue-violet mountain range somewhere in New Mexico or Arizona.

David valued this piece more than any other in his collection. It was painted by his mentor, Yuri Zykov, a contemporary Russian master. He had taken a workshop with Zykov, a man with the weather-beaten face of an old sea captain who smoked a pipe and wore a black Gavroche artist cap. Half-way through the first day of the workshop, David knew he had to continue to study with this brilliant painter.

As his eyes followed the bold strokes and directional movement of the big shapes in the painting, he was reminded of how his mother had also studied with a great master. Emile Gruppe, a New England landscape painter who established The Gloucester School of Painting in 1940 with his mentor, John Fabian Carlson. Gruppe was a legend in his own time, and David's mother beamed with pride whenever she spoke of the man who taught her how to paint.

Crossing his arms, David stepped back from Zykov's painting and examined it from a different vantage point. The piece was so powerful it made him question his own painting skills.

Who am I kidding? I'll never be as good as this guy. Having a one-man show in a major art museum is a pipe dream. A goal I'll probably never achieve.

A voice brought David out of his reverie.

"Yes, I'm still here." He walked around his studio, listening to the person on the other end of the line.

"Agitated? Why is she agitated?"

Overwhelmed by what he was hearing, he began rubbing the back of his neck.

"Inject her with what kind of drug?"

He frowned when he got his answer. "Just something to calm her down." He rolled his eyes. "Can't you be a little more specific?"

He grew annoyed when the caller didn't answer his question. "Listen to me, can't you give her a pill? Another dose of her Ativan?"

Running his hand through his thick dark hair, he let out a long, deep audible breath. "No," he said. "Absolutely not. You do not have permission to inject my mother with any drugs."

The more he heard, the more frustrated he became. He seized a ballpoint pen and clicked it repeatedly.

"No, I don't care how safe it is. And I've never seen my mother in an agitated state. Are you sure you're talking about Zelda Reid?"

Thunder roared overhead.

He strained to hear the caller. "She did what? Can you please repeat that?" He shook his head as he heard the words.

"Spit in an aide's face?"

He tossed the pen towards his desk. It landed with a smack, right on top of the pristine lid of his MacBook Pro. He threw up his hands in an "I give up" gesture.

"Yes. Yes, I'll be there as soon as I can."

David whipped off his artist's apron, flicked a switch that turned off the music and lights, and rushed out of his studio.

Wipers frantically thumped back and forth as they attacked the wall of water on the windshield. David leaned over the steering wheel, struggling to see the pavement in front of him. At intersections, he stopped and squinted, trying to make out the names on the street signs.

Not that street.

Not that one either.

There it is. Sea Pines Drive.

He turned onto the slick blacktop road. His silver Lexus SUV rolled along, sending waves of water into the air as it approached its destination. After passing what seemed like an endless stretch of ornate iron fence with stacked stone columns, he spotted the elegant sign next to the front gate that read "Haven at Stone Cliff - Nursing and Rehabilitation Center".

Driving through the open gate, David steered his car up a gently sloping hill. Halfway to the top, he stepped on the brake. He peered through the windshield, listening to the steady, rhythmic strumming sound his wipers made as they cleared away the water.

Through a weakening shield of rain, Haven slowly emerged. Perched atop the seaside village of Stone Cliff, Maine, the gothic building loomed above him. And as the rain tapered off, silent flashes of lightning against the night sky gave the enormous stone structure a sinister appearance. One that made his skin crawl.

No wonder she's agitated, he thought. *I'd be agitated too if I were stuck inside that place.*

David nudged the gas pedal, and the Lexus finished its ascent to the top of the hill.

After parking, he grabbed his umbrella and climbed out into the storm. The wind was howling, an ominous bay so loud and frightening it could send an African lion running for the deepest, darkest part of the jungle. He knew his umbrella would be ripped to shreds, so he tucked it under his arm and ran through the rain toward the front entrance.

Once inside, he stood there shaking the water from his hair, eyeing the colossal solid oak double doors he had just come through. He brushed the drops of rain from his face and from the sleeves of his leather bomber jacket, and then turned toward the lobby.

Last renovated in the 1950s, the atmosphere inside Haven was dark and somber. A classic red leather Chesterfield sofa with high arms and a studded back was flanked by tall drape-covered windows that towered above the black-and-white marble floor. The couch, its red leather worn and cracked, shared a mahogany coffee table with two matching Chesterfield armchairs.

The only light in the dreary room came from a French brass floor lamp with a cream-colored shade and an identical table lamp at one end of the sofa; the brass on both pieces tarnished to a deep brown with a few golden tones peeking out. In the dark corners of the room, the shapes of vintage chairs, tables, and lamps sat quietly, undisturbed —inanimate objects that seemed as if they were sleeping the big sleep.

Musty air filled his nose as he made his way across the lobby. He passed a deserted reception area, an antique metal cage elevator, and a grand sweeping staircase. Then he turned a corner and headed down a gloomy corridor. Hearing a scream, he quickened his pace.

"Let me go! Mary, help me!"

David raced down the hallway and darted into his mother's room.

Zelda was thrashing about, swinging her arms at three nurses' aides. She was biting them. Kicking them. Scratching them. Screaming. Crying.

"You're evil," Zelda said. "Evil! I hate you all."

David stared in disbelief. "Mother, stop it!"

Zelda looked up. The instant David's face registered, her scowl disappeared.

"David!"

Delighted that her son had arrived, Zelda calmed down. She smiled at the aides as if she had just been playing a game with them.

"My son is here," she said. "He's come to take me home."

David sat beside his mother on her bed, his arm wrapped around her. She was exhausted, crying softly.

"David, please get me out of here."

"Once you finish your therapy, I'll take you home."

"No, I want to go home now."

"The doctor has to release you," he said, taking her hand in his. "He won't do that until you finish your therapy."

"But I'm afraid."

"There's nothing to be afraid of."

"Yes, there is. There's spooks in here." Her eyes searched his face for a reaction.

He grinned and shook his head. "There are no spooks in here."

"I saw one," she whispered.

"It was a dream. Or your imagination." He stood up and helped her get underneath the covers. "Now lie down and go to sleep."

"Don't leave me," she said, clutching his shirt-sleeve.

"I'll stay a little while longer. We can watch TV together."

"Okay," she said happily, settling back into her pillow.

David sat on a chair next to the bed, pointed a remote at the television and a picture leapt out of nowhere and onto the screen.

Zelda gave him a sweet smile, and then turned her attention to the program on the TV.

A little girl was standing next to a Christmas tree with her father. "Do you believe in angels?" she asked, reaching out to touch a strand of silver tinsel.

David watched the scene unfold. It was from the movie *The Christmas Box* based on the novel by Richard Paul Evans.

A few minutes later, he glanced at his mother. Her eyes were closed, already fast asleep. As he rose from his chair, Dawn Mitchell, a black nurse's aide, entered the room carrying a neatly folded stack of clean clothes.

"Thanks for coming to our rescue," Dawn said, a cheerful smile on her face.

"Sorry for what she put you through. She's always been the most loving, gentle person. That kind of behavior is totally out of character for her."

"Well, it is typical behavior for most people with dementia," she said.

"That is so sad."

"It sure is. By the way, your mother keeps calling out for someone by the name of Mary. Who's Mary?"

He thought about it for a few seconds. "I have no idea."

Dawn opened a closet door and began hanging Zelda's clean clothes on the wooden rod.

David removed his brown leather jacket from the back of the chair and slipped it on. As he bent down to pick up his umbrella, a pain shot through him. He grabbed his lower back, wincing in agony, and squeezed his eyes shut. An instant later he opened his eyes, and it was then that he spied the painting on the floor, partially hidden by a nightstand.

He straightened his body and shuffled over to it. This time he crouched instead of bending. He picked up the picture and examined the frame. Frowning at what he saw, he stood up.

"How did this fall off its hook?" he asked.

Dawn turned away from the closet, her gaze traveling to the painting he held. "The rooms on this floor were painted a few days ago. One of the painters must have taken it off the wall."

"It hit the floor hard," he said, pointing to a deep groove in the gold-leaf frame. "See here. Big dent."

Dawn scrutinized the damaged frame. "Hmm. Clumsy painter? Maybe dropped it?"

Edgar Fitzgerald peeked into the room. When he saw Dawn, he entered. A listless, burly Irishman in his mid-forties, he looked as if he had already grown weary of life.

"Dawn, me da's sheets smell horrible," Edgar said. "Could you please change them for him?"

"Sure. I'll take care of it right now." Dawn smiled at Edgar and left the room.

Edgar looked at the painting in David's hands. "That's a gorgeous picture. If I didn't know better, I'd say it was an original by John Singer Sargent."

"Good eye. It's a copy of a painting by Sargent." David gestured toward his mother's bed. "My mother painted it years ago. Are you an artist?"

"Na. I dabbled around in oils a few years ago. Got frustrated and gave up. But I still love great art."

David returned the painting to its place on the wall. A sudden boom of thunder roared overhead, and the frame rattled.

"Is your ma in here for keeps?" Edgar asked.

"No. For therapy."

"What happened to her?"

"Well, this idiot heard his cell phone ringing when he was helping her walk to the bathroom. He left her side to grab his phone, and she fell and broke her hip."

Edgar shook his head. "What'd you do to that idiot? I would've strangled him."

"Oh, I torture him every day."

Edgar was puzzled. "How do you manage that?"

With a disheartened look, David said, "That idiot was me."

CHAPTER 2

When David returned home that night, the wind was still raging. He walked into his studio and stood there in the dark, listening to the windows rattling in their frames. Water droplets clung to the tips of his hair and nose and dripped onto the immaculate hardwood floor. Shivering, he peeled off his wet jacket and hung it on a brass hook by the door. When he snapped on the lights, the studio and its exquisite furnishings seemed to leap out at him.

The room personified David Reid. He was a perfectionist, and the studio reflected his high ideals. A huge oak easel stood like a giant in the center of the room, its varnished wood gleaming, a magnificent landscape painting held firmly in its grip.

Elegant floor-to-ceiling windows on the north wall kept direct sunlight at bay; the view of the backyard gardens and great forest beyond obscured now by reflections of objects inside the room. An old sugar maple and cast iron work table, covered with watercolor sketches, sat close to one end of the windows as if waiting for daylight to return so work could resume.

White bookshelves, crammed with art books and literature, shared a section of the studio with a gallery of stunning, extravagantly framed paintings. And at the far end of the room the rustic fieldstone fireplace, a bed of glowing embers popping and hissing in its black iron grate, was flanked by a big chestnut brown recliner and matching sofa.

It was an extraordinary world, this room, this dream studio he and his wife had designed. But no matter how breathtaking the studio was, it was not enough to remove the gloomy look on his face. He sauntered toward the easel, hands stuffed in the pockets of his blue jeans, intent on scrutinizing the painting he had worked on all day. But as he approached the canvas, he glimpsed a small body curled up on the sofa next to the fireplace.

Wrapped up in a brown-and-white western style blanket was his seven-year-old daughter. Hannah was wearing her favorite jade green fleece pajamas and looked so peaceful. The spitting image of her mother, she had the same lustrous brown hair, perfect turned-up nose, and rosy complexion. Even though she was a rough and tumble tomboy, she looked like a little princess to him.

He walked over and gently shook her arm. "Hannah."

The girl's eyes opened. She peeked out of the narrow slits, and then shut them. "No, I don't want to get up yet."

"What are you doing in here?"

Hannah's eyelids snapped open. "Daddy, where were you?" She wrapped her arms around his neck and hugged him.

"I went to visit Gram. Why are you sleeping in here?"

"The thunder scared me."

"Why didn't you climb into bed with Mommy?"

"I did. But she fell asleep. Then I heard a wolf howling outside the window."

David smiled. "That was the wind, Hannah. Not a wolf."

"No, I'm sure it was a wolf." She cuddled up to him. "And when I woke Mommy up to tell her about it, she got mad and told me to go to sleep. Or go back to my own bed. So I came in here to be with you."

The lights flickered and went out. Now it was pitch dark, darker it seemed than when he had entered the room.

"Don't worry," Hannah said as she reached under her blanket and pulled out a big silver flashlight. "I have this." She pushed up on the flashlight's sliding bridge switch. Nothing happened. She tried again. Same result. Nothing.

She frowned. "I fell asleep with it on."

Thunder boomed so loud the house shook.

"Not again!" She clamped her hands over her ears.

An eerie silence followed the single blast of thunder. They sat there together, staring into the darkness.

"Daddy, I'm scared."

"There's nothing to be scared of."

"Yes, there is. There's a wolf out there."

David chuckled. "You know what?"

"What?"

"You and your grandmother are two of a kind. You're just like her."

"Good. I'm glad," she said. "Because Gram is the best person in the whole world."

After David had tucked Hannah into her bed, he returned to his studio. He sat on the stool that faced his easel and stared at the landscape painting in front of him. The painting he was so enthused about earlier that night suddenly meant nothing to him.

He glanced across the room at another easel.

It was his mother's single masted studio easel. It stood there, near one of the towering windows, abandoned, an unfinished still life painting propped up on it.

It can't be over for her, he thought. *It just can't be.*

David drifted; lost in his thoughts, to the day his mother fell and broke her hip.

It was a chilly September day. Hannah was in school. And Kathy had just left to show a house in Camden. David and Zelda were enjoying the afternoon together in his studio. He was painting at his easel. She was reading a book by the fireplace.

The doorbell rang.

David dropped his brush into a tin can, the wooden tip clanking as it struck the bottom of the can.

"Someone's at the door, Mother," he said. "Now you sit there. Whatever you do, don't get up."

"I won't," she said.

David hurried to the front door and swung it open.

It was the UPS man. A wiry young man with a grating voice and a bandage taped across the bridge of his nose.

"Perfect timing, Eric," David said, his eyes fixed on the box in Eric's hands.

Eric gave the package to David.

David looked at the sender's name. Dick Blick Art Supplies. "Dick Blick to the rescue." He glanced up at Eric and was surprised to see the bandage.

"You get into a fight?"

"Nope. Ran into a door."

"Really?"

"Yep. Couldn't see a thing. Banged right into the bathroom door."

David grinned and shook his head. "Well, thanks for always being so prompt. I really need this. I'm down to about a thimble full of Gamsol."

"Whatever that is." Eric handed a black signature pen to David.

"It's odorless mineral spirits. Used to thin oil paint."

"I see." Eric watched David scrawl his name across the screen of his UPS mobile device. "Still selling lots of paintings?"

"I wish. This lousy economy has given my business a big boot in the butt."

"Sorry to hear that."

"Thanks," David said, gripping the doorknob. "Well, take it easy."

"You too." Eric made a move to walk away but stopped. "You should see the other guy," he said.

"What?"

Eric pointed to his nose.

"Oh yeah?" David shot him a knowing smile.

Eric tucked his UPS device under his arm and smacked his fist into the palm of his left hand. "Yeah."

"I hope the fight was over something worthwhile."

"It was. Nobody gets away with flipping me off." Eric waved to David. He turned on his heel and strode down the sidewalk toward the UPS delivery truck.

David closed the door and raced back into his studio. He was relieved to see his mother sitting on the sofa, still immersed in her book.

"You doing good, Mother?"

He heard her sniffle.

Is she crying?

He walked over to her. "What's wrong?"

She ignored him.

A teardrop splashed onto a page in her book.

"The poor little kitten died," she said, her voice cracking. And then she broke down and wept.

To see her cry was more than he could take. He knelt beside her, tears glistening in his eyes. "It's okay, Mother. It's just a story."

"No, that kitten was real. These are stories that actually happened." She continued to weep; then she handed him the book. "Here, take this. I don't want to read it anymore."

He looked at the cover. It was *Chicken Soup for the Cat Lover's Soul*. A book Hannah had given to her after her cat died.

"You miss Fluffy, don't you?"

She nodded her head, but still wouldn't look at him.

"Hannah's been asking for a kitten. Maybe we should go to the humane society and adopt one."

"No," she said. "I told you before. I don't ever want another cat."

"But your next cat could live for many, many—"

"I *do not* want another cat," she said firmly, her thoughts weighted down with grief. She pulled a balled-up piece of white tissue from her sleeve and wiped her nose.

He took her hand and sat with her a few minutes, trying to comfort her. "Are you all right now?"

"Yes, but I need to make a trip to the bathroom," she said, reaching for her walker.

"Hold on. I'll get that for you." He grabbed the walker and positioned it in front of her.

Pushing herself up from the sofa, she rose to her feet and grasped the soft contoured handgrips.

"Very good," he said.

He took hold of the pink and blue pinstriped gait belt and assisted her as they walked out of the studio and down the hallway toward the bathroom.

Then the phone rang.

David stopped. He patted his pockets, searching for his cell phone. "Damn. I left my phone in the studio. And I'm expecting a call from the Legacy Gallery in Scottsdale."

The phone rang and rang. That insistent "Answer me now!" ring.

"Can you wait right here, Mother? Just for a minute. I need to get that."

Zelda stopped and stood there, hunched over her walker.

David released the gait belt and sprinted back into the studio. He picked up the phone. The incoming number was from Chase Bank.

Not another call from Chase Credit Card Services.

Ever since I signed up for—

A loud thud startled him.

And then came the most terrifying scream he had ever heard.

"Oh dear God—NO!" he shouted. He raced out of the studio. When he entered the hallway, he saw his mother lying on the floor, screeching in agony.

He darted toward her.

"Oh my God!" he said. "Oh my God!" He dropped his phone, kneeled beside her and took her hand in his.

Tears were flowing down her cheeks. Her lips trembled as she cried out. "David, help me. I can't stand the pain."

"I'm sorry, Mother. I'm so sorry."

She looked into his eyes, and then passed out.

With sweat trickling down his face, he frantically searched for a pulse. Feeling a weak throb in her neck, he snatched up his phone and cursed it as he punched 911 into the keypad.

David closed his eyes and tuned out the horrible memory.

Work was out of the question. He was tired and needed to sleep. He rose from his stool and crossed the studio to shut off the lights when he heard the howl. Flipping off the row of light switches, he peered out the windows at the backyard and the wall of trees in the forest beyond the yard.

He heard another howl, this one leaping in volume.

With the moon breaking out of the clouds, he caught a glimpse of an animal wandering around at the edge of the forest.

It was a coyote.

He watched the blonde canine circle a birch tree. In a sudden burst of speed, it scrambled into the backyard, its bushy tail swishing back and forth.

It howled again and then gazed at the house.

David flicked one of the light switches on. Then off.

Now the coyote looked directly at him, its ears pointed and erect.

He slowly moved toward a French door that led to the redwood deck, eased the door open, and confidently stepped out onto the deck.

The coyote stared him down.

David locked eyes with the animal.

Finally becoming intimidated, the coyote sniffed the ground, relaxed its ears and sat down. It tilted its head and looked at David as if it was hoping for a tiny morsel of food.

David smiled at the sight of the beautiful animal. Then he knew what he had to do. He squared his shoulders and took a step forward.

"Get," he said, waving his arms forcefully. "Get!"

The coyote let out a whimper and bolted back into the forest.

CHAPTER 3

Three men stood on the seaside bluff, looking back and forth between the mighty Atlantic Ocean and their portable easels. David Reid was one of the men. Hearing the shrieks of gulls overhead, he looked up and saw the seagulls wheeling and soaring across the clear blue sky.

David smiled, delighted to be standing in that spot, surrounded by the spectacular beauty of the New England Coast. He glanced at his painting, then looked down at the enormous waves sending white froth into the air as they slapped against craggy, moss-covered rocks. As he applied another stroke of color to his canvas, he felt his French easel lean to the right.

Loose screw, he thought.

He bent down and inspected the right leg. Sure enough, the screw in the middle of the leg was loose. As he tightened the brass wing-nut, he admired the rich golden color of the old beechwood. Time had turned the finely crafted easel into a work of art, and he treasured it.

David recalled the day he received the easel. It was the day he turned eleven years old.

As soon as he got home from school, his mother led him into the living room. When he saw the easel, he felt his heart skip a beat. He scrambled up to it and was thrilled to see it was one just like his mother's. An original Jullian, the finest French sketch box easel in the world.

The memory brought a smile to his face.

As David stood back up, he felt the muscles in his lower back tighten. He drew in a deep breath and blew it out, then leaned backward with his hands on his hips to stretch the stiff muscles. While holding that position, he thought about his first plein air excursion. An event which took place two days after his eleventh birthday.

He was dragging his painting gear along a narrow dirt trail using a folding metal luggage cart. The cart thumped back and forth, hitting ruts in the dusty path, and he kept checking it to make sure nothing tumbled to the ground. Glints of sunlight, reflecting off the chrome frame, caused tiny spots to jump around in front of his eyes like he had caught a pop from a camera's flash.

Up ahead of him, his mother gallantly made her way down the trail, searching for an ideal spot to set up their easels. After two years of suffering, her depression was gone. A newly acquired passion for painting had given her a new lease on life. She was more vibrant and carefree than David had ever remembered. And seeing her so happy made him feel invincible. Like nothing bad could ever happen to them again.

Stopping in her tracks, she gazed out to sea with her right hand above her eyes, shielding them from the sunlight. She turned to face him, clinging to the leather handle on her folded sketch box, a bulging red backpack peeking over the top of her shoulders.

"This is it, David," she said, beaming with joy. "We can set up right over there." She pointed to a spot a few yards from the edge of the bluff.

They veered off the path and walked through tall, sun-struck weeds to the location his mother had chosen. The roar of the sea was profound, the rumble of the fierce waves striking a chord inside David that sent goosebumps running up and down his arms. The fresh sea breeze felt wonderful; it ruffled his hair, and when he licked his lips, he could taste the salt.

His mother helped him set up his new easel, and within a few minutes, he was squeezing thick, juicy colors onto his palette. He picked up a brush, dipped the tip into a mound of sumptuous blue oil paint, and made a timid little mark on his canvas. Unsure of how to continue with the magnificent seascape he imagined he could create, he glanced over at his mother.

She stood there, her hair caught in the wind, looking down at the white breakers rushing to shore.

As much as David loved Audrey Hepburn and Elizabeth Taylor, he thought his mother was more beautiful than either one of them. The mesmerizing seascape had a hold on her, but she snapped out of the trance. She turned to the gray-toned canvas on her easel, grabbed her largest flat bristle brush and began to paint, trying to capture the moment at a frenzied pace—like a person who feared the waves would suddenly stop their violent attack on the rocks, the sea would turn calm, and the light would drastically change.

After she had thrown down the big, bold shapes of her painting and blocked in the lights and the darks, she eased up and relaxed.

"How's it going?" she asked David.

"Having fun . . . but it's a mess," he said, grinning at her.

She walked over to check out his painting.

And that was the moment it happened.

A fierce gust of wind blew her painting off the easel. The canvas performed unbelievable somersaults as it tumbled through the grass and weeds, weaving wildly at a feverish pace.

She chased it toward the edge of the cliff. Two feet away from the brim, the canvas came to rest. She reached down to pick it up, but the wind snatched it away from her and sent it sailing over the cliff.

David raced to her side, worried that she might fall over the ledge, and together they watched the painting descend.

The wind seemed to enjoy itself as it played with the canvas—letting it go into free-fall, then pulling it back up a bit. Like a maestro, it controlled the painting, releasing it from its grip so it would drop toward the crashing waves, then stepping in to stop it—to let it float along on another uplifting current. This went on longer than David could have imagined. Went on until becoming bored with its game, the wind let go, and the canvas hit the surface of the water.

David stared at his mother, afraid she was going to break down in tears. But she didn't cry. Instead, she burst into a roar of laughter so loud and boisterous he thought she had lost her mind.

She held her sides and sank to her knees, doubling up with laughter.

Taken by surprise, David watched her laugh, his right hand clutching a small paint brush. She had worked so hard on that piece. And now it was gone, claimed by the wind and the sea.

He looked down at the ocean. The canvas was being tossed from one massive, white-frothed wave to another.

His mother climbed to her feet. She stood beside him, looking down in silence at her lost treasure.

"I'm so sorry, Mother," he said, biting his lip to stifle a sob in a way that caused them both to begin laughing.

Now she laughed so hard tears ran down her cheeks.

He looked back down at the painting and, for a brief instant, felt a crazy urge to dive off the cliff and retrieve it.

Am I insane?

Why would I think of doing such a thing?

Father would say the devil put that idea in my mind.

But I know better—because the devil doesn't even exist.

He turned back to his mother.

She wiped her eyes with her fingertips and looked back down at the canvas, watching it bounce along the crests of the waves.

Her laughter abated. She met his gaze, a grave look on her face.

"That is one reason you shouldn't use a stretched canvas outdoors," she said. "Always use a hardboard panel."

"Like the one on my easel?" David asked.

She nodded. "Like the one on your easel."

The image of her beautiful young face stayed with him for a few more seconds and then vanished.

David's mind returned to the present moment. He squinted at his painting, applied a few more strokes, then removed the linen panel from the easel and slid it into a wet painting carrier. After swiftly packing up his gear, he lugged it toward Andrew Shepard.

Andrew was refining his painting. Sporting a pair of Gucci black-rimmed eyeglasses and a light five o'clock shadow, he had a British accent that made women swoon.

David stopped next to Andrew and examined his painting. "Very nice. Now don't work it to death."

"I won't," Andrew said. "Wish your mother a happy birthday for me."

"Will do. See you later." David walked away from Andrew and waved to Charlie Peters, a white-haired, jovial man in his late-fifties.

Standing close to the edge of the bluff, Charlie gave David a comical salute. With his palm facing outward and his eyes bulging like a buffoon, he pressed his lips together and delivered a smile that stretched from ear to ear.

Benny Hill. David grinned. *Looks just like him.*

David strolled toward his sparkling clean Lexus, parked on the grassy shoulder of a dirt road. Across the road, a lush wooded area was ablaze with autumn's colors. Birds sang in the trees. Leaves fluttered in the gentle wind.

David reached his car, stopped and looked up at the woods. Red and yellow leaves shimmered in the sunlight. Then a sudden rush of wind swept through the trees. The leaves hung on for dear life, but many broke free, rising and falling with the wind's current.

It was Hannah Reid's first visit to Haven. David watched his only child skip through the parking lot. She was happier than the day he and Kathy had taken her to Six Flags New England. That was only three months ago; when life was beautiful, and everything was humming along just fine.

Inside Haven, several elderly residents lingered in the hallway that led to Zelda's room. The frail old men and women reminded David of the windswept leaves clinging to the branches of the trees near the bluff. Some of these people were hanging on for dear life. Others had given up hope and were about to let go.

Harvey, a sad, inconsolable man with loose, saggy skin beneath his chin, sat in his wheelchair, staring up at David as he wove his way through the maze of elderly people, his arms filled with beautifully wrapped gifts.

The next face David saw belonged to Mabel, another wheelchair-bound resident with short, curly white hair and a face covered with spiderweb-like wrinkles. He gave her a kind smile, but she didn't return the smile. Her vacant, pale blue eyes showed that she was numb. Her stupor brought on, David thought, by the realization that soon she would no longer exist.

David turned around and waited for Hannah and Kathy to catch up to him.

Harvey blinked back tears when he saw Hannah approach her father, holding onto a large pizza box.

With the face of an angel, Hannah was too young to realize she was a budding beauty. Flustered by the old man's tears, she turned her gaze to Kenneth, a portly man, struggling to make his way down the hall with the aid of his walker. With a lively, determined look on his face, Kenneth winked at Hannah.

She smiled shyly at him.

"How old are you, sweetheart?"

"Seven," Hannah said. "How old are you?"

"Seven—ty." Kenneth chuckled.

Kathy Reid, a stunning woman in her forties who looked no older than thirty, was trailing far behind her husband and daughter. Toting a six-pack of A&W root beer, she quickened her pace to catch up with them.

"David, I just saw Sharon Petralia," Kathy said. "Her husband's in a room down the hall."

"Carl? He's only forty-eight. Was he in an accident?"

"No. Brain tumor."

He gasped, eyes wide. "Oh, no."

"He had a stroke. His doctor told him it was a transient ischemic attack. But then a tumor showed up on his CAT scan."

"He's the same age as me." David looked into Kathy's eyes. "You think you have all the time in the world. And then—wham!"

"Mommy, what's a tumor?" Hannah asked.

"I'll explain it some other time. But right now, we've got to get the pizza to Gram before it gets cold."

The family resumed their walk down the long, gloomy corridor.

Arriving at Zelda's room, the Reids walked in to find Franklin, an obese man with a bright red face, sitting in a wheelchair, watching TV.

"An aide whisked your mum off to the dining room," Franklin said. He bit into a chocolate chip cookie and began chewing. "She'll be back to fetch me any minute now."

Astonished, Kathy turned to David. "I called here this morning. I told the nurse not to feed her lunch. Told her we were bringing in a pizza."

David shook his head in dismay. "Set everything down. We'll go get her."

David entered the dining hall with a smile that disappeared when he saw his mother.

Hannah, beaming with joy, raced ahead of her parents and scurried up to her grandmother.

Zelda's head was lowered. She stared into her lap as tears rolled down her face.

Ethel, a chubby, sour-faced woman sat across the table from Zelda. She was scowling at her so viciously it seemed she was daring Zelda to raise her head.

"So what are you waiting for?!" Ethel said. "This is my table. Get out of here. You're not my friend. You're nobody's fucking friend!"

David walked over to Zelda and put his hands on her shoulders. "Mother, it's all right. Don't cry. This lady doesn't mean what she's saying."

"I do so mean what I'm saying!" Ethel said, fiercely. "Get her the hell out of my sight. She doesn't belong here."

David looked around. He spotted an aide. It was Taylor Hanson. He gestured for her to come over to him.

Taylor ambled across the floor toward him, her purple Nike running shoes squeaking like sneakers on a basketball court. If she picked up her feet, the irritating noise would stop. But she glided along, and David could see by the subtle grin on her face that she enjoyed annoying people.

"Why are you just standing over there while this woman is abusing my mother?"

"I didn't know there was any problem, sir."

Ethel looked at Zelda with hatred burning in her eyes. "All of your friends are dead. And soon you'll be dead too!"

Hannah was shocked. She watched in disbelief as her grandmother wept. Her face scrunched up and she, too, began to cry.

"From ten feet away, you couldn't see or hear what's going on here?" David asked.

"No, sir."

David glared at Taylor. Disgusted, he grabbed the handles on Zelda's wheelchair, backed her away from the table and quickly wheeled her into the corridor. He stood outside the dining room, waiting for Kathy and Hannah to join him.

Hannah was sobbing as she walked out of the dining area. He watched as Kathy bent down to comfort her.

"This is a horrible place," Hannah said. "Why does Gram have to live here?"

At that moment, David detected the pungent odor of urine. He helped his mother stand up and, as she stood there grasping the shiny metal rods below the chair's padded armrests, he examined her to see if she had wet her pants. Her pants were dry, so he touched the black vinyl seat. It was dry too, so he sniffed the seat. The smell overwhelmed him.

David glanced at Kathy.

She was watching him with a baffled look on her face.

He stood up, shaking his head. "Mother's pants are dry, but the seat on this wheelchair stinks so bad it's enough to knock you out."

An empty pizza box and a half-eaten birthday cake were on the bedside dresser, surrounded by cans of root beer.

Zelda slowly unwrapped one of her presents. She had not yet recovered from the incident in the dining hall. Nor had Hannah, who hiccuped softly between stifled sobs.

David forced a smile. "I think you'll love this one, Mother. It's from Hannah."

Kathy leaned in to help Zelda rip off the wrapping paper. Her nose wrinkled in disgust. She turned to David and whispered, "You thought that seat smelled bad? Take a whiff of her hair."

A few moments later David was waiting for Nurse Jennings to finish a phone call that had interrupted their talk. He drummed his fingers on the tile countertop and looked out at the people who were sitting in the lounge. Most of them were sleeping in their wheelchairs; others were facing the TV with dazed looks on their faces.

"Hey, there—David," a voice from behind him called out.

David turned to see Edgar Fitzgerald pushing his father's wheel-chair, guiding the elderly man toward the lounge.

"Hello," David said with a warm smile.

Edgar gestured toward Nurse Jennings. "Keep an eye on that one," he said in a soft, low voice. "She's worse than Nurse Ratchet."

Just what I need, David thought. He turned in time to see Jennings hang up the phone.

"And I'm not exaggerating," Edgar said as he wheeled his father away.

Nurse Jennings strolled over to David. She was in her fifties, attractive and well-groomed. However, she had a tough, no-nonsense demeanor about her akin to that of an Army sergeant. "Sorry for the interruption. Go on."

"Thank you," David said. "After the fiasco in the dining room, I noticed the smell of urine on the seat of my mother's wheelchair."

"The seats on the wheelchairs are scrubbed down every night. But I'll make sure your mother's chair receives extra attention tonight."

"I appreciate that. Now, one more thing. When was the last time my mother had a shower?"

Jennings scanned a chart. "She refused her shower on both Monday and Thursday of this week.

"No, no. She cannot refuse a shower. Her hair needs to be washed."

"We cannot force a resident to do anything they don't want to do."

"Then bribe her. Tell her if she takes a shower, you'll give her a nice cold bottle of root beer."

"We are not permitted to bribe a resident."

As politely as possible David said, "Well, I'm her power of attorney, and I'm giving you permission to bribe her." He cracked a captivating smile.

Unmoved by his charm, Nurse Jennings frowned at him. "I'll see to it that your mother gets her showers."

On the way back to his mother's room, David thought about the things he had seen and read on Haven's website.

First off, he was greeted by a home page that featured a large, pleasing image of a young woman, a little girl, and an older woman. They were absolutely beautiful, wearing big bright smiles with perfect white teeth, the camera capturing them in what had to be one of the happiest moments of their lives. The high-resolution image filled the screen.

Wonder if I could get a hacker to replace that photo with one taken today of my wife, daughter, and mother? That would be a more accurate portrayal of this place.

As he walked along, he recalled statements Haven had made on their website:

"Provides the highest quality care by employees who seem like family."

Yessir. That aide in the dining room seems just like a family member—a family member from a dysfunctional family, but not from our family.

"Enjoy a shower before bed? We can make it happen."

But only if your loved one holds a gun to our heads.

"State of the Art Historical Building."

Dreary nineteenth-century seaside hotel last renovated in the early 1950s.

"Nurses and Aides respond quickly to meet residents' needs."

That'll be the day.

"Provides a homey family atmosphere."

It's not a home. It's a prison.

The more he thought about the deceit, the angrier he got.

Are other nursing homes misleading the public like this? If so, how are they getting away with it?

Zelda had trouble falling asleep that night. Her heart beat frantically at the thought of going back into the dining hall the next morning. She worried that she might have a stroke if Ethel ever spoke to her like that again.

What did I do to upset her? she wondered.

And by asking herself that question, she got the answer. She realized why Ethel had lashed out at her.

The poor woman is probably just as distressed about being in a nursing home as I am. She just wants to go home.

Zelda clasped her hands, closed her eyes, and whispered a prayer.

"Please, God, forgive Ethel for cursing at me today. She's just homesick. Give her strength. Bless her and her family. And please find a way to restore my son's faith. Forgive him for turning his back on you. Please, I beg you, save my David's soul. Amen."

CHAPTER 4

I t was a cold autumn night. A battered, old pickup truck lurched along a road in Stone Cliff, a quaint village located a few miles southeast of Rockland. Inside the truck, a small boy stared out the passenger window, on the lookout for the house he loved so much.

"There it is, Dad. Stop!" he cried out.

His dad shifted down. Resting his foot on the brake, he hunched over the steering wheel so he could get a good look at the house.

"Isn't it beautiful?" The boy glanced at his father, then turned his attention back to the property.

Nestled among towering pine trees was an exquisite log home. A swirl of white smoke rose from the massive stone chimney. Light illuminated the windows and its warm glow, reflected up from the wooden porch, lit up the gleaming reddish-orange logs.

"Yep. It sure is."

The boy was fascinated. "Can we live in a house like that someday?"

"Maybe someday, son."

"If you win the lottery?"

"Yep. If I win the lottery."

The boy smiled.

His dad returned the smile, shifted back into gear, and hit the gas.

Inside the log home, Hannah Reid peeked out her bedroom window and watched as the noisy truck faltered and wheezed, and finally took off, leaving a blue cloud of exhaust in its wake.

Two sets of French doors and a row of solid wood casement windows lined the walls in the dining room of the Reid's home. Above the stylish oak table, a rustic timber beam hung below the pine planks that covered the cathedral ceiling.

Over the stereo sound system "Good Life" by OneRepublic was playing softly. David loved the song, but it made him feel so sad at that moment. Sad because, yes indeed, "the window closes oh so quick."

"Honey, this roast beef is terrific." David stabbed another tender, juicy piece with his fork. "Did you buy this at Shaw's?"

"No," Kathy said, wiping her mouth with a napkin. "At French and Brawn's Marketplace in Camden."

"Let's stick with them. The last roast we had wasn't as tender or tasty as this."

"I agree." Kathy picked up her glass and took a sip of red wine. She noticed that Hannah was just sitting there, sulking, picking at her food. "Hannah, you haven't touched your dinner. What's wrong?"

Hannah looked up with a frown. "How much longer does Gram have to live in that awful place?"

"Until she finishes her therapy and can walk again," David said.

Hannah dropped her fork onto her plate, crossed her arms, and sat back in her chair.

"Honey, it's only temporary," Kathy said. "The head nurse told us she'd take care of all the problems and make it a more comfortable and happy place for Gram."

"Yeah. Sure," Hannah mumbled.

At the same time the Reids were having dinner, Zelda was sitting on a shower bench, shivering as Dawn Mitchell gently scrubbed her back with a soapy washcloth.

"I'm cold," Zelda said. "I'm cold."

At that, Taylor Hanson lifted the shower hose up and shot a stream of water straight into Zelda's face.

"Ow!" Zelda said, squeezing her eyes shut.

Dawn frowned. "Stop that, Taylor!"

Taylor lowered the hose. But an instant later, she raised it back up and launched another jet of water at Zelda's face.

Zelda screamed.

Taylor laughed.

And Dawn could only stare at Taylor, wondering what had happened to her to make her so mean and hateful.

Moments later, as Hannah was reaching for a salt shaker, a drop of water landed on her nose. She glanced up at the ceiling. "Look. The roof's leaking again."

David looked up.

A big dark stain covered two of the pine planks above the table. In the center of the damp patch, another water droplet had formed. Tilting his head to one side, he watched the translucent bead grow larger.

"Not again," Kathy said. "David, we need to just bite the bullet and get a new roof."

"Shell out thirty-one thousand dollars for a new roof? We can't even afford new tires for my car."

"We could save money by choosing asphalt shingle instead of cedar shake—"

"No. No asphalt shingle."

The water pellet lost its grip and fell, smacking Hannah in the eye. She blinked the water away and giggled.

They all watched as another water bubble emerged.

David stood and tossed his cloth napkin onto the table. "I'll have to get up there and patch it again."

Kathy grimaced. "That is not a good idea. What if you—"

"I'm not going to fall. I'll be very careful." He walked away from the table.

"I know you'll be careful," Kathy said, bounding out of her chair. She followed him, the heels of her trendy shoe boots clicking against the hardwood floor. "It's just—I'm afraid you'll hurt your back again."

In the utility room, Kathy watched David open one drawer after another as he searched for his heavy-duty flashlight.

"You know I'll never be able to sleep," he said, "worrying about how bad it might be up there."

"David, you need to relax and put it out of your mind. Let's find a movie to watch on Netflix."

"I can't concentrate on a movie with this problem hanging over my head. And, besides, tomorrow it's supposed to rain. Might even snow. Then I won't be able to get up there at all. Right now is the perfect time."

David opened another drawer. He pulled out a big yellow flashlight and flicked it on to test the batteries. Satisfied with the intense beam of light, he snapped it off.

"I don't want you wandering around on top of the roof at night. That makes no sense."

"It would make perfect sense if you were me." He flashed a smile and winked at her as he slipped on his coat.

Kathy stared at him with her arms folded, a solemn expression on her face.

When he saw her stern look, he switched off the laundry room lights, turned the flashlight back on, and held the light under his chin. Looking like a ghoul, he grinned at her. "Wish me well on my journey up to the top of this mountainous roof," he said, imitating Vincent Price. "For if you don't and I fall to my death, I will haunt you forever."

David placed a ladder on the east side of the house and shook it to make sure it was steady. As he made his way up the metal steps, a raindrop smacked the top of his head. He stopped and waited. Feeling no more rain, he continued his ascent. When he reached the top, he carefully stepped sideways to dismount the ladder.

Pointing his flashlight down in front of him, he squinted as he surveyed the slope of the roof, the beam of light dancing over the cedar shake shingles. He moved slowly, sweeping the light from side to side, searching for the source of the leak.

Just when he spotted what might be the problem, a torrent of rain began to fall. He looked up and big raindrops pelted his eyes. Perplexed, he stood there staring at the sky, the cold rain drenching him. And then he shouted, "How many other bad cards can you possibly deal me?"

As he inched his way back to the ladder, he slipped and fell. His flashlight flew out of his hand, clattered across the wooden shingles, hit the lip of the downspout, and tumbled off the edge of the roof.

Having fallen on his hands and knees, he stared at the spot where the flashlight had vanished. He rolled over onto his back, examined his bruised palms, and then gazed up into the black sky.

"I got the message," he said, blinking away the rain that splashed into his eyes. "But did you have to take my flashlight too?"

Thunder roared overhead. A mighty blast.

What are you doing? David thought. *There's nobody up there, you fool.*

He squeezed his eyes shut and lay there on the hard shingles, feeling the sting of the raindrops as they bombarded his face.

And then the rain stopped.

Someone turned off the faucet, he thought as he stood up. Then he criticized himself again for acting like a damn fool, a fool who believed someone could actually be in charge of the rain.

———

Fifteen minutes later, Kathy was wiping off the kitchen countertops. David staggered in, his hand over his heart, his face flush with fear.

"What's wrong?" Kathy asked.

He closed his eyes, wavering as if he were about to faint.

"David?" She dropped her dishcloth and grabbed his arm.

"Chest pain," he said, so nervous and shaky he could hardly speak. "Call nine-one-one. I think I'm having a—a heart attack."

It was midnight, and they were still in the emergency room at the Pen Bay Medical Center in Rockport.

David lay in bed, staring up at the ceiling, focused on the worst case scenario—that he would need open heart surgery. Kathy sat beside his bed, cradling Hannah in her arms. She twirled the child's hair around her fingers as she slept, the girl's face resting comfortably against the soft gray cashmere of her mother's V-neck sweater.

A short, dark-skinned doctor pulled back a white curtain and entered the small area where they had been waiting for over three hours.

"Mr. Reid, I'm pleased to say you did not suffer a heart attack," the doctor said, his accent indicating that his native country was most likely India. "There is no damage to your heart muscle."

"So what caused that intense chest pain?" David asked.

"Anxiety. You had an anxiety attack."

"Thank God," Kathy said, letting out a sigh of relief as she tightened her embrace on her daughter.

The doctor looked up from his chart. "May I ask what you were doing right before you felt the chest pains?"

"I was up on the roof of our home trying to locate a leak."

"At night?"

"Yes. At night," David said.

"So you were experiencing frustration with the roof problem?"

"Yes."

"Are you on any medications right now?"

"Paxil . . . which is supposed to prevent anxiety attacks."

"I'm very familiar with Paxil. When did you begin taking it?"

"A few days before the stock market bottomed in March."

"When was the last time you checked your stock portfolio?"

"Pardon me?"

"When did you last check your stock portfolio?"

"Right before we sat down to dinner tonight."

"So . . . you've taken quite a hit financially?"

"To say the least."

"And the cost of roof repairs was weighing heavily on your mind?"

"Yes."

The doctor was silent as he jotted notes on the paper attached to his clipboard.

David looked at Kathy.

She frowned and shook her head.

He knew she was disappointed that he was still obsessively checking their stock portfolio on the internet.

The doctor removed the sheet of paper from the clipboard and handed it to David.

"This is a prescription to increase your daily dosage of Paxil. I feel it's still the best medication for you. However, you cannot expect the drug to do all the work for you. You need to learn how to relax. And free your life of as much stress as possible."

Reaching into the pocket of his white smock, the doctor pulled out a brochure and held it out, his dark, red-rimmed eyes suggesting he was near the end of a very long shift. "This will help you deal with your stress."

Kathy drove them home from the hospital.

While navigating the car down Main Street in Rockland, she glanced over at David. Sure, she was upset with him. But she could never stay upset for very long. Was it that Cary Grant dimple in his chin that made her love him so much? Or his warm, loving eyes? That charming smile? His heart of gold?

It was everything, she thought as she turned her gaze back to the road. She loved every single thing about her husband. The day David walked into her life was the day she experienced a miracle. God loved her so much that he sent her this wonderful man.

Sensing her eyes on him, David turned to her. "Sorry."

"For what?"

"For creating another expense we can't afford. Wait'll we get that hospital bill. It'll probably be more than what it would've cost to hire a roofer to make the repairs."

"David," she said. "Stop thinking about money. Our stocks will go back up again. It's just going to take a little time."

"Like ten or twenty years?" he said, managing a smile.

"Who cares how long it takes? Wall Street doesn't rule our lives. We do. You do. Every time you pick up a paint brush, you take control of your destiny. Of our destiny. We'll make it through these hard times. Trust me. Everything will be fine."

CHAPTER 5

Emily Harding walked toward the nurses' station, her blue corduroy handbag dangling from her right shoulder. She stopped to take a quick sip of caramel mocha from a large Starbucks cup. She could hardly believe her good fortune. She had graduated from Kennebec Valley Community College two weeks earlier and had already landed a job as an LPN.

Now that she was making good money, she could buy things she could never afford before. New living room furniture, a newer car, the latest version of the iPhone, and as many cups of Starbucks coffee as she pleased.

Emily was elated. But when she entered the nurses' station, Nurse Jennings glared at her, and her heart sank.

"Taylor told me you called Zelda Reid's son last week and asked him for permission to give her an injection of Lyzapine. Why did you do that?"

"I didn't tell him it was an antipsychotic drug. I said it was just something to calm her down."

"You're not supposed to call families for permission. Doctor Jamali prescribed the drug. It's your job to administer it."

"But in school, they said you should always—"

"I don't care what they said in school. You'll follow my instructions from now on. Do you understand?"

"But being in a strange environment frightened and confused the woman. That's why she got agitated. One of my instructors at Kennebec warned us about the dangers of using chemical restraints on elderly people. He told us to use kindness and love instead of—"

"Well, we don't have time for kindness and love," Jennings said, squaring a small stack of papers on her desk. "Next time just give her the damn shot."

―――――

The next afternoon Nurse Jennings looked up from her computer and saw Katie Weber pushing Zelda past the nurses' station. Jennings swiveled around in her chair.

"Where's that diet cola?"

Katie glanced at Jennings with a puzzled look on her face.

"The one I asked you for over an hour ago?"

Bringing the wheelchair to a halt, Katie took a deep breath and blew it out. She ran a hand through her shiny red hair. "I couldn't leave Marion alone on the toilet."

Jennings sneered at Katie. "I don't give a crap about Marion."

Surprised by the nasty comment, Katie's jaw dropped.

"Go get me the cola. And a slice of that pizza in the fridge."

"But that pizza belongs to Thomas Fitzgerald."

"He'll never miss one piece."

"No, *he* won't. But Edgar might."

"Get me the cola. And the pizza. And hurry it up, will you?"

Katie stared at Jennings in astonishment. "I'll get it for you in a few minutes. I just finished helping Zelda with her lunch, and now I need to—"

Jennings folded her arms and shot her a dark look.

Katie sighed. "I'll get your soda right after I change Zelda's shirt. She spilled orange juice on it."

"No," Jennings said. "Get it for me right now."

"Fine." Katie started down the hall with Zelda in tow.

"Leave Zelda here. I'll keep an eye on her until you return."

Katie backed up the wheelchair and parked it beside the workstation. She watched as Nurse Jennings pivoted her chair to face the computer, taking Zelda out of her sight.

Katie opened her mouth to object, but thought better of it. She turned and hurried down the corridor.

"Help me, please. My butt hurts."

That sounds like Zelda, Dawn Mitchell thought as she made her way toward the end of the long hallway.

"I'm getting up."

Yep. That's Zelda.

Dawn rounded the corner just in time. She saw the frail old woman standing in front of her wheelchair, teetering back and forth, on the verge of falling.

"Zelda! No!" Dawn ran up to Zelda, caught her just as she took a clumsy step forward, and gently lowered her back into the chair.

Nurse Jennings spun around in her chair and looked at Dawn. "What's going on?"

"Zelda nearly fell."

Jennings gave Dawn an indifferent look. "Get her into bed,"

"It's only twelve forty-five. She's not supposed to go down for her nap until two o'clock."

"Put her in bed right now."

"Her son said she's been spending too many hours in bed. He wants her to—"

"Who's the boss here—her son or me?"

"But he—"

"Put her to bed," Jennings growled. "And then give Mabel her shower."

Dawn turned on her heel. Wrapping her hands around the wheelchair's rubber handgrips, she pushed Zelda away from the nurses' station and down the hall towards her room.

Nina Petrovski, a thin, stern Russian aide walked out of room 117. She heard the irritating noise coming from the far end of the corridor. The sound of a resident moaning.

Shirley Fischer again, Nina thought.

As she moved closer to room 124, the moans increased in volume.

"A'm thirs—ty," Shirley called out. "Ha—lp me."

That woman drive me nuts. Why she not die and give us peace? Big mistake leaving Russia. I need go back.

Nina walked into the old woman's room and stood with her hands on her hips.

"What is wrong now?"

Shirley lifted her head from her pillow. "I need a drink of water."

Nina found a glass, filled it with water, and stirred thickening powder into it. She handed the cloudy mixture to the elderly woman.

Shirley raised the glass to her lips, took a sip, and spit it out. "I want water. Not this trash."

"Cannot drink water without being thickened. Could choke and die."

"I won't choke," Shirley shouted. "Now give me some water."

"Cannot do that. All liquids need be thickened. Doctor orders."

"I don't care what the doctor says. I'm thirsty. Gimme some water."

"Need thick liquids. Or you get water in lungs."

Shirley dangled her arm over the bedrail and released the cup. It shattered on the floor, leaving a pile of thick liquid mingled with fragments of glass.

Nina shot a dagger look at Shirley. The old woman moaned the entire time Nina cleaned up the mess.

After Nina left Shirley's room, she went to the snack lounge to get a Coke. She found Taylor there, retrieving a tiny bag of potato chips from a vending machine.

"Taylor, does woman in room one twenty-four ever stop moaning?"

"Rarely."

"Does it ever bother you?"

"Not at all." Taylor smirked. "It's music to my ears."

Nina frowned. "I would like strangle her."

Zelda felt better. She had eaten a bowl of vegetable soup for lunch and was finally out of that uncomfortable wheelchair. And now her favorite aide, Dawn Mitchell, was tucking her into bed.

"Are you comfortable, Zelda?" Dawn asked.

"Yes."

"Well, get some sleep. I'll see you later."

"I love you," Zelda said.

"I love you too, sweetheart." Dawn took Zelda's face in her hands and kissed her on the forehead. "It's kind of chilly in here. Would you like another blanket?"

"No, I'm fine."

"Okay. Enjoy your nap." Dawn walked to the door, reached for the light switch and hesitated. She looked over her shoulder at Zelda.

"Do you want me to leave one of the lights on?"

"No, honey. You can turn them all off."

After the lights had gone out, Zelda lay there in the dark room, staring at the closed window blinds, thinking how she should have asked Dawn to leave on the small lamp on her dresser. She stared at the silhouette of the lamp. Then she thought about how ironic it was that she couldn't remember what movie she watched last night, but she could remember events from years ago—events she hoped and prayed she would forget. Like the day when Joseph died.

Two days before Thanksgiving, they had gone hunting.

Just the three of them, out marching through the snow-packed woods on a frigid November morning in 1970, wearing red plaid wool coats, softly laughing as Joseph whispered jokes to David.

"How do you catch a unique deer?" Joseph asked.

"I don't know, Father," David said. "How do you?"

"Unique up on it!" Zelda laughed.

"Hey, no fair," Joseph said, turning around with a feigned scowl on his face. "You're not supposed to deliver the punch line unless you're the one telling the joke."

"Sorry." Zelda giggled.

Joseph turned back to David. "So how do you catch a tame deer?"

"Hold out an apple?" David asked.

Joseph laughed. "No, tame way—"

"Unique up on it," Zelda said, blurting out the words.

"You!" Joseph snarled. "You ruined it again!" He took a step toward her, his boot crunching in the snow. But before he could touch her, she burst into laughter and dashed away.

And then Zelda fell asleep. A deep sleep that kept her from stepping into the horrible part of that memory.

CHAPTER 6

Big clouds drifted across the sky that warm September afternoon, their billowy rounded tops towering high above their flat bases.

On the north side of Haven, David steered his mother's wheelchair down a bumpy sidewalk. Leaves gently rustled overhead. Sun-dappled shadows danced across the gray stone walls of the ivy-covered building, and David paused to study the colors in the shadows.

An image worth painting, he thought. *Yes, especially if I include that magnificent arched window.*

When he rounded the northeast corner of the building, he could hear the sound of the surf, thrusting itself against the rocks. And between the trunks of the oaks and the spruce trees, he could see the blue-gray ocean in the distance, its frothy waves hurling toward the shore of a nearby headland.

Zelda jostled in the chair as its tires bounced over ruts in the old concrete, but she never complained.

"Sorry about the bumpy ride, Mother."

"I don't mind. It feels so good to be outdoors." She glimpsed an old building to their left, nestled in thick overgrowth and partially covered with vines. "Look at that. A carriage house."

"Yes," he said, noticing how the structure reflected the style of the main building, the same pitched roof and ruddy stone walls, the same conical tower and pointed arched windows.

"Horses used to rule the roads back then," she said. "Back when I was a child."

But now the only sign of a road near the carriage house was small sections of worn red brick peeking up through the onslaught of grass and weeds.

David veered off the sidewalk and onto a path that led to the gardens. Gravel crunched beneath the wheels as they made their way down the footpath. The gentle breeze from the sea tousled their hair, and the smell of fresh salt air invigorated him. He looked up at the treetops. Birds merrily chattered as if they had no idea winter was on its way.

"I love to hear the birds sing," Zelda said.

"I do too. But the one right above us sounds like it's talking. Not singing." He brought the chair to a halt and crouched beside his mother. "Listen carefully. Tell me what you think it's saying."

She listened for a moment, and then said, "It's a finch."

"Yes. A purple finch."

"And it's saying . . ." Zelda squinted her eyes, concentrating on the bird's loud, repetitive language, trying to imagine what message it might be passing on to other birds. "Come join me," she said. "Let's spend this wonderful day together."

He smiled at her. "That's what I think it's saying too."

She patted his arm. Then, scrunching up her eyes, she peered at something further down the path. "Is that a greenhouse?" she asked, pointing to a structure mostly hidden by shrubs and trees.

He tried to make out the object.

Sunlight glinted off panes of glass that peeked through the thick foliage.

"Sure looks like it," he said. "Let's check it out."

He took control of the wheelchair again and pushed it down the dusty path. The closer they got to the building, the more he could see bits and pieces of it. When the greenhouse finally came into full view, he stopped and stood there, studying the grim, decaying structure, thinking how once it had been a vibrant place that encouraged the growth of beautiful flowers, fruit, and vegetables. In his mind's eye, he could picture the greenhouse as it was a hundred years ago when Haven was a grand seaside hotel.

Employees swarmed inside the big glass structure, cheerfully helping guests choose between African violets or lilies, Chinese hibiscus or orchids. Some workers were spraying luscious green ferns with sparkling fresh water while others packed fertile soil around plants in terra cotta flowerpots.

David pushed his mother past the wall of glass panes, foggy and yellow with age, half-covered with ivy and weeds.

"It's a shame, isn't it?" she said. "To neglect a building like this. To just let it deteriorate."

"It sure is," he said as he walked up to one of the windows. Shielding his eyes with his hands, he looked inside.

He was amazed to see that the building housed thriving plants despite being abandoned by its current owners. Unruly trees, reaching for the sun, had forced their limbs through the glass panels on the roof. Vines curled their way around the structure's rusty metal beams. A climbing hydrangea, exploding with the desire to expand and dominate, spread itself over a large section of the south wall, covering the glass with its glossy heart-shaped leaves.

On the floor, he saw a pile of broken clay pots and an overturned birdbath, its pale gray concrete bowl cracked and stained. A broken door, hanging on by one hinge, had jagged strips of dry red paint peeling away from its wooden panels.

A blue jay flew by, and he followed it, watching it sweep through the air like a tiny plane performing an aerobatic maneuver. Then he lost sight of the bird. Determined to find it again, he narrowed his eyes and searched among the twisting limbs and vines, among the red and gold leaves dangling from the branches that hung below the glass ceiling.

A flutter of its wings gave the bird away.

He spied it, perched on a branch near a smashed window. Stepping back, he turned to his mother. "Want to take a look?"

She nodded, her face lighting up in anticipation.

He scooted her as close as he could to the wall of glass. She looked inside and took it all in. "You know, it's incredible. The way nature won't give up. The way it can remind us of just how small we are."

"Yes. Nature doesn't need people," he said.

She continued to study the scene before her. "It's beautiful."

He nodded. "Like great art."

"Exactly," she said with a laugh.

The blue jay was still roosting in the same spot. David pointed in its direction. "Look up there."

"What?" Zelda glanced up. "What is it?"

"A blue jay. Resting on that branch right up there."

She searched for the bird.

"Do you see it?"

"No."

"Look a little bit more to your right."

"Oh, I see him now," she said, whispering as if the bird might hear them and fly away. "He's lovely. But why is he still hanging around here? Winter's just around the corner."

"Maybe he wanted to stay behind to watch the leaves change color."

"Oh, David." She laughed.

They watched the bird in silence, fascinated by its beauty.

"Do you know it's been said a blue jay carries the blue of heaven on his back?"

"Never heard that before," he said. Feeling a muscle in his back tightening, he lifted his arms over his head. Twining his fingers together, he pushed his palms upward and carefully stretched. As he gazed up at his outstretched hands, he saw something on the roof. Something he knew would please his mother. "Looks like that bird better be on its way soon."

"Why?"

He pointed up at the ceiling. "Enemy waiting in earnest."

She smiled when she saw it.

A gray cat, stretched out on its side, was sunning itself on top of the glass roof.

"A kitty," she said, tenderly.

———

David maneuvered the wheelchair away from the greenhouse, around waist-high hedges, and entered the garden area. Statues, plants, and flowers that were still in bloom surrounded them.

He noticed Edgar sitting on a bench in front of a hedge, talking to a middle-aged woman. Two wheelchairs were parked near the bench. Edgar's father was in one of them. An elderly woman was in the other.

Edgar saw David and waved him over.

David wheeled his mother over to the bench.

"Come out for a stroll, did ya?" Edgar said.

"Yes," David replied. "I had no idea it was so pretty back here. For a place that's been so neglected, it's amazing how enchanting it is."

"Aye. Being able to bring our folks out here is about the only perk this place offers. Nothing like fresh air and the sound of the sea to pick up your spirits."

Edgar introduced the woman sitting next to him to David and Zelda.

"David, Linda and I were just discussing how it's against the law to use physical restraints on nursing home residents. What's your take on this matter?"

"Well, if I found out that someone was physically restraining my mother, I'd throw a fit. So I agree. It should be against the law."

"How would you feel if you walked in and found your mother in her wheelchair with a gait belt attached to the front of it? Put there to prevent her from getting up and falling?"

David pondered the thought. "I'd feel relieved. Glad the staff devised a way to protect her against another fall."

"Well, my friend, that will never happen," Edgar said. "Because, according to our lawmakers, that is a physical restraint."

"How can they classify that as a restraint? There's nothing cruel about it. It's just a means of protection."

"Oh, but those officials look at it from another perspective. If a gait belt is attached to the front of a wheelchair, the resident can't get up and fall."

David was stunned. "Are you saying our government officials hope they'll fall?"

"Aye. Our government claims their law prevents needless suffering. But what it really does is increase the odds of a broken hip and a quicker death."

David felt like someone had just slammed a golf club into his skull. His ears began ringing. His head throbbed. The color drained from his face. He looked at his mother and was relieved to see that she was looking up at the trees, paying no attention to the conversation.

"That can't be true," David said as he pushed Zelda's chair toward a flowering joe-pye weed to get her out of earshot. "It can't be. It's absurd."

"Oh, but it is true. And it's the law." Edgar leaned forward and wiped drool from his father's mouth.

"The government is supposed to protect its citizens." David's left eye started twitching. "Why would they make such a law?"

"Because our government wants to eliminate elderly people as quickly as possible."

"Why in the world would they want to do that?"

"Think about it. An old person dies. And that brings an end to what?"

Confused, David just stared at Edgar.

"It brings an end to social security checks, David. And an end to Medicare and Medicaid payments to the nursing home."

"Doesn't make any sense," David said. "A nursing home loses income whenever a resident dies. So isn't it in their best interest to keep their residents alive?"

Edgar shook his head. "Listen. If an old person falls, and that fall leads to their death, the facility's management doesn't blink an eye."

"But no body, no money."

"These homes quickly fill the space." Edgar sighed and took a deep breath. "Everyone is in the dark until a loved one enters a nursing home. Then the lights snap on, and it becomes crystal clear. For the ones who care that is. For the ones who stay on top of things. Trouble is most residents don't get many visitors. Their relatives are too busy these days. Too busy to watch over old folks who have one foot in the grave. And those are the residents who suffer the most."

"So you're saying *all nursing homes* are bad news. Every one of them?"

"No, not all of them. I believe there are people out there in charge of some facilities who have scruples. Or a deep faith in God. A handful of individuals in this entire country, mind you, who are heroes instead of greedy scums."

David felt his heart flutter. "But for the most part, they're—"

"Scums," Linda said. "Heartless people who get big bonuses for every life they help bring to a timely end."

David sank onto the bench next to Edgar. He glanced over at his mother.

Zelda was watching a yellow butterfly flutter around the pink and purple joe-pye blossoms. The sight brought a smile to David's face.

Even at eighty-four, Mother is still so beautiful.

"Now here's the icing on the cake," Edgar said. "While physical restraints are illegal, chemical restraints are not."

"Chemical restraints? Do you mean drugs?" David asked.

Edgar nodded. He leaned back against the narrow wooden slats on the bench and crossed his legs. "If an elderly person gets agitated, instead of using kindness and love to calm them, doctors prescribe injections of antipsychotics to sedate them. And antipsychotics are not only very expensive drugs—they're very dangerous ones. Drugs that can cause sudden cardiac death."

"Or send a person down a rabbit-hole they can't climb back out of," Linda said. "And that's what they did to my mom in a nursing home in Camden." Tears filled her eyes. "She's never been the same since that ordeal."

"They gave her mom injections of Lyzapine three times a day for over two weeks," Edgar said. "Without Linda's knowledge or permission."

Linda wiped her nose with a tissue. "And that drug pushed Mom into the final stage of Alzheimer's. Just look at her."

Slumped in her chair like a rag doll, Linda's mother stared vacantly at the ground.

"A month ago she was a different person," Linda said. "Happy. Laughing. Carrying on intelligent conversations with people."

"That doctor ignored the black box warning the manufacturer put on the drug's label," Edgar said. "A warning that there's a high risk of stroke or heart failure if given to elderly people with dementia."

Linda tossed her soiled tissue into a trash can next to the bench. "Lyzapine is supposed to be used to treat schizophrenia and bi-polar disease," she said. "And yet they're using it on elderly men and women who are frightened half out of their minds by sudden changes in environment and routine. The doctor who prescribed the drug didn't give a damn if it killed my mother. Or turned her into a vegetable. He felt it was more important to protect the aides from getting scratched or bitten. So he ordered them to inject Mom with Lyzapine."

"Compare that to two fighters in a boxing ring," Edgar said. "One of them gets to use a sledgehammer to protect himself. The other is given a safety pin."

An alarm went off in David's mind as he remembered the call from the nurse the night of the severe storm. The nurse who wanted permission to inject his mother with something to calm her down.

Linda stood and stretched. "All we can do is pray for a miracle. And hope that God will deliver us from evil."

I wouldn't count on that, David thought. He got up, brushed off the seat of his pants and walked over to his mother.

What a depressing conversation.

And a pitiful way to spend such a gorgeous day.

"Well, we've got to get going. Want to show Mother around the garden area. And take in the view of the ocean before she goes in for her nap."

"Yes. Nap time," Linda said. "Out of the wheelchair and into the bed. A vicious circle it is. No wonder these poor people lose the will to live."

David feigned a smile. "Goodbye. Enjoy this nice weather." And then he pushed the wheelchair down the path, away from Edgar and Linda.

I'm not going to focus on all that garbage. My mother will be going home soon, and we'll be finished with this place forever.

While David was driving home that afternoon, he thought about what Linda had said: *All we can do is pray for a miracle. And hope that God will deliver us from evil.*

Pray for a miracle, he thought, remembering how his father had done just that for him when he was five years old.

It was in December 1966. His mother had noticed he was walking with a limp. He couldn't put his right heel down on the ground without feeling pain. But he never complained. He just kept playing, loping along as if nothing was wrong. The next thing he knew he was confined to a hospital bed two days before Christmas. Too young to know why he had been taken from his home and placed in a strange place, he wept and wept. He just wanted to go home.

The first night in the hospital, he cried himself to sleep. But he woke up when he felt a hand on his head.

His eyes opened wide. "Father!" he cried out.

"Shh," Joseph Reid said, putting a finger up to his lips. "It's very late. Past visiting hours." He handed David a 1954 mint condition Jimmy Olsen comic book, a Superman coloring book, and a brand new box of Crayola crayons.

Thrilled, David eagerly accepted the gifts. "Oh, thank you so much!"

"You can color pictures tomorrow, but right now you need to lie back down, close your eyes and get some sleep. I shouldn't have woken you up, but I wanted to see those baby blue eyes."

"Father, this Jimmy Olsen comic is from your collection, isn't it?"

Joseph smiled. "It's yours now."

"I'll take good care of it."

"I know you will, son."

David smiled as he lay back down on the pillow. He pulled the white cotton bedspread up to his chin and then watched his father clasp his hands together. Bowing his head, he began to pray. He prayed to God. Pleaded with Jesus. Begged them for mercy.

And when David heard his father's voice crack and saw tears escape from his tightly closed eyes, he became frightened. Afraid he was going to die and never go home again.

When David opened his eyes the next morning, he could still hear his father's quiet, gentle voice: *Please God, heal my little boy. He's so young and innocent. Please make him well so he can come back home to his mother and me. I'll do anything if you'll just heal my boy.*

After a few moments of staring up at the ceiling, David sat up in bed. Filled with pent-up energy, he climbed to his feet and discovered that his right foot no longer hurt. He could walk again without pain. He grew so excited that he jumped up and down on the mattress.

A sour-faced nurse walked into his room, saw him leaping on the bed, and said, "Stop that or I'll give you an enema!"

"Look at me," David said. "I can walk again—there's nothing wrong with my foot."

The nurse stared in awe, watching him jump up and down with the energy and stamina of a bucking bronco.

"And it was God who healed me!" he said. "Not the doctor. It was God!"

"Stop that," the nurse shouted. "You stop that jumping at once!"

"Whee—thank you, God, for healing me!" David said as he bounced up and down on the bed.

A few years later, David learned he had been diagnosed with rheumatoid arthritis. And it was a miracle he had been healed.

He gave testimony of his healing experience at every opportunity. He praised the name of God for four years. But when he was nine, he stopped praising God.

That was a fluke. Pure luck that I woke up and was fine. A misdiagnosis by an inept doctor.

CHAPTER 7

Gamon's Thai Kitchen was a small, austere restaurant in a fifty-year-old shopping plaza badly in need of renovation. The owners kept the place clean and tidy, so the poor condition of the building and its undesirable location meant nothing to its frequent customers. Customers that included not only many of the wealthiest people who lived in Rockland, but people from Rockport and Camden as well. People who would drive for miles to savor the taste of the most delicious Thai food in the state of Maine.

Light wisps of cold rain swept through the air as David and Kathy walked out of Gamon's, carrying sacks of food.

"This'll be a nice surprise," David said as they headed for their car.

"I know. I can't wait to see her face," Kathy said. "Too bad Hannah's going to miss out. She loves this Chicken Pad Thai."

"Well, I'm glad she's spending the day with Matthew and his family. The less time she spends at that nursing home, the better." David pulled open the passenger door for Kathy. She stepped around him so she could climb into the car and slipped on the slick pavement.

"Watch it," he said, catching her arm and holding it tight.

Once she was safely seated, he squatted and touched the glistening blacktop. "We've got ice. I don't believe it. Ice. And it's only the first of October."

"Tomorrow's the first."

"Ice in September then. Even more unbelievable. Why did we ever choose the Penobscot Bay area over Carmel?"

"Housing prices," she said. "Remember?"

"Yeah," he said with a laugh, sidestepping a small area of icy pavement. "Lowest price house—$1,295,000. And it had only two bedrooms and one bath."

A teenage girl walked past him, slid across the narrow strip of ice and fell. David moved toward her, slipping and sliding. He reached for her hand. She grabbed it and, as he tried to help her up, they both lost their balance and fell.

"Ouch!" David said, moaning in pain as he hit the ground.

"I'm so sorry," the teenager said.

"Not your fault. I'm okay." He rolled over, slowly got up on his hands and knees and stood. He held out a gloved hand to the teen; she took it and climbed to her feet.

"Are you all right?" he asked.

The girl nodded and thanked him, and then carefully picked her way through spotty patches of ice on her way to the restaurant's entrance.

David climbed into the driver's seat.

"Are you okay?" Kathy asked as he slammed the door shut.

"I bruised my knee," he said. "I'll survive."

She looked down and saw that his right knee, poking through a hole in his trousers, was skinned but not bleeding.

"David . . ."

"It's no big deal. Really. And it was kind of fun slipping and sliding around like that. Made me feel like a kid again." He smiled at his wife as he turned on the ignition. She smiled back, relieved.

"Well, thank goodness you didn't hurt your back."

Unfortunately, pain was pulsing through his lower back. He had twisted it during the fall, but the stinging pain from his scraped knee was worse than the back pain. So, thanking his lucky stars, he backed up the car and drove out of the parking lot.

David and Kathy arrived at the Haven Nursing Facility thirty minutes later, three times longer than it should have taken them. But at least they arrived unscathed. Others had not been so lucky. A Chevy Malibu, creeping along in front of them, slid and smacked into a parked car. A Ford pickup weaved over the center line and nearly struck them head-on before sliding back into its lane. The truck skidded sideways and then rammed into a telephone pole. Another sliding car, filled with laughing teenagers, bounced up over the curb and plowed into a blue mailbox. The teens were still laughing when David stopped to make sure no one was hurt.

In Haven's parking lot, David noticed the moon climbing over the distant mountains. He squeezed Kathy's arm and pointed at the huge pink orb hanging above the foggy mountain range.

"Oh, isn't that beautiful?" she said.

"It's incredible. Makes me want to grab my brushes and paint it."

He slipped his arm around her waist and they carefully walked toward the entrance of the facility. Luke Gronski, a husky aide, threw open one of the doors and pushed a young man outside.

Kevin Fitzgerald, a scruffy but handsome man in his late-thirties, was in a drunken stupor. He stumbled out, then awkwardly turned around to face the aide. "I'm a chain smoker. When I lit up in me da's room I didn't even realize what I was doing . . ."

"You lit up because you're drunk," Luke said. "You're always drunk. Don't ever come in here again like that or you'll never set foot in this place again."

"Just try to keep me from seeing me da, and I'll rip your bloody head off!" Kevin said, shaking his fist at the aide.

Luke grinned and shook his head apologetically at David and Kathy as they passed him and entered the building.

Walking side by side, they made their way down the dimly lit corridor, carrying the Thai food. They entered Zelda's room and stopped when they saw her.

Zelda was slouched back in her wheelchair, her mouth wide open, eyes staring blankly into space.

David dropped the takeout bags onto a chair and rushed over to her. "Mother!" he said, gently patting her face.

Zelda didn't move. Her eyes were glassy, unblinking.

He reached for her shoulders and cautiously shook her. "Mother!"

She didn't respond.

"Kathy, get a nurse," he said. "I think she's had a stroke." He turned to his wife and saw the worried look on her face. She dashed out of the room.

David patted Zelda on the cheek again. Her eyes were still open. But now she began to snore. He tried to rouse her again, but she did not respond.

A short, chubby nurse charged into the room, rolling a metal cart containing a vital signs monitor.

"Going to check her vitals," the nurse said.

Kathy slipped her arm through David's. They watched, helplessly, as the nurse hooked Zelda up to the medical equipment.

"She started snoring a minute ago," David said. "Strangest thing I've ever seen."

"Not so strange to me. I've seen it plenty of times," the nurse said, studying the monitor in front of her. "Her vitals look good. She's fine."

"Fine?" David said. "How can you say she's fine? She looks like she's in a coma."

The nurse ignored David as she removed the cuff from Zelda's arm.

Zelda stirred.

Kathy took her hand.

Zelda blinked, and then stared into Kathy's eyes.

"Mom, it's me. Kathy."

"Oh, please, Kathy. Help me wake up. I can't wake up." Zelda moaned, too groggy to keep her eyes open for more than a few seconds.

David moved closer to the nurse. "What drugs have you people given to my mother?" He noticed the name tag pinned above her left breast: Betty Gerhart, LPN.

The nurse ignored him and wheeled the cart toward the door.

"Did you hear me? What fucking drugs have you given to my mother?!"

"I heard you," she said. "And foul language will get you nowhere with me."

The nurse left the room.

David followed her into the corridor. "Betty, I asked you a simple question. You ignored me. I'm sorry for swearing but this is my mother we're talking about."

Betty Gerhart turned to face him, a big frown on her face. "I don't know what drugs your mother was given. And even if I did, I'm not permitted to divulge that information. You'll need to speak to Nurse Jennings." She did an about-face, grabbed the handle of the cart, and marched down the corridor, wiggling her fat butt.

"Thank you," David said. "That's all I wanted to know."

What a nightmare, he thought. *How could they do this to my mother?*

He stared at the lame excuse for a nurse until she turned a corner and disappeared.

What gives these people the right to tamper with my mother's health? To conduct drug experiments on her like a lab rat.

And then it hit him.

Did they give her pills or a shot?

He returned to his mother's side and pushed up her shirt sleeve. His jaw dropped. He stepped back, staring in disbelief at several purple bruises on her upper arm. In the center of each black-and-blue mark was a circular imprint, evidence that a syringe had been used.

David always believed nursing homes were supposed to take good care of their residents and keep them safe.

But no, they're not safe.

My mother was sent to a nursing facility for therapy and proper care. But letting her enter this place was the same as throwing her to a pack of wolves.

The shiny steel door slid open. David stepped off the elevator and onto the lower level of the Pen Bay Medical Center. He headed down the hallway toward the Mental Health Services Division. On the walls were beautiful paintings that made the corridor look like an art gallery. He passed one painting after another but, blinded by anger, he didn't even notice them.

At the end of the hall, he entered the Mental Health Services unit and found the door to the office of Dr. Bashir Jamali. He walked into Jamali's waiting room and sat down. Two hours passed before he was called in to see the psychiatrist.

"What can I do for you, Mr. Reid?" Jamali asked.

"Why did you give Lyzapine to my mother?"

"To calm her down," he said, his cheerful mood making David feel like he was facing one of the most incompetent doctors he had ever met.

"That drug is not an antidepressant." David frowned. "It's an antipsychotic. Used to treat people who have schizophrenia and bio-polar disease."

The smile faded from Dr. Jamali's face. "I am well aware of that."

"Are you also aware that the instructions for prescribing the drug clearly state that Lyzapine is not to be given to elderly people with dementia?"

The doctor replied in broken English. "We use very low dose. Very safe that way."

"Safe?" David was furious, but he kept his anger in check. "Roscoe Pharmaceuticals, the manufacturer of the drug, has a black box warning on Lyzapine. Their instructions explicitly state that it can increase the risk of death in elderly people with dementia."

"We only give low dose."

"Roscoe doesn't say a low dose will not harm elderly people. They say not to give it to them. Period."

"Low dose not enough to cause harm."

"Did you hear me? Elderly people with dementia who are given

Lyzapine are at a high risk for stroke, heart failure, diabetes, and pneumonia."

"There was no other way the nursing staff could calm her down," Jamali said. "She could have hurt herself or one of the aides."

"So you chose to play Russian roulette with my mother's life?"

"She will be fine," the smile returned to Jamali's face. "Wait a month or two. She will be fine."

"She'll be fine? Her dementia has gotten worse thanks to your wonder drug."

"I'm sorry to hear that."

"Sorry? That word can be so absurd. Especially in cases like this. You think saying you're sorry will erase everything you did or suck out the poison you pumped into her brain?"

Dr. Jamali was speechless. Beads of sweat formed on his forehead.

"Some of the side effects are the very same symptoms you were trying to treat. So you only made matters worse. Plus you put her at high risk of death. What gives you the right to do that?"

Jamali just stared.

"Don't you consult family members before giving their loved ones dangerous drugs?"

"My colleagues give the drug to their patients all the time. It is very safe drug."

"And if your colleagues told you they put their patients on a boat and send them over a waterfall to cure migraine headaches, would you do the same?"

"Is not same thing. And I do not have time to waste talking about shoving people over waterfalls."

"Maybe you'd prefer the cliché then?"

"Excuse me?"

"If all your colleagues jumped off a cliff, would you?"

"Ridiculous." Jamali scowled at David.

"It is the same thing. You endangered my mother's life by giving her that drug."

"Is not dangerous."

"Have you ever heard of reckless endangerment?"

"Does not apply to me."

"It doesn't?" David laughed. "What if I hit someone in your family with my car and caused them to suffer permanent brain damage? Would you sue me? Would you win the lawsuit? Of course you would win. Because that would be classified as reckless endangerment."

Once again, Jamali was speechless.

"My mother is not the same person she was before you tampered with her health. If she doesn't return to normal soon, you better prepare yourself for a reckless endangerment lawsuit." David stood up and turned to leave.

"You will not be able to touch me. I did nothing wrong."

David turned around and grinned at Dr. Jamali. "We'll see about that," he said calmly. Then he walked out of the doctor's office, gently closing the door behind him.

CHAPTER 8

"**B**oston sucks!"

Kevin Fitzgerald sneered at Paul Ebner. "You love the Yankees. Good for you," Kevin said, spraying off the deck with a hose. "But keep your opinions of the Red Sox to yourself."

Ebner, a big brute of a man with mean eyes and a tattoo of a wicked owl covering his muscular neck, let out a hearty laugh. "I've said it before, and I'll say it again—Boston sucks!"

"One more time and I'll knock your block off." Kevin twisted the nozzle on the hose and dropped it, the boat gently rocking on the rolling waves.

Ebner pulled a large olive-green lobster out of a basket. "You and who else, ya little shrimp?"

"Him," Kevin said, pointing at the jumbo-sized lobster Ebner was holding.

Ebner laughed so hard his whole body shook. His belly bounced up and down. Tears leaked from his eyes. "Boston sucks . . . you little twerp."

Kevin glared at Ebner.

Ebner kept on laughing.

Kevin snatched the lobster away from Ebner so fast that the big bully's face registered shock. As Ebner opened his mouth to speak, Kevin swung the lobster around and hit him in the face with its huge claws.

Ebner cried out in pain. "I'll kill ya, you little bastard!"

Kevin was five foot ten. Far from little. Just because Ebner was six foot five, he looked down on everyone as little wops, little shrimps, little creeps, little coons, little kikes; whatever the ignorant, insecure racist felt like using to insult the other workers.

Kevin swung the lobster at Ebner again, hitting him in the side of the head. Bits of broken shell sprayed in all directions.

Ebner reeled backward, nearly losing his footing.

Kevin didn't wait for a reaction this time. He rammed into the big brute, knocked him off his feet, and beat him so badly that when his fury abated he was astonished to see thick strands of blood dripping from his hands.

The shower head spit steady streams of warm water onto Kevin's face. Even though he just got fired from his job on O'Riley's lobster boat, he felt great.

It always feels good to put someone in their place, he thought. Only, in Ebner's case, that place should've been the bottom of the sea.

After he toweled off and dressed, Kevin dropped to his knees in his father's bedroom and looked under the bed.

"Rusty. Come on," he said to the big orange tabby, its green eyes glowing in the dark, dusty space beneath the box springs.

"Come on out of there."

The cat stared at Kevin like he had never seen him before.

"Come on, kitty."

The cat did not move.

"Do you want to go see Da?"

Rusty meowed. He crawled out from under the bed and circled Kevin's legs, rubbing his lithe body against Kevin's blue jeans.

Kevin picked up the cat and hugged it. He gave it a kiss on the top of its head, and then searched for the cat carrier.

The traffic light at Tillson and Main promptly changed from yellow to red. The bright blue '69 Camaro screeched to a halt.

Inside the vehicle, an orange tabby wailed in protest.

Kevin Fitzgerald glanced over at the cat carrier on the passenger seat. Rusty looked up at him through the bars of his temporary prison. The cat let out a deep, throaty growl and wailed again.

"It's okay, boy," Kevin said. "We're not going to the vet's. We're going to see—"

BAM!

The impact of another car took Kevin's breath away. Pummeled from behind, he rocked forward and then slammed back against his seat. The cat carrier tumbled onto the floor. Rusty screeched and cried. The big cat moved around in the tight quarters, frantically trying to find a way out of his wobbling cage.

Kevin reached down and pulled the carrier up. He looked inside. Rusty was not injured, just scared. The cat hissed at him. It tried to reach through the bars so it could swipe at him.

"Simmer down. You're okay."

Kevin set the cage back onto the passenger seat, swung his car door open, and ran back to the car that had just hit the rear end of his vintage Camaro. Madder than a rabid dog, he yanked the driver's door open and shouted. "Are you blind or—"

He shut his mouth the moment he saw the frail, elderly gentleman behind the wheel. The man looked up at Kevin, his eyes glazed, in shock over the accident he had just caused.

"Are you okay, sir?" Kevin asked, patting the old man on his shoulder. He bit his lower lip as he pictured his da sitting in that seat.

The man blinked twice, and then gazed up at Kevin. "Just a bit shook up. My foot. It slipped off the brake." Now he blinked away tears. "I'm so sorry."

Kevin left the man for a moment to inspect the point of impact. He was surprised to see that neither car had suffered much damage. Just a few scratches and dents on the bumpers. From the jolt he had received, he imagined his Camaro's rear end would be crumpled up. With a sigh of relief, he trotted back to the old man.

"You have nothing to worry about. Only minor damage to our bumpers. No need to call the police or insurance companies."

"Oh, thank God."

"But I do want you to follow me to the hospital. I think you should be examined to make sure you weren't hurt."

"That's not necessary."

"Well, I think it would be a good idea if you—"

"No, no. I don't trust hospitals," the man said. "Been through hell and back with all of them. They've caused me enough trouble to keep me miserable for the rest of my life. I'm going home."

Kevin stared at the man's wrinkled old face. He knew he was right. The very thought of the problems hospitals and nursing homes had created for his family was enough to turn his stomach. "Then how about if I follow you home to make sure you get there okay?"

"I appreciate your kindness, son." With glistening eyes, the old man grasped Kevin's hand and shook it. "Thank you."

Kevin strutted down one of Haven's dismal corridors, toting the cat carrier and breathing in the smell of urine he knew did not come from Rusty's cage. He turned a corner and saw Kathy assisting Zelda with her walker. He stopped in front of the door to his da's room, wondering if the two women would like to see the cat. Feeling certain they would, he approached them and held up the carrier. Without a word he smiled and pointed at the furry orange face behind the thin metal bars.

"Oh, Mom—look," Kathy said.

Rusty meowed, trying to reach them with his paw.

"Zelda and Kathy, meet Rusty, me da's cat."

"Oh, he's a precious one," Zelda said.

"Aye. We love the little guy."

Kathy laughed. "Little guy? He's huge!"

"Most orange tabbies are big, fat, lazy cats," Kevin said. "Most of them are aloof, too. But not this guy. He's very affectionate."

Kathy watched the cat rub his face against the bars. "I'll bet your dad will be thrilled to see him."

"Aye. Rusty here is Da's best buddy."

When Kevin pulled Rusty out of the cat carrier and handed him to his father, tears welled up in Thomas Fitzgerald's eyes. The old man snapped out of his daze. He hugged the cat, his face pressing into its soft, furry cheek. Rusty began purring loudly, like a finely-tuned engine. Then Thomas sneezed. The cat's ears turned back and flattened. It looked all around. The old man laughed. He reached up and stroked Rusty behind his whiskers. The cat relaxed and started purring again.

Nurse Jennings entered the room, saw the cat, and frowned.

"Pets are not allowed in this facility." She glared at Kevin. "Remove that cat immediately."

Kevin's face fell. "But me da—"

"No animals in the rooms." Jennings reached down and snatched the big cat away from Thomas.

Startled by her callousness, Thomas began to weep. "No, please. I want Rusty . . . I want Rusty." He held up his hands, begging for the cat to be returned to him.

"Sorry," Jennings said. "But rules are rules."

Seeing his father cry overwhelmed Kevin. At first, his eyes brimmed with tears. Then his face flushed with anger. He scrambled over to Jennings and pulled the cat out of her arms. "Keep your filthy mitts off his cat!"

"Then get it out of here. Now."

"He has a right to see his cat. You can't deprive him of that."

"What part of "No Animals Allowed" do you not understand?"

"Show me the sign," Kevin said, wiping his nose with his shirt sleeve. "Where is it? This sign that says *no animals*."

She crossed her arms and stared at him.

"The home me ma was in allowed residents to visit with their pets."

"Well, they have their rules. And we have ours. No animals are allowed at Haven. Animals carry germs."

"And people don't?"

She scowled at him and then marched out of the room.

"Miserable bitch," he said in a low voice.

She walked back into the room.

"I heard that." She stood there for a moment, contemplating her next move, and then boldly walked up to him, her face mere inches away from his. "You are the biggest troublemaker who's ever walked into this place. Take your cat and leave."

———

Kevin could still hear his father crying when he reached the end of the corridor. He stopped and stood there listening, holding Rusty like a baby. When the cat began crying, he put it up against his shoulder and rubbed its back. He felt like collapsing. Like giving up.

Edgar came around the corner and stopped short when he saw Kevin. "Kevin, what's wrong?"

"Jennings won't let Rusty visit Da."

"What? Why not?"

"She said it's against the rules. She kicked us out of his room."

"She did, did she?" Edgar removed his backpack, slid out his laptop, and glanced in both directions. "Give me the cat."

"What are you going to do?"

Edgar held out his hands. "Quick, give me the cat."

Kevin handed Rusty to his brother.

Edgar stuffed the cat into the backpack and zipped it up just enough to allow Rusty to peek up at him. "Now go home and rake all those leaves. It's your turn, you know."

"I swear I'll get even with that evil bitch someday."

"Forget about her. Go rake the leaves."

Seething with anger, Kevin watched his brother stroll down the hallway toward his father's room. Then he remembered he left the cat carrier on the bed. He darted down the hall.

"Forgot the cat carrier," he said as he approached Edgar. "Can't let that witch see me walk out of here without it." He passed Edgar, then turned back to face him.

"Oh, and I got fired from O'Riley's boat today," Kevin said. "That big goon, Ebner, provoked me, so I smashed him in the face with a lobster."

Edgar was dumbfounded. He didn't know whether to curse Kevin out or laugh. He chose to laugh.

Kevin wiped his eyes. As upset as he was, he still managed a weak smile.

CHAPTER 9

Against the cold blue twilight, the windows of a contemporary oceanfront home glowed with warm golden light. The owner of the stunning property was Kathy Reid's broker, George Hoffman. And that night George was celebrating his birthday with a group of friends, relatives, and realtors.

In the large, opulent great room, people mingled as they enjoyed bacon-wrapped scallops, shrimp, and stuffed mushrooms with red or white wine. Lush green sycamore trees, living inside a huge atrium on the west wall, towered above the guests.

David took a sip of red wine as he eyed the gorgeous trees and flowering plants in the glass-enclosed structure.

"So how old is George now?" David asked, turning his gaze to a distinguished-looking young man standing beside him.

"He turned forty-three today," Mark Farley said.

Five years younger than me, David thought.

He looked around the spacious room; at the breathtaking view of the ocean and sky outside the wall of glass, at the gleaming white marble floor, the white sofas and chairs, the sunburst chandeliers, the sparkling glass tables, and big white columns.

"He's sure done well for himself."

"He certainly has," Farley said, "But he worked his butt off to get here."

"Made it all on his own?"

"Every dime. Got into real estate when he was only nineteen."

"And he made millions just by listing and selling real estate? Or did the big money come from opening his own brokerage?"

"The big money came from investing wisely."

"In the stock market?"

Mark laughed and shook his head. "I said he invested *wisely*."

"In what?"

"Real estate. Apartment buildings, duplexes, strip malls." Dressed in a gray, tailor-made Italian suit, Farley raised his wrist and glanced at his white gold Cartier watch for the third time in the last ten minutes.

"Nice watch."

"Yeah. I love it. But if I don't close an escrow soon, I'll be forced to sell it."

David shook his head. "Sorry to hear that."

"Oh, well. Easy come, easy go. Things will come back around. Hey, did you know George and Marilyn are leaving for Paris Monday morning?"

"Really? Wow. Paris. How I miss that place."

"You've been to France?"

"Several times. With my painting buddies."

"I'll bet you guys had a blast. Are you planning to go back?"

David nodded. "Someday." He took another sip of wine. Feeling his cell phone vibrating, he pulled it from the inside pocket of his suit jacket and looked at the caller ID.

"A trip to France and Italy are at the top of my list," Mark said. "I'm hoping to—"

"Excuse me, Mark. Important call here." He pressed the phone up to his ear. "This is David Reid." Having a hard time hearing, he squinted his eyes as if doing so would silence the chatter and music in the noisy room. "Oh, no." He closed his eyes and took a deep breath. "Pen Bay?" He paused as he listened. "Okay. I'll head over there right now." He ended the call and glanced at Mark. "Sorry. I've got to leave," he said, slipping the phone back into his pocket. "Nice talking to you."

Mark started to speak, but David had already turned and walked away.

David made his way through the crowd, searching for Kathy. When he spotted her, he rushed to her side.

"Kathy, Mother's in the hospital."

"Oh, no. What's wrong?"

"She's got pneumonia."

"Oh, my God. Grab our coats. I'll go find Hannah."

"No, I want you two to stay and enjoy the party. Don't say a word to Hannah about this. I'll go to the hospital and see you later tonight."

A calm, refined nurse escorted David into his mother's room, then quietly retreated.

Zelda was lying in bed, an oxygen mask attached to her face, her chest rising and falling with each breath.

David moved closer to her. One look at her pallid face and he crumbled. Choking back tears, he sank into a chair beside the bed.

Why didn't I spend more time with her?

Why did I let painting rule my life?

For an hour he sat there wishing there was some way to turn back the hands of time.

This can't be the end of the line for us, can it?

He hammered himself with memories of how rude and inconsiderate he had been to his mother. He thought about the time he had scolded her for calling him three times one afternoon while he was working on his website.

She was just lonely and didn't know what to do with herself.

She had lost interest in afternoon TV shows due to constant reruns and commercials. Shortly after that routine had been broken, she showed the first signs of dementia.

Then there was the time he was trying to unclog her toilet.

After several unsuccessful attempts with a plunger, he looked at her and frowned. "Next time, call the maintenance man," he snapped. "This is his job, not mine." He checked his watch. "Great. I'm out of ultramarine blue. And Cooper's art supply closes in ten minutes. Now I'll have to wait until tomorrow to finish my painting."

Snapping at her just because I was out of blue oil paint. I even threw the wet plunger onto the carpet in her hallway, splattering the white door with dirty-looking water because I was so frustrated with trying to unplug that toilet.

Then there was the time she had walked into his studio while he was painting.

He frowned. "Mother, I can't visit with you now. I've got to finish this piece today."

She moved closer to him, opened a small cloth bag, and pulled out an old palette. "I just wanted to give you this."

He looked at the object and recognized it.

"Emile's palette?" he asked.

"Yes." She nodded, tears springing to her eyes. "I want you to have it."

"Whoa," he said as he accepted the lovely, antique palette. "Emile Gruppe's palette." He examined the piece of precious wood. "I can't take this. It's your greatest treasure."

"No, you're my greatest treasure," she said.

Overwhelmed with love, his eyes sparkled.

"Tell me again," he said. "The story of how you came to own Gruppe's palette."

"Well, I was watching Emile paint during a workshop. One of the other students stepped up and said he wanted to buy the demo painting, and Emile sold it to him. I felt like I missed out. So later I asked Emile if I could buy his palette. And he said, 'My palette? Why on earth would you want this beat-up old thing?' And I told him, 'So I can treasure it for the rest of my life.'

He smiled the sweetest smile and hugged me. Then he handed me the palette, blobs of paint still clinging to it. I tried to pay him, but he refused. 'I can't take money from you for that,' he said. 'It's yours now, and when you look at it, remember me.' "

David nearly wept.

Oh please, don't let our time together end now.

A few minutes later, in sheer agony, David walked out of the room. He paced back and forth in the hallway. He didn't know which way to turn. Suddenly a thought entered his mind. An idea that caused him to come to an abrupt stop. He pondered the thought, and then raced out of the hospital.

David removed his jacket and dropped it on the floor as he entered his studio. He sat on the stool in front of his easel and stared at the painting before him.

Half-finished, but lovely, the painting glowed with colorful light-filled passages.

He drew in a deep breath and picked up an X-Acto knife from his tabouret. He stared at the knife. Then at the canvas. Back to the knife. He shook his head and laid the knife back down. As he wiped his sweaty palms on his jeans, he changed his mind. He snatched up the knife and thrust it into the center of the canvas. Twisting and turning the razor-sharp tip, he ripped the painting to shreds.

Pleased with himself, he yanked the tattered canvas from his easel and carried it across the studio. Jerking a door open that led to the redwood deck, he stepped outside and sent the canvas flying through the treetops.

Then he went into his mother's bedroom.

He switched on the lights and looked around, taking it all in.

A brass bed. Her beautiful Amish handmade quilt. A heart-shaped pillow on her bed with gold letters embroidered over red velvet spelling out "Forever Yours." An antique dark mahogany dresser.

On the dresser: Her gold wedding band. A white leather-bound Bible. Several framed photos. A Bose Wave music system.

David pressed the touch pad on the Bose. "O Mio Bambino Caro" from Gianni Schicchi began playing. He listened to the music as he looked down at the photos. One by one, he picked them up.

Zelda, a rare beauty at thirty-seven, plein air painting, the immense Rocky Mountain Range behind her. Zelda with her husband and her only child, David at age five. Zelda with 12-year-old David sitting in front of their Christmas tree. Zelda with Kathy and Hannah, standing in front of the Cinderella Castle at Disney World. Zelda and David, a recent happy moment.

David picked up the red velvet pillow from the bed and sank into an armchair. He stared at the words "Forever Yours." As he hugged the pillow, a tear rolled down his cheek. He wiped his face with the back of his hand and closed his eyes.

Within a few moments, he was standing in a cemetery on a cold winter day. He watched as an intense burst of wind sent a wreath swirling through the air. The wreath hit the ground and tumbled along until it joined a pile of wreaths and dead flowers on a two-foot-high mound of dirt covering a fresh grave.

Suddenly he was consumed by blackness. There was absolute silence. He could not feel himself breathing. Could not feel his heart beating. His eyes adjusted to the pitch black world. He could now see something. In gray, dim light the face of his mother was turned up towards heaven. Eyes closed, head resting on a satin pillow, at peace now in her coffin. Then her eyes opened. She whimpered and cried when she realized where she was.

"David, help me!" she screamed.

He woke up with a start. Sitting in the armchair, he frantically looked around the room. Realizing it was just a nightmare, he took a deep breath to calm himself down.

CHAPTER 10

It was a bright, cheerful day. The spotless Lexus crawled through the early morning traffic.

Through the passenger window, Hannah watched the cars creeping along beside them. She saw a driver staring at his cell phone, paying no attention to the car in front of him. *Doesn't he know he shouldn't be texting while driving?*

The car rolled forward, and the man looked up from his phone. He slammed on his brakes just as his car was about to smash into the rear end of a new BMW.

Some adults are so stupid. They know they shouldn't do something, but they do it anyway.

David squinted against the harsh sunlight. He popped open the glove box, pulled out his black Ray-Ban sunglasses and slipped them on.

Hannah watched her dad, hugging her book bag as they approached her school. "Now that Gram's doing better, can I visit her after school?"

"Let's give her a little more time to recover, honey."

Hannah frowned. She peered over at the next car that came up beside them. This driver was paying attention to his driving. Doing exactly what he should be doing. *Boring.* But then she noticed a girl sitting in the seat behind the driver. The girl was looking out the window, peeking through strands of long blonde hair that were combed down over her face with only the tip of her nose showing. The girl waved at Hannah.

It was such a weird, unexpected sight that at first Hannah was too startled to move. "Look, Daddy," she said. "Look at that girl."

David glanced over at the girl. He shook his head and smiled at Hannah. "Very funny."

At that moment, the girl pushed her hair back away from her face, gave Hannah a big smile, and waved.

This time Hannah waved at the stranger, giggling with delight.

Wait'll I tell Gram about this!

At the nurses' station on the south wing of Haven, Nurse Jennings was on the phone.

David drummed his fingers on the counter as he waited for Jennings to finish the call. He turned and looked into the lounge. It was filled with residents.

Wheelchairs were lined up against one wall. Feeble, motionless old men and women were sitting there. Some with heads drooping like wilted flowers. Others staring lifelessly into space. The sight of the helpless, over-medicated people was nearly as heart-breaking as the starving, traumatized Jews he had seen in photos of Nazi concentration camps.

Out of the corner of his eye, he glimpsed Edgar pushing his father along the corridor towards the lounge. Edgar nodded to him as he approached.

"How's it going?" Edgar asked.

"Not good."

"So what else is new?"

"Does the staff here ever follow instructions you give them?"

Edgar laughed. "Never."

"This place is unbelievable." David glanced back to see if Jennings had finished her call. She was still on the phone. And it seemed to him she was taking her time just to annoy him.

"Let's go," Thomas Fitzgerald said, his worn-out voice cracking. "Let's go."

David turned back to Edgar and his father.

"Give 'em hell," Edgar said to David as he walked away.

David smiled wryly and then looked back into the lounge.

A long string of drool hung from the crooked mouth of a skinny old man, half-asleep in a tattered wingback chair. A big, heavy man wearing a wool beanie hat hooted with laughter at something on television. Then he abruptly stopped laughing and froze like a statue.

David turned back around as Jennings hung up the phone.

She looked up to find him glaring at her.

"How can I help you?"

"I've got two problems," he said. "The first is that, once again, the seat of my mother's wheelchair smells like it's been soaking in piss for a week."

"I'm sorry to hear that."

"No apologies would be necessary if you people would just clean off the seat after you change her pants."

"As I told you before, all wheelchairs get scrubbed every night."

"Let me get this straight. Someone pees their pants. Sits in it for three or four hours. One of your aides come along, changes their pants, and then puts them right back into the wheelchair without cleaning off the seat? What kind of sick joke is that?"

"Sorry, but our aides are overworked as it is."

"Then hire more aides!"

"What is your second complaint?" she said sternly.

"I've been assisting my mother with her walker today, and she doesn't seem to be making any progress. In fact, she's doing worse."

"I'm sorry you feel that way," Jennings said with an icy look.

"When's her next therapy session? I'd like to be there to watch the therapist work with her."

"Her therapy has ended."

"Pardon me?"

"Her therapy sessions ended last Friday."

"Why in the world would you stop her therapy?!"

"The therapist said she's mentally incapable of reacting to her cues. So she ended your mother's therapy sessions."

"My mother's hard of hearing. Is the therapist aware of that?"

"It has nothing to do with her hearing. It's the Alzheimer's," she said with all the sympathy of a robot.

"My mother has to be able to walk before she can come home. What are you going to do about that?"

Nurse Jennings smiled. A self-satisfied, arrogant smile.

"Don't give me that smug look. If you don't get her back into therapy immediately, you'll be hearing from my lawyer."

Nurse Jennings didn't bat an eye. With the smile still plastered on her face, she looked down at some paperwork spread out before her and calmly began sorting it out.

───────────

It was a quarter after six that evening, and so dark David couldn't see a thing through the kitchen window. He went back to peeling the papery, gold skin from a yellow onion, letting the thin slivers drop into the sink near the mouth of the disposal. Placing the onion on a butcher block cutting board, he picked up a chef's knife and sliced through the firm white flesh. As he prepared to quarter the onion, he looked over at Kathy.

She was standing in front of their Jenn-Air range, stirring strips of sizzling chicken in an iron frying pan as the ventilation fan whooshed in the hood above her head. On the granite countertop next to her was a bowl of white rice, and a large platter filled with diced peppers, sliced tomato, and small chunks of broccoli.

"You know, it seems like the staff at Haven is doing everything in their power to keep Mother there," David said as he quartered the onion. The pungent smell filled his nostrils and stung his eyes. He picked up his glass of Sauvignon Blanc and took a sip, trying to blink away the blinding tears.

"More than likely they don't want to lose the income your mom generates," Kathy said, keeping her eyes on the skillet.

The logic behind her remark stunned David. "They could never get away with that," he said. "Could they?"

"Of course they could."

He raised the knife in front of his face and examined the sharp blade. "Then someone needs to rectify that situation."

Kathy turned around and saw him staring at the knife. "Thinking about chopping them up into little pieces?"

"If I could get away with it, I probably would." He lowered the knife, popped a tiny piece of onion into his mouth and winked at her.

CHAPTER 11

David weaved in and out among the pedestrians ahead of him, rain thumping against his black nylon umbrella. His shoes were squeaking, and his socks were soaking wet from sloshing through the pools of water on the sidewalk. He was relieved to see the building that housed his destination: the Maine Department of Health.

When he reached the top of the concrete steps, he shook the water from his umbrella and ducked just in time to avoid getting skewered by a passing umbrella held by a young woman. He followed the woman into the building, walking alongside the trail of water left by her folded umbrella.

He made his way to the row of elevators. On the ride up to the fifth floor, hope filled his heart. He felt that the supervisor would help him. Would assure him that a mistake had been made. And that Haven would be fined for every infraction.

He was wrong.

It was now raining so hard that a wall of water obscured the view outside the window of Rudolph Mandel, the health services supervisor. A finicky little man in his forties, Mandel had shiny brown hair parted on the right and beady, evil-looking eyes. With a thicker mustache, this man could pass as Adolf Hitler.

"So . . . you're saying you can't help us?" David asked.

"I'm saying you have no evidence to support your complaints against Haven."

"What about the photo my wife took of my mother looking like a zombie after they gave her injections of an anti-psychotic drug? A drug that could have killed her. Or the digital recording I made of my conversation with the facility's doctor? Telling me he can ignore a pharmaceutical company's black box warning and do as he pleases."

"I'm sorry. But the results of our investigation show that the staff at Haven has done nothing wrong."

David stared at Mandel in disbelief. "Then I have one last question for you." He waited for Mandel to respond.

"Go on," Mandel said.

"How much money do these corporations pay you to dismiss complaints against them?"

Mandel sneered. "Get out. *Now.*"

David rose from the chair, extended his right arm in the air with a straightened hand and clicked his heels together. "Heil Hitler!" he said as he gave Mandel a Nazi-style salute.

Outraged, Mandel sprang to his feet. "How dare you!"

"No, how dare *you*—you corporate-owned little prick! You worthless fuckin' traitor!"

David slammed the door shut as he left, shattering the frosted glass window pane bearing Mandel's name.

The rusty tines of the rake bent when David dragged it across the leaves. He swept them into a huge pile near a row of white birch trees on the east side of the property. Stopping to rest for a moment, he scanned the front yard, assessing the amount of work left to be done. Hearing a rustling sound from the mound of leaves behind him, he turned and saw the tips of a pair of antlers sticking out from the colorful pile.

"Oh, my gosh," he said, feigning shock. "There's a deer in this pile of leaves!"

Now he heard giggling.

"Go away, deer. Shoo!"

The giggles grew louder.

"I'll go get my gun if you don't leave now," he said. "Then you'll be sorry."

The antlers disappeared beneath the shimmering leaves; crisp, broken leaves that shifted and crackled, and finally settled.

A great idea came to him.

He had been drawing earlier in the morning with graphite pencils. He always used a small sandpaper block instead of a sharpener so he could get a flat edge on his pencils. He patted the pockets of his jeans. There it was. In his right pocket.

"On second thought I think I'll just . . . oh, where is that pack of matches?" He searched his coat pockets. "Not in my coat. Oh yeah. I remember now. I put them in the back pocket of my jeans." He dropped his rake on the ground and pulled out the sandpaper block. "Yep. Here they are. One match tossed into this big ol' heap of leaves, and you'll be running for the hills, Mr. Deer."

The stack of leaves was as still as a rabbit frozen with fear.

David ran his fingernail over the narrow strip of sandpaper.

Scared by what sounded like a match striking against the rough edge of its container, two deer leaped out of the leaves and sprinted across the yard.

David bent over, roaring with laughter.

Hannah spun around. "Daddy, you're not supposed to burn leaves!"

She looks so cute in that costume, he thought.

Her neighborhood friend, Laura West, stood beside her, brushing the leaves and dirt from her outfit.

He stopped laughing and looked at them with a stern face. "You two will ruin those costumes before Halloween even gets here.

Change clothes this instant. Your mom will have a fit when she hears about this, Hannah."

"But Mommy said we could."

"She did, huh?"

"It was her idea."

"Well, it's deer hunting season. And do you know what would happen if I chased you two through those woods," he said, pointing to the forest behind their house.

Hannah's eyes widened with fear. "The hunters might shoot us?"

"Yes. So I don't want you wearing those costumes unless you're going from house to house on Halloween."

"Okay, Daddy."

"Yeah. We won't put them on again till Halloween," Laura said.

Hannah lowered her head and shuffled off toward the house with Laura following close behind.

David watched them for a few seconds. "Wait. Maybe we can have a bit of fun. I've always wondered if a deer would attack me if I tried to chase it."

The girls turned around. "What?"

"If you were a deer," he said, taking a few steps toward them. "Would you attack me or run away?"

He bolted toward them.

The girls took off, screaming and laughing. Around the house once, twice, three times. Then David collapsed on the lush green lawn, the two children tumbling down on the ground next to him.

Kathy found them there, lying on the grass. She glanced at a patch of lawn, still littered with leaves. "David, when are you going to finish up the yard?"

"I'm done for now."

"Are you planning to visit your mother later this evening?"

"No, I'm exhausted. I'll go see her tomorrow."

"Can we go out to dinner?" Hannah asked. "And take Laura with us?"

"I'm too tired to drive anywhere."

"I'll drive," Kathy said. "And you can just sit back and relax."

"Sounds good to me. But first I'm going to have an appetizer." David glanced at Hannah. "Venison." And then he grabbed her. She cried out in laughter as he tickled her and pretended to chew on her arm.

"Bah, this deer tastes awful," he said, munching away at her brown sleeve.

Delighted, Laura watched them with envy. "Your dad is so funny, Hannah. I wish my dad acted like this."

David studied the chess board, contemplating his next move. He moved his bishop to an undefended square. As soon as he lifted his hand from the piece, he knew he had made a mistake. He kept his eyes glued to his bishop, hoping Kathy wouldn't notice his blunder.

Kathy attacked his bishop with one of her white knights. She grinned and added the bishop to her collection of black pieces that stood near the side of the board.

"I hate this game. I can never beat you. Let's play Monopoly instead."

Kathy laughed. "You hate Monopoly."

"Well, I'm tired of losing. At least I have a chance of winning when we play Monopoly."

David's eyes darted around the board searching out his next move. He leaned forward, rubbing his forehead with his fingertips. Then, hearing the voice of a child talking about seeing dead people, he looked over at Hannah and Laura. Snuggled up together on the couch across from the fireplace, they were peeking over the tops of sofa pillows, frightened by what was happening on the TV.

"Isn't that movie too intense for those kids?" he said.

"It's *The Sixth Sense*. It's not so bad. Now if it were *Saw* or *Nightmare on Elm Street*—

"Let's play Monopoly," he said, sitting back in his chair. "This game is giving me a headache."

"Okay," Kathy said, collecting her pieces and placing them in a box on a large footstool near the square wooden game table. "You know, I still find it so hard to believe—" She dropped her king on the carpet, reached down, and snatched it up.

"Hard to believe what?" David asked.

"That the Health Department dismissed our complaints against Haven."

David shook his head in disgust. "Who would've ever imagined they'd blow off all twelve grievances."

"Aren't they supposed to protect nursing home residents by invoking fines for negligence and abuse?"

"Obviously not."

CHAPTER 12

Edgar Fitzgerald lifted the fork up to his father's mouth. Thomas accepted the piece of grilled chicken, smiling as he chewed the tender white meat.

"Good, huh?" Edgar said.

Thomas nodded.

Noticing a spot of salad dressing on his father's chin, Edgar scanned the bed table for a napkin. Spotting a stack of them on the dresser below a wall-mounted TV, he walked over and picked one up. But when he turned around, he couldn't believe his eyes; his father was pouring Pepsi into his grilled chicken salad.

"Da, no!"

He raced over to the table and grabbed the can from Thomas. But it was too late. The salad Edgar had brought in from his father's favorite restaurant was now submerged in a lake of Pepsi Cola. Edgar looked at the mess in the plastic take-out container and then glanced at his father.

Thomas was now staring blankly at the TV which was playing an episode of *Leave it to Beaver.*

Edgar wiped the dressing from his father's lips and sank into the chair next to him. He told himself it was no use.

Da will never recover. He'll never be able to live at home again. He's in the final stages of dementia. He won't last much longer.

A few moments later, Thomas roared with laughter.

Beaver had just fallen into a giant bowl of soup on a billboard.

Edgar perked up. "Beaver's funny, isn't he, Da?"

"Aye." Thomas chuckled. "He's a goofy kid. But I love him."

Edgar was thrilled. Feeling optimistic, he sat back in the chair, folded his arms, and looked back up at the TV.

Maybe Da will get better.

Maybe the end won't come for years.

Please, God. As long as I can be with him, I don't care where he lives.

———

It was 8:35 p.m. when Edgar noticed his father's eyes had closed.

"Da, do you want to go to bed now?"

Thomas opened his eyes and slowly nodded.

Edgar pushed the call button. Then he waited. And waited.

After forty-five minutes had passed, he walked into the hallway. There were no nurses or aides anywhere in sight. He groaned and ran his hand through his hair. He looked up at the light above the door. It was on; emitting a dull yellow glow.

He stomped back into the room. His father was asleep in his wheelchair, his head tilting awkwardly to the right. Edgar paced back and forth across the floor.

Damn them.

He ran his hand through his hair again.

Damn them all to hell.

What if Da was choking? He'd be dead long before anyone walked into this room.

He looked down at the floor as he paced and saw a brown smudge on the linoleum.

Is that poop?

He scanned the floor and noticed a few more brown specks.

More poop. Or maybe it's chocolate.

He went into the bathroom, ripped a few paper towels from the metal container hanging on the wall, moistened one with water, and returned to the spot on the floor. Kneeling down, he wiped up the largest brown stain and then held the paper towel up to his nose.

It's shit.

He scanned the floor and saw dust balls and a thin orange strand that looked like string. He touched the stringy object with a dry paper towel. It was hard. And brittle.

A piece of spaghetti? You've got to be kidding me.

This place should be as clean as a hospital.

These aides must've been raised in pigpens. Or they're just too damn lazy to clean it up.

Edgar had been waiting for one hour before he stomped back out into the corridor. Catching the sight of an aide leaving a room at the far end of the hall, he called out to him.

He didn't hear me. Or is acting like he didn't hear me.

He stuck his fingers between his lips and whistled as loud as he could. The loud, shrill whistle got the aide's attention, and probably woke up every resident on that hall.

Luke Gronski ran down the hallway toward Edgar.

"Are you crazy? You can't whistle like that in here."

"What else could I do to get your attention? You ignore my da's call light. His buzzer is sounding off and you ignore that too."

"I'm not ignoring anything. I'm trying to take care of twenty residents all by myself. What's the problem?"

"My da fell asleep in his wheelchair. He needs to go to bed."

"Is that all?" Luke frowned. "He isn't sitting in wet pants? Hasn't fallen on the floor? And you're acting like it's an emergency?"

"Well, what if it *was* an emergency? What if he was alone and started choking? He would die before you got to him."

"It's like this in all nursing homes. They're all understaffed."

Edgar crossed his arms over his chest and glared at the aide.

"Do some research. Google nursing homes," Luke said. "You'll see that I'm right."

Edgar cleared his throat and opened his mouth to speak, but Luke spoke first. "I'm doing my best."

Edgar's arms dropped to his sides. "I guess most baby boomers are in for a rude awakening."

"I'm afraid so. Corporate America has us all by the balls."

Edgar eyed the aide's name tag. "I'm sorry, Luke. Now can you please help me get my da into bed?"

Luke nodded, and Edgar followed him into his father's room.

"One time I got scolded for putting Da in bed by myself. I was told it was against Haven's policy. Why would that be against their policy? He's my da, for goodness sake."

"Because you could hurt him and then Haven would be liable."

"Is that so?"

"Yes," Luke said.

Edgar shook his head. It was ridiculous. "They should be more concerned about being liable for reckless endangerment and neglect."

Edgar helped Luke walk his father to the bed. Thomas was so weak his legs kept buckling under him.

"Mr. Fitzgerald, do you need to use the toilet before we lay you down?"

Thomas shook his head. "Sleep. I want . . . sleep."

The two men lowered Thomas into bed. Edgar removed his father's slippers while Luke checked the man's pants.

"He's dry," Luke said. He pulled up the bed rail and placed a cushioned mat next to the bed to help prevent the old man from getting hurt if he tried to get out of bed and fell. "I guess that's it. See you later." Luke headed for the door.

"You forgot something," Edgar said.

Luke turned to face him. "What?"

"To raise the head of the bed."

Edgar walked to the foot of the bed. He bent down, seized the metal handle and turned it. "Just *please* remember to do this when I'm not here."

"Dang. I always crank that up. Sorry, I forgot this time."

"Well, please remember from now on. If my da were to throw up, he could drown in his vomit."

"He's not sick. So that's nothing to worry about."

Satisfied that the head of the bed was now in the proper position, Edgar let go of the crank. "Sometimes sickness comes on suddenly. And you puke. Da threw up at home while sitting in his wheelchair. Looked like black coffee grounds. The blood thinner he was taking caused an ulcer. The doctor told us that had he been lying in bed, he most likely would have suffocated."

"Oh . . ." Luke said.

"So please don't forget to crank up the bed. I've already asked the nurses several times to make sure all aides know to do this."

Luke shrugged. "Okay. But if he's not on that drug anymore, the chances of that happening again are—"

"Not slim," Edgar interrupted. "It happened one other time when I had Da in my workshop with me. Lucky he was sitting in his wheel-chair instead of in bed taking a nap. I was carving a piece of black walnut when all of a sudden he told me he felt like he was going to faint. Then he said he was going to puke. I grabbed a towel and ran over to him. He cried out for help. Then his eyes rolled back, and he passed out. Brown liquid started pouring out of his mouth. Freaked me out. Called nine-one-one. Rushed him to ER. Turned out to be a vasovagal syncope."

"A vaso—what?"

"Vasovagal syncope."

"Never heard of that."

"It's something caused by a drop in blood pressure. Followed by a faster, then slower heart rate resulting in poor blood and oxygen flow to the brain. And that results in temporary loss of consciousness."

"Wow," Luke said, anxiously. "I'll try to remember to crank the bed up from now on. Well, I've got to get rolling now." He turned toward the door.

"Luke."

Luke looked over his shoulder at Edgar.

"Please don't *try* to remember." Edgar said, his voice pleading, desperate. "*Always* remember."

Luke nodded. "Don't lose any sleep over this. Your dad's in good hands." He hurried out of the room.

"Oh, how I wish I could believe that," Edgar whispered.

Edgar stood there, thinking about the time his fiancé went into the hospital to have a D&C. After surgery, she was left alone in a recovery room. A nurse walked in about twenty minutes later to check on her and found out she was dead. Olivia had thrown up and drowned in her own vomit. The love of his life. Gone forever.

He quickly dismissed the thought. He moved around to the side of the bed and looked down. His father's eyes were shut. Edgar bent down and kissed his cheek.

Thomas opened his eyes.

"Goodnight, Da. I love you."

Thomas grinned. "I love you too, you little shit."

Edgar's face lit up. He watched his father close his eyes again and stepped away from the bed. Elated, he strolled toward the door, looked back at his father one more time, and then headed down the corridor. As he walked, he heard a weak voice calling out for help. He stopped and peered into a room.

"Help me."

Edgar crossed the threshold and stepped into the room. "Hang on. I'll go find an aide."

"No, don't call the aide!"

Edgar walked over to the bed and looked down at the old man.

"Please call the police. They're the only ones who can help me."

"Sir, you've more than likely had a nightmare. Now go back to sleep."

The man reached out to Edgar with outstretched arms. The dim light from the corridor provided just enough light for Edgar to see the purple bruises on the man's wrists. A closer look revealed more bruises on his forearms.

The elderly man pushed up the left sleeve of his nightshirt and pointed to a big black and blue bruise on his upper arm. "He beats me all the time. You've got to call the police."

"Who beats you?"

"The aide."

"The one on duty tonight?"

The old man nervously glanced at the entrance to the room. Seeing no one there, he nodded. "Yes."

Edgar examined the man's bruises, and then looked over his shoulder at the empty doorway. Feeling certain the aide had returned to the far end of the hall, he turned on the bedside lamp. "Can you roll over on your side for me?"

"I can't. Too weak."

Edgar rolled the man over. His eyes widened when he saw the huge bruise on the man's right side. "That aide did this to you?"

"Yes."

"Why?"

The old man coughed. A nervous, dry cough.

"Because I take too long on the toilet." He coughed again, this time violently. "I get constipated. It takes a while for me to go. And he gets impatient and—" The old man broke down and wept. "He twists my wrists. Slugs me in the arms. Hits me in the side."

Overwhelmed with anger and frustration, Edgar headed straight for the nurses' station. The nurse on duty was Nurse Jennings. He told her how the man was crying out in pain but didn't mention that he said he was abused by the aide.

"What man?"

"One down the hall from my father's room."

"You must mean Mr. Sassaman," she said. "He has shingles. He's in pain all the time."

Edgar was puzzled. "Shingles? What's that?"

"A disease that affects your nerves. It causes burning, shooting pain. Constant itching. A rash. Blisters. Pretty much a life of hell."

That night Edgar ran a search for shingles on his computer. He learned that when a person is infected with the disease, a rash appears on one side of the body. Within a few days the rash turns into red fluid-filled blisters that ooze and crust over. He clicked on images of the rashes and blisters caused by shingles. The photos made him nauseous, but not because the pictures were repulsive but because he had been told a lie.

He slumped back in his chair, a wave of helplessness and distress sweeping over him.

One side of the body. Not both sides of the body.

Red fluid-filled blisters. Not big purple bruises. That aide is physically abusing Mr. Sassaman.

An hour later Edgar woke up in his computer chair.

Exhausted, he shuffled into his bedroom and opened the closet door. While searching for a nightshirt, he noticed one of his father's shirts; a navy blue Boston Red Sox T-shirt he had borrowed from him last year. He pulled the wire hanger from the wooden rod and looked at the shirt.

It felt so soft. Gently removing the shirt from its hanger, he could smell the familiar scent of his father. The clean, fresh aroma of Old Spice, still lingering after all those months.

Tears filled Edgar's eyes and, with a sob, he buried his face in the shirt.

I want my da back. I want things to be the way they used to be.

His shoulders shook as he thought about his father living in such a miserable place.

That place is an institution. A prison for innocent people.

Da worked so hard. He deserves better.

All those old people deserve better.

Edgar stepped away from the closet, his father's shirt still pressed up against his wet cheek.

He stood next to his bed and thought about how hard his father had worked to make a better life for his family. How Thomas had moved the family from Galway, Ireland to Pennsylvania and slaved away at Bethlehem Steel for years so he could earn enough money to buy a lobster boat and relocate the family to New England. How he and his two sons learned the lobster business together and made a good living at it, so good that Thomas was able to buy a nice home for his family in Rockport.

Everything was going well for the family then. They were living inside a dream world. But then the bomb dropped. His mother was diagnosed with Alzheimer's.

Rebecca Fitzgerald ended up in a nursing home in Camden. The exorbitant fees were so high that the facility drained them of everything they owned. First their savings, then the house, and finally the boat.

The boys and their father had to hunt for a place to rent. They wound up in an old, dilapidated two-story house on the outskirts of Rockland. When their mother passed away, Thomas became so depressed that he ate less and drank more. Then he started falling. So often that at first they thought it was because he was drunk. But eventually, they learned the falls were caused by dementia.

Wandering off in the middle of the freezing winter nights led to Thomas battling constant bouts of pneumonia. But it was a stroke that swept him away; off to Haven at Stone Cliff, and into a dreary room where he would surely die.

The next morning Kevin came downstairs and found Edgar at the kitchen table, hunched over a cup of steaming coffee, a sour look on his face.

"What's up with you, bro?" Kevin asked.

"Got a hell of a headache. Thanks to that hellhole in Stone Cliff."

Kevin poured himself a cup of coffee and sat down at the table.

The two brothers talked about the problems they had encountered at Haven so far. Their fruitless efforts to get their father into another facility due to long waiting lists. And the disturbing truth that most nursing homes in the United States were pretty much the same.

"America. The greatest country in the world." Kevin spat on the floor. "There. That's what I think of America. We should've never left Ireland."

There was silence for a few minutes.

Edgar stared out the window at the pink clouds in the dawn sky. Kevin sat there, his head lowered, clenching his hands.

"Oh, my God." Kevin kicked back his chair and jumped up. The wobbly old chair tumbled backwards and smacked up against the refrigerator. "I can't be late for my first day on Bennett's boat." He scrambled across the kitchen and up the stairs.

CHAPTER 13

Struggling against the freezing wind, bundled-up pedestrians ambled along the sidewalk, coat lapels and scarves shielding them against the bitter cold.

David Reid marched up the steps of a building with a sign mounted on its brick façade. The sign said "McKinley & Jensen Law Firm".

Inside the building was the elegant office of a very successful lawyer. James McKinley, a suave, impeccably dressed attorney with piercing green eyes, tapped a pen against his yellow legal pad as he shook his head.

"I'm sorry, David, but a lawsuit against Haven would just be a waste of money."

"Are you telling me a doctor can ignore a black box warning from a pharmaceutical company and not be penalized for it?"

"It happens all the time. The only way an MD could get hammered is if the patient dies. And even then the plaintiff has to have evidence to prove the doctor was at fault."

"So the law doesn't care about preventing a death? They prefer to wait until a person dies before they'll take action?"

"I know it doesn't sound logical. But that's the way it is."

David stared at the pen in McKinley's hand. It was a blue Tibaldi Bentley fountain pen. The elegant writing tool, made in Italy, was gorgeous. Solid brass base with rhodium plating and an 18-karat gold nib.

Several weeks ago David saw the Tibaldi on Amazon while searching for a pen to sketch with. The Tibaldi was priced at $1,200. And here was McKinley, tapping it against his legal pad as if it were a BIC ballpoint pen, the kind that comes in a box of sixty for $4.95.

"Since you're this angry with Haven, I recommend you move your mother to another nursing home."

David looked up. "I've got her on the waiting lists of three other facilities," he said. "Unfortunately it could be weeks before a spot opens up."

"Have you considered private in-home care?"

"Yes. But we can't afford that right now. We're barely keeping our heads above water as it is."

McKinley stared at his expensive fountain pen. "Sorry to hear that. If it's any consolation, my wife and I have had to tighten our belts." He looked up, and his eyes met with David's. "Before the market collapsed we were spending money like there was no tomorrow."

You probably still are, David thought.

"I don't understand why doctors are allowed to ignore the black box warnings on Lyzapine. And why should drug manufacturers like Roscoe Pharmaceuticals even bother posting those warnings if the doctors just shrug them off?"

"I'll admit it seems ludicrous. But that's the way it is."

"That's the way it is?" David said, nearly exploding with anger. "I'm sick of hearing that bullshit phrase. What—we're—we're all supposed to cling to those words and accept them, knowing the harm those drugs are doing?"

McKinley shrugged. He doodled some more on his legal pad, fascinated by how beautifully the Bentley made smooth black marks as it glided over the paper.

"So patients are being betrayed by the governmental agencies that are supposed to protect them. And there's nothing we can do about it?"

"Right. You can't fight city hall."

"Like hell you can't," David said. "This love affair between the pharmaceutical companies and our government has to end."

"I'm telling you, you can't fight these big corporations. They'll squash you like a bug." McKinley rapped his pen against his desk blotter.

David stared at the pen as if it were an intruder who kept interrupting his train of thought.

Embarrassed by his habit of repetitive pen tapping, McKinley pulled open a desk drawer, carefully set the exquisite writing instrument in its black velvet-lined case, and gently closed the drawer. "David, let's say your mother were to fall at Haven. And to die as a result of that fall. Now that would be a case of wrongful death caused by negligence. And we might be able to win a case like that."

"Might? So even if negligence leads to death, the chances of getting justice are still slim?"

McKinley tilted his head to one side and then raised his hands in a gesture of uncertainty.

David leaned closer to McKinley's desk. "I want them to be punished. And prevent my mother's death by doing so. What's the point of a lawsuit after she's dead?"

"Well, when death is involved, there's usually a chance of suing for a substantial amount of money."

"Money? I don't want money. I want my mother with us for as long as possible."

David's shiny black oxfords left footprints in the freshly fallen snow, creating a pale rose-colored path on the bricks as he walked across the public square. He glanced up at a statue he nearly passed by without noticing and stopped. Shoving his hands deeper into his coat pockets, he stood there, studying the sculpture.

It was a statue of Lady Justice clutching a long double-edged sword in her right hand. A set of scales were suspended from her left hand, dangling on chains and in perfect balance.

He recalled seeing the statue many times in the past. But this was the first time he noticed that Lady Justice was blindfolded.

Why is she blindfolded?

And then a logical answer came to him. The blindfold was supposed to represent objectivity. People felt that justice should be meted out objectively, without fear or favor, regardless of money, wealth, or power.

How absurd. There is no justice in this country.

Corporate America is in charge of the United States.

Therefore, this statue is a sham.

David felt like climbing onto the statue's pedestal. He wanted to yank the sword from Lady Justice's hand and strike it against the stone scales, smashing into them until the broken pieces ended up as a heap of rubble at the base of the statue.

But instead, he walked away. From the statue. And from the justice his mother was entitled to.

CHAPTER 14

Halloween was only three days away and yet brilliant white snow sparkled in the sunshine, making the Reid's property look like a scene on a Christmas card.

David stood in the driveway, leaning on his snow shovel. Hearing a groan, he scanned the trees surrounding his home. And then he saw it. A big gray limb, covered with heavy snow and ice, creaked as it bent down, quivering from the burden placed upon it.

He held his breath as he imagined the hefty limb slamming into his house.

The limb let out one last high-pitched groan, then broke off with a sharp crack, collapsing onto the ground. It sent powdered snow high into the air above it, missing the house by mere inches.

David blew out the pent-up air trapped inside his lungs, a foggy white vapor briefly obscuring his face. He was at the end of the driveway, nearly finished with his chore. Thrusting his shovel back into the mound of ice-crusted snow, he scooped some up and tossed it into the yard alongside the driveway.

"Daddy!" Hannah called out, her boots crunching through the snow as she ran toward him. "Can we go visit Gram today?"

David stood there, his hands resting on top of the shovel's handle.

"Oh, I don't know, Hannah. It's getting late. And you have school tomorrow."

"Please," she said.

He thought about it for a moment. "I need to finish this job first. Maybe after dinner."

"But Mom has to show houses this evening."

She looked so disappointed. He couldn't resist the chance to make her happy. "Then I guess it'll be just you and me, kiddo."

"Yippee!" Hannah spun around and skipped up the freshly shoveled path that led to their garage.

The dim hallway was littered with old, worn-out-looking people in wheelchairs, stranded there along the walls, looking like broken-down cars by the side of a road.

A landscape print in a shoddy frame, hanging on the wall three doors down from his mother's room, caught David's eye. He stopped to inspect the image. It was a faded reproduction of *The Skiff* by Pierre Augusta Renoir.

"Come on, Dad!" Hannah jerked on her father's hand, then she released it and raced ahead of him.

David backed away from the painting and followed Hannah down the corridor, glancing at the name cards next to the door of each room.

Hannah nearly bumped into Edgar as he came out of his father's room. Edgar backed up against the wall to let her pass and flashed a tentative smile at David.

Zelda was sitting in her wheelchair, staring at the TV. She looked up at Hannah, who bounded up to her, breathless, as happy as a kid who had just been given a new puppy.

"Oh, my goodness," Zelda said, happily. "It's my little peanut!"

David walked in and watched as Hannah gave Zelda a big hug.

"I've missed you so much, Gram."

David joined them. He bent down and kissed Zelda on the cheek. "How're you doing, Mother?"

"Wonderful. Now that you two are here. Where's Kathy?"

"Mommy's showing houses. Big, expensive ones to a man who writes songs for movies."

David smiled at his mother. "A composer from LA. Writes motion picture scores."

"For Disney movies," Hannah said.

"Disney and other studios, too." David removed his coat and hung it on the back of a chair. "I am so thirsty. Do you guys want a soda?" he asked.

"Yes! Root Beer for me." Hannah laughed with excitement.

"Me too," Zelda said.

David inserted five coins into the slot of a vending machine and then pressed a big square button. A plastic bottle rolled down the discharge chute and landed with a thud. He collected the bottle from the mouth of the machine and tucked it under his arm.

As he fed more coins into the opening on the burnished chrome plate, he saw Edgar approaching the machine next to his.

"Watch that machine," Edgar said. "It'll steal your money. Never gives me the correct change."

"Thanks for the tip." David inserted another coin into the slot.

"How's your ma doing?"

"Much better."

"Why did she have to go to the hospital?"

"She had pneumonia."

Edgar's expression turned grim. "Me ma died of pneumonia."

"Sorry to hear that."

Edgar stared blankly at the vending machine in front of him. "Died in a hellhole just like this one."

David walked into his mother's room carrying three bottles of soda. He stopped in his tracks when he saw Hannah and Zelda clutching onto each other, trembling with fear.

"Daddy, I'm afraid!" Hannah cried out.

"What's wrong?"

"I just saw something—something really scary!"

David glanced at the television. "Something on TV?"

Hannah shook her head.

He looked around the room. At the walls, the ceiling, and the floor. "So what did you see? A spider?"

"No, it was a spook," Hannah said. "Crying by the bathroom door."

Hannah clung onto Zelda, who was wiping her nose with a tissue.

David set the soda bottles on the bed table. He took Hannah's hand in his and led her out of Zelda's earshot.

"Honey, what you saw was most likely a hallucination. Do you know what a hallucination is?"

"No," she whimpered.

"It's something you see that's not there."

"No, he was there. Gram saw him too."

"Gram's on medications that can cause hallucinations. Her fear most likely rubbed off on you and made you believe there was something there too.

"No, I saw him. He was there! He was there!" She pointed toward the bathroom door. "Right over there!"

David kneeled beside Hannah, took her trembling hands in his and gently squeezed them.

"It's okay, Hannah. Calm down. What did he look like?"

"Like a . . . like a sad old man. And he said something to me."

"What did he say?"

"He said—I can't find my way out of this place. Please, show me the way."

She frowned at the thought of the frightening moment, burst into tears, and collapsed into her father's arms.

Bewildered, David tightened his embrace on his daughter.

CHAPTER 15

David stood in front of the freshly stretched canvas, examining it to make sure there were no creases. He inhaled the scent of pine rising from the canvas frame and smiled. He loved that piney aroma, almost as much as he loved the smell of fresh oil paint.

He walked around his worktable with a small tack hammer, tapping down the corner folds to make certain the canvas would have a clean, professional finish. As he was tapping down the last fold, he heard a horrifying scream. He rushed out of his studio and into the hallway.

There was another scream, this one less intense than the first.

David bolted down the hall toward the location where the sound was coming from. It was Hannah's bedroom. He entered the room and looked around.

She was not on her bed.

Not at her desk.

Another ear-splitting scream. The shriek came from inside her closet.

David yanked open the closet door and saw Hannah sitting on the floor with her arms wrapped around her knees.

She was crying, half-buried by clothes hanging from the closet rod.

"Hannah, what's wrong?" he asked.

She didn't move. She just kept weeping.

Kathy sprinted into the bedroom, her face pale with fear. She joined David in front of the closet and peered down at Hannah. When she saw that Hannah was all right, she exhaled a sigh of relief. "What's the matter, honey?" Kathy asked.

David pulled aside the clothes covering Hannah's face and knelt down.

Hannah stopped crying. Her face was red. Tears trickled down her cheeks.

"Hannah, why are you sitting in here?" David asked.

"I'm hiding."

"From who?"

Hannah started to weep again.

"Please don't start up with that silly ghost business again," Kathy said. "There's no such thing as ghosts."

"I'm not hiding from a ghost. I'm hiding from the wicked people who work at Haven."

Kathy placed her hand on David's shoulder and kneeled down beside him. She looked into Hannah's eyes. "Why do you think they're wicked?"

Hannah's lips trembled as she opened her mouth to speak. "Because they're not helping Gram," she said, choking back sobs. "And if they don't help her, she'll never be able to come home."

The next night was Halloween. But Hannah wanted no part of it.

When her mother suggested she get into her Halloween outfit and go out collecting treats with her friends, Hannah locked herself inside her bathroom and refused to come out. With the bathroom key stuffed snugly inside the tiny pocket of her blue jeans, she sank onto the floor next to the bathtub, ignoring her mother's demands to open the door.

After Kathy gave up and walked away, Hannah turned on the

faucet just enough so it dripped water into the tub. She sat there counting the drops of water, mesmerized by each crystal clear droplet. Counting was her way of blocking out things. Things she did not want to think about. And it worked until she got up to forty-seven. At that moment she heard noises outside and stopped counting.

Pulling back one of the pink cotton curtains that blocked her view, she peered out the window.

The twilight sky was now deep blue, but she could still make out the silhouettes of two dark figures walking down the side of the road, swinging black buckets back and forth. As the figures moved closer, the buckets turned white. And so did the figures. And it became clear to Hannah that they were ghosts. Horror-stricken, she watched the big white ghouls twirl around and around, dancing happily as they approached her house. One of the ghosts had a white face that looked like an alien, its bony eyebrows arched up and its huge mouth a gaping black hole.

The other ghost was the corpse of a pirate. He limped along with the aid of a cane; his hat pushed back on his head, the long, lace-trimmed sleeves of his white coat billowing in the wind. Hannah could see his chalky white face, his evil sneer, and his black eyes in the dim moonlight and when he looked her way, she clamped a hand over her mouth.

She released the curtain and turned away from the window. Her whole body shuddered with fear, her teeth clattering against each other. She started to cry but, hearing the sound of the doorknob creaking, she suddenly stopped. Seizing the clear glass knob, she held it tight. But she was no match for the powerful force on the other side of the door.

The door burst open.

And there was her mother, holding up a small brass key. "You're not the only one with a key to this room."

"Mommy," she cried. "Help me!" Hannah wrapped her arms around her mother's waist.

"Now what's wrong?" Kathy asked.

"There's ghosts outside." Hannah wailed. "Ghosts from Haven. And they're coming to get me."

"It's just some kids, sweetheart."

The doorbell rang.

"Don't answer the door, Mommy!"

"They're just coming for some of those Snickers bars."

"No, they're not coming for candy." Hannah squeezed her mother's waist as tight as she could. "They're coming for me!"

Kathy crouched down beside Hannah. "It's okay, darling," she said, with growing concern. "I won't open the door."

It was a cold, bleak afternoon. Dark gray clouds passed over the school, casting their shadows over the playground, over the heads and faces of a few curious children who stopped to look up at the intimidating sky. But the rest of the kids were too involved to notice the clouds. They were busy enjoying the new playground equipment.

Inside the school it was silent. As quiet as if it were midnight. With the windows closed tight against the chilly November air, it was another world. A world that third-grade teacher Elaine Bates cherished.

Bates calmly inspected a student's paper, turned it over, and began to check another paper. Gazing up, she was surprised to see Hannah.

The only one left in the classroom, Hannah was seated at her desk with her head buried in her arms.

Bates removed her reading glasses and strolled back to Hannah's desk.

"Hannah, why haven't you gone out to recess? Are you sick?"

Hannah raised her head. Her eyes were bloodshot. She looked exhausted.

"No. I'm thinking."

Concern registered on Bates' face. "What are you thinking about?"

"I'm trying to figure a way to help him."

"To help who?"

"The ghost I saw at the horrible place where my gram lives. I'm trying to figure a way to get him out of there."

Bates was stunned. Her hand touched the side of her face near her lips.

"Can you help me, Mrs. Bates?" Hannah blinked, and a tear slid down her cheek. "I need to get my gram out of there, too."

Bates had no idea how to respond. She glanced out the window and stared down at the school yard. Children were playing on the jungle gym, swinging from bar to bar to get to the other side of the structure. Other children were chasing each other around the play-ground, laughing and scrambling, enjoying a game of tag.

Bates looked back at Hannah.

Hannah's eyes crinkled up. She began to sob. "Please help me, Mrs. Bates."

Inside a professional office building, an 82-year-old gentleman, well-dressed with thick, neatly styled white hair, shuffled down the corridor. Seeing a sign that read "Dr. Benjamin Graber – Psychiatrist", he opened the door and entered the office.

The man spotted an empty chair next to Hannah and sat down. David and Kathy were seated on the other side of Hannah, leafing through magazines.

Hannah looked up at the gentleman.

He smiled at her.

She smiled back then looked down at the floor. His shiny brown loafers caught her eye. She stared at them for a moment, then looked back up at him.

"If you go to a nursing home, they'll steal your shoes," Hannah said. "And if you poop your pants, they'll make you sit in it all day long."

Flabbergasted, the elderly man's mouth gaped open.

Moments later the Reid family was sitting across the desk from the psychiatrist, a brilliant-looking man with dark wavy hair, and a neatly trimmed beard and mustache. He had his hands clasped together as he studied Hannah's face.

"Hannah, you didn't see a ghost," the doctor said. "You were frightened because your grandmother was frightened. She told you she saw spooks in her room. You wanted to believe her, to please her. So you created a ghost in your mind. You saw what you wanted to see."

Flanked by her parents, Hannah leaned rigidly forward.

"No, I saw him. He was real."

The doctor shook his head. "Yes, you saw him. And he was real. But he wasn't a ghost. You simply saw an actual man in the dim light of the room. An elderly man who was confused. A man who couldn't find his way back to his room. A man who was simply asking for help."

"No, it was a ghost. The ghost of an old man. And he was crying by the bathroom door."

The doctor unclasped his hands and adjusted his round rimless spectacles. "Tell me more, Hannah. What did this ghost look like?"

"He was black . . . and white and gray. Like the people in those old, old movies. And he was flickering a little bit . . ."

The psychiatrist looked stumped. He exchanged glances with David and Kathy. Then he fixed his gaze on David. "David, you said it was very dim in that room. Where was the light coming from?"

"From a small lamp near the bed. And from the TV set."

"Is the TV in that room a new flat panel model or an old box set?"

"Old box. With a big clunky remote."

The doctor smiled with satisfaction. "Hannah, the flickering from that TV screen in the darkened room must have affected the appearance of that old man."

Hannah firmly shook her head. "The TV was not flickering. It was a ghost. I know what I saw. It was a ghost."

A few moments later David was sitting alone with the doctor.

"At this point, I feel that hypnotherapy would be the best treatment for your daughter."

"Hypnosis?"

"Yes."

"That sounds too creepy to me. Is there any other way?"

"David, actual hypnosis is nothing like what you've seen in movies or on TV. Subjects in a hypnotic trance are not slaves to their masters. They have absolute free will. And they're not in a semi-sleep state, they're in a heightened state of awareness."

"So the medical profession embraces this kind of treatment?"

"Yes. It's a widely accepted practice. The hypnotic state makes a person more likely to respond to suggestions. Hypnotherapy can help some people change certain behaviors. It can also help change their perceptions and sensations. And it's very useful in treating pain."

"So you're going to suggest to Hannah that she never saw a ghost. And she'll end up believing you and will forget about the entire incident?"

"There are no guarantees it will work. But it's the only way we can possibly erase that traumatic experience from her mind."

"I'll talk it over with Kathy. See if she wants to proceed." David stood up and extended his hand to the doctor.

"One thing though, David," the doctor said as they shook hands.

"Yes?"

"If I succeed, you must promise me one thing."

"What?"

"That you will never take that child to Haven again."

Hannah was curled up in the back seat of the car, sound asleep. As David maneuvered the vehicle through heavy traffic, he glanced over at Kathy.

"Seriously?"

"Yes," Kathy said.

"Who was this guy again?"

"Jim Gordon. An agent who retired a couple of years ago. David, you're getting too close to that car. Keep your eyes on the road."

David quickly turned his attention back to the traffic. "Did he tell you exactly what happened?"

"Yes. His wife bought him tickets to go see this psychiatrist who was planning to hypnotize a whole audience of people who wanted to quit smoking."

"And it worked for him?"

"After twenty years of being a chain smoker, he said he never touched another cigarette."

"What did the hypnotist say that made him quit smoking?"

"He doesn't know. He said one minute he was listening to the man on stage and the next minute he was leaving the auditorium with everyone else."

CHAPTER 16

Through the kitchen window, David watched Matthew Starke gather some snow in his hands. Forming the snow into a big round ball, the energetic third-grader placed it on the ground. He rolled it along an unspoiled snow-covered section of the yard, keeping an eye on the size of the ball as it grew larger and larger.

Across the yard, Hannah stood next to the big white base of what would soon become a snowman, smoothing out the lumps on the sides with her wool mittens.

Kathy joined David at the window and handed him a cup of coffee.

"Be careful," she said. "That's really hot."

Swirls of steam rose from the cup.

"Smells delicious," David said.

Together they looked on as the two kids lifted the heavy white snowball and placed it on top of the big round base.

"After five days of absolute peace," Kathy said, "I do believe the ghost is gone forever."

David studied Hannah's happy expression as she frolicked in the snow. "I didn't think hypnosis would work but, obviously, it did."

He took his first sip of the coffee, wincing as it seared his lips.

The black silhouettes of trees standing against a pink and purple sky signaled the end of the day. Kathy called the kids in for dinner. As they raced each other to the bathroom to wash their hands, Matthew stopped to admire the paintings hanging on the walls in the hallway.

"Wow, these paintings are awesome. Did your dad paint them?"

"Yes," Hannah said with great pride.

"Do you think he could teach me how to paint like this?"

"I think he just teaches grownups how to paint."

Matthew stood there, gaping at the magnificent paintings.

"I asked him last year if he would teach me how to paint. And he said that someday he would. Since he's never brought it up again, I think someday means when I'm like twenty years old or something."

"Well, maybe he just forgot."

Hannah took Matthew's arm and tried to pry him away from the paintings. "Come on. I'm hungry," she said.

"Hannah!" Matthew refused to budge.

"What?"

"I would love to learn how to paint like your dad. Will you please ask him if he'll give us lessons?"

"Okay. I'll ask him when he's in a really good mood."

"That would be great!"

"But don't count on it. For the past few months, he's been totally stressed-out."

"Why?" Matthew asked as she pulled him into the bathroom.

"You know how grown-ups are. They always worry about the same thing."

"What?"

"Money," she said, squirting soap into her palm. "Now hurry up and wash your hands."

Seated at the dining room table, David unfurled a white cloth napkin, laid it across his lap, and picked up a shiny fork.

Hannah studied her father's face. "Daddy, my friend Skylar told me her family prays before dinner every night."

There was silence for a moment.

"Well, good for them," David said. He speared a piece of pork roast and put it into his mouth. He chewed it slowly, savoring the flavor.

"Then if it's good for them," Hannah said. "It should be good for us, shouldn't it?"

David glanced at Matthew who was waiting for his reaction. "I guess so," he said. "Go ahead. Say your prayer."

Hannah bowed her head. So did Kathy and Matthew.

"Our Father who art in heaven," Hannah said.

Matthew and Kathy joined Hannah in prayer. "Hallowed be thy name."

David put another slice of pork into his mouth. He watched the three of them pray as he chewed.

"For thine is the kingdom, and the power, and the glory, forever and ever. Amen." They opened their eyes and began to eat.

Hannah looked at her father. "Why didn't you pray with us, Daddy?"

David ignored the question. He dipped a spoon into his pile of mashed potatoes and gravy, scooped some up, and brought the spoon to his mouth.

"Daddy, why didn't you?"

"Hannah, stop asking so many questions and eat your dinner."

Hannah frowned and stared down at her plate.

Kathy glared at David.

David gave Kathy a grave look as he took a sip of wine.

"Oh, I forgot something," Hannah said. She bowed her head, clasped her hands together and closed her eyes. "Please, dear Lord, help my gram get better so she can come home soon. Amen."

Hannah's words brought a lump to David's throat. He stared down at his plate, his eyes glistening.

Before turning in for the night, Kathy opened Hannah's bedroom door to check in on her. In the sliver of dim light from the hall, she could see her daughter thrashing about, her blanket a twisted mess.

"Nooo—stay away." Hannah mumbled softly in her sleep. "Stay away from my gram. Get away."

Kathy walked over to the bed to get a good look at Hannah. Drenched in sweat, she began to groan. "No. Stop it. Get away."

Kathy gently shook her, trying to wake her up.

"No, leave me alone. No!"

"Hannah, it's me. Mommy."

Hannah woke up, her eyes filled with fear.

Kathy hugged her. "You're okay, sweetheart. You were just dreaming."

"No, I wasn't dreaming. I was there. At that wicked place. They're hurting Gram," she said.

"Who is?"

"Those nurses. And the bad ghosts. They're making Gram sick. She'll die if we don't get her out of there."

"Honey, you were dreaming," Kathy said, her heart beating wildly. "We've been through this before. Remember? There are no such things as ghosts."

Hannah lay back on her pillow. Her eyes searched the room, looking for something and not finding it. She stared up into her mother's eyes. "What about the Holy Ghost? Is there such a thing as the Holy Ghost?"

Kathy was stunned. She closed her eyes and took a calming breath. When she looked back down, her little girl's eyes were shut.

Hannah had drifted off into sleep like someone who had just spouted off some incoherent remarks and fell back into the spell of a coma.

Kathy buried her face in her hands and quietly wept.

The next afternoon, while cleaning Hannah's bedroom, Kathy found some drawings on her desk. She smiled at the first picture. It was a black and white kitten, very well rendered for a girl Hannah's age.

Wow. David needs to see this.

The second drawing was one of their house and the trees and bushes surrounding it.

This is great. David must be giving her lessons while I'm out showing homes. Strange, though, that he never mentioned this to me.

The third drawing was of a collie asleep on a porch, sunlight falling on the dog's head, its body in the shade.

I shouldn't be snooping like this. Maybe she's planning to give me these for Christmas.

She decided to stop looking through the drawings. She made a movement to put them back where she found them, hidden beneath a stack of books, but then temptation got the best of her.

She peeked at the next picture.

Her eyes widened.

She pulled the paper out so she could get a better look.

It was a drawing of a nurse stabbing an old woman in the throat with a knife. Hannah had used colored pencils on this drawing. Bright red blood flowed out of the old woman's neck and onto her white nightgown.

Kathy's hands shook as she slid out the next drawing.

It was a picture of an elderly woman lying on the floor next to a wheelchair, curled up in a ball to protect herself from a nurse's vicious kicks.

The next drawing showed more abuse by the staff. And the next one was even worse.

Kathy stood beside David's desk, watching him sift through the pile of drawings.

He sat back in his chair and looked up at her. "Well, the hypnosis didn't work. For some reason, she's pretending to be all right. And she's probably doing these drawings as a way to ease her anxiety."

"We need to confront her about this. Right now."

David studied one of the drawings. "No, I think it'd be best if we let the psychiatrist do that. Let's make an appointment to meet with him as soon as possible."

The doorbell rang.

Kathy left the studio, opened the front door and found Joyce West, their next door neighbor, standing on the front porch.

"Hi, Joyce. Oh, my gosh, I'm so sorry. I said I'd return your mixer right after I baked that cake."

Joyce frowned at Kathy.

"Hold on. I'll go get it right now." Kathy turned to leave but stopped when Joyce spoke.

"I'm not here for the mixer," Joyce said, her jaw clenched. "I'm here to talk to you about your daughter."

Kathy tensed up. "Come on in." She led Joyce into the living room, and they sat down. "What's the problem?"

"Laura is upset. I've never seen her so disturbed. She won't stop crying."

"Why? What did Hannah do?"

"She told Laura to make sure that her grandpa never moves into a nursing home."

Kathy closed her eyes and shook her head.

"Hannah told her that if Papa goes into a nursing home, she won't be able to see him again until she's twelve years old. *Five years* from now."

"I'm sorry. We made up that age restriction to keep Hannah away from Haven for a while. She had a bad experience there and we—"

"Then she told Laura that if he dies before she reaches that age, she'll never get to see him again."

"Please tell Laura that Hannah was confused." Kathy started wringing her hands. "Tell her the truth—that, if her grandpa ever winds up in a nursing home, he'll get the very best of care."

Joyce glared at Kathy. "A few weeks ago we told Laura that her grandfather isn't able to take care of himself anymore. We told her he needs to move into a home with other people his age."

"Oh, my." Kathy didn't know what to say next.

Joyce went on, describing in detail the evening she sat her daughter down at the kitchen table to explain the situation with her grandfather.

"Listen carefully, Laura. Papa isn't able to take care of himself anymore. He may need to move into a home with other people his age."

"You mean he'll have to sell his house and move into an apartment?"

"Well, it's kind of like an apartment."

"Close to us?"

"Yes, of course. Just a few minutes away."

"Justin's grandma lives in an apartment building for seniors only. Is that the kind of apartment Papa will be moving into?"

"No, honey. It's a home for elderly people. It's called a nursing home."

"Nurses live there?"

"No, they work there."

Laura thought about it for a moment. "Papa's sick, isn't he?" Tears sprang to her eyes. "He's going to die, isn't he?"

"No, honey—no."

"Yes he is. He's going to a hospital to live."

"It's not a hospital, Laura. It's a nursing home."

"If it's got nurses in it, then it's a hospital."

"It's not a hospital."

"Grandpa has cancer, doesn't he?"

"No. Absolutely not."

"Then what's wrong with him?"

"He's just old, Laura. And he needs help. Help with things he can't do for himself anymore."

"He's going to die, isn't he?"

"No. Not for many, many more years."

"No, he'll die in there. I know he will. He hates hospitals. And he hates doctors and nurses. Please, don't put him in there. Please don't. He can come here to live. I'll take care of him."

"You can't take care of him. You have to go to school."

"Well, you can take care of him, can't you?"

"No, I can't. You know I work in Daddy's office in the mornings. Then I have to come home to clean and cook, and—"

"Tell Daddy to hire a secretary. Please, Mommy. Please. Quit that job. Tell me you'll take care of Papa." Tears streamed down Laura's red, flustered face.

Joyce told Kathy how she and her husband resolved the problem later that evening. They brought up some nursing home websites and showed Laura pictures of beautiful facilities and the happy faces of residents and their family members.

That made Laura happy. And eager to visit her grandfather once he got settled into the home of his choice.

"Then Hannah comes along," Joyce said, "and convinces Laura that nursing homes are evil places."

"How did she convince Laura of that?"

"By showing her posts on blogs about nursing homes on the internet."

Kathy freaked out. "She did what?!"

Joyce frowned, this time more deeply than before, furrowing her thick, beautiful eyebrows.

"Did she tell Laura about anything she saw at Haven?"

"Yes," Joyce said, shifting her position on the sofa. "About how some old witch swore at her gram and made her cry. About how they make people sit in wheelchairs soaked in—in—in urine. And if you want to know the truth, she used the word 'piss' not 'urine'. She also said they never give her gram a shower. They just let her go around with stringy, stinky hair."

"Anything else?"

"Isn't that enough?"

Kathy felt a mild wave of relief sweep over her.

But then Joyce's expression revealed that there *was* something else. "Oh, there is one more thing. But it's so absurd. So ridiculous that I dismissed it immediately after Laura mentioned it."

"What?"

"Hannah told Laura that Haven is haunted. Can you believe that? And she said she saw a ghost there."

Fear rose up in Kathy. She felt her face flush.

"That kid sure has a vivid imagination," Joyce said as she stood up. "More than likely she gets it from her father. Most artists see things that aren't there."

———————

Kathy and David agreed not to bring up anything about ghosts during their talk with Hannah. It was 8:45 p.m. when they walked into Hannah's bedroom and found her sitting in front of her computer.

"Shut that thing off," Kathy said. "And take a seat on your bed."

A Facebook page vanished as Hannah put her iMac into sleep mode. She crept over to her bed and sat down on the bright pink comforter that covered the mattress.

"Hannah, why on earth would you tell Laura West that nursing homes are evil places?" David asked in a low, calm voice.

"Because they *are* evil places," Hannah said.

"And why do you think they're evil places?"

"Because the people are mean."

"How so?"

"They won't let kids my age visit their grams or poppas."

David rolled his eyes. "Hannah, rules are rules. And employees who work in these nursing homes cannot allow people to break the rules or they could be fired."

"But it's not fair."

"Well, not everything in life is fair."

Hannah's lower lip quivered. Her eyes flooded with tears.

"You'll get to see Gram soon," David said.

"When?" she asked with a stubborn look on her face.

"As soon as it's humanly possible."

Later that night, David asked Kathy to call the psychiatrist first thing in the morning and make an appointment for them to see him immediately.

The next afternoon they were sitting in the doctor's office, flipping through the pages of magazines while Hannah kept herself entertained with a toy construction set.

The receptionist slid back a glass window and peered out into the waiting room. "Reid."

David and Kathy stood. "Come on, Hannah," Kathy said, gesturing for Hannah to join them.

"Oh, Mom. Can't I play a little longer?"

"No," Kathy said. "Now, come on."

"Mrs. Reid," the receptionist said, "the doctor would like to meet with you and Mr. Reid first. Hannah can keep playing until he finishes up with you two."

"Hurray," Hannah said, quickly returning to work on the miniature construction site.

"Okay," Kathy said, taking David's arm.

The receptionist pushed the window back into place, sealing off her workspace from the waiting room.

"So you see, traumatic events can be buried or suppressed in the subconscious," the doctor said, shifting his weight in his chair and sharing a reassuring smile. "Hypnosis pushed the memory of that horrific event into Hannah's subconscious."

"Then why didn't it stay buried?" David asked.

The doctor raised his eyeglasses, rubbed the bridge of his nose, then adjusted the thin plastic temples. "With some people it takes more time than with others. It all depends on the kind of event that was experienced."

"Well then in Hannah's case, we're talking about a very frightening, unique event," David said.

"Not necessarily. Ghost sightings are common events. Millions of people claim to have seen ghosts. And UFO's. Not to mention demons. Bigfoot. Creatures from the black lagoon."

The doctor paused and studied their faces. "Do you know more Americans believe in space aliens than in God?"

David was silent. *Count me in.*

"That's nonsense," Kathy said. "Where did you ever hear such a thing?"

"Many polls have proven it to be so."

"Then millions of people will have a rude awakening when they die," Kathy said with a disgusted look on her face.

"Kathy." Dr. Graber stared into her eyes. "Do you believe in ghosts?"

"I believe in spirits," she said. "I believe that when we die our soul, our spiritual body, leaves our earthly body and goes to—"

David interrupted. "Let's stay on the subject at hand, shall we, doctor?"

"All right. Has Hannah been acting more in control of herself?"

"Yes. She's calmer. More self-assured," David said.

Kathy sat quietly, waiting to hear more.

"Except for that bad dream she had, has there been any more emotional incidents since I hypnotized her?"

"No," Kathy said.

David shook his head.

"Good. And we achieved all that without drugs," the doctor said, his cheerful expression reflecting his confidence.

"But what about the ghost?" David said. "Is there a way you can convince her it was just a delusion?"

"Yes. By hypnotizing her again."

David sighed. Kathy tightened her hold on his arm.

"Oh, come on now." The doctor chuckled. "It's not brain surgery, you know." His chair squeaked as he leaned forward. "This time I'll use a reprogramming method. Instead of trying to bury that memory, I'll convince her she just imagined it. That the apparition never existed."

"How sure are you that you can convince her of that?"

"Ninety-nine percent sure."

CHAPTER 17

The blustery storm the night before had delivered three more inches of snow to the village of Stone Cliff. But just before dawn the winds had died down, and the snow stopped falling.

It was a peaceful afternoon. Everything frozen, still as stone.

David closed his car door, pushed a button and all four door locks were rapidly sucked down with a force that always seemed magical to him. He turned, squinting against the harsh light, and chided himself for leaving his Ray-Bans on the kitchen countertop. The sunshine, reflecting off the snow-covered ground, created a bright, dazzling world; one he hoped wouldn't trigger a migraine.

Slipping and sliding on the slick, glassy spots on the surface of the pavement, he crossed the parking lot toward the entrance of Haven.

When he stepped inside the building, it was like stepping from day into night. His eyes slowly adjusted to the gloomy lobby and when he could see again, the first thing that came into view was a dreary oil painting of a ship at sea. He studied the picture, wondering how long it had taken for the cracks to appear in the paint that surrounded the sea-going vessel, the paint that gave the viewer the impression of violent waves. He squinted as he tried to read the artist's signature in the lower right-hand corner of the canvas. The name had been carelessly scraped into the dark blue paint; carved in so recklessly that he could not solve the mystery of who the painter was.

His wet boots squeaked against the marble floor as he made his way through the lobby. He passed the empty reception station and entered the first corridor. At the end of the hall was a T-intersection. He turned right and saw Kathy walking along with Zelda, holding onto a gait belt attached to his mother's waist.

Hunched over with her rear-end sticking out, Zelda took two steps, wobbled, and then stopped.

Taylor Hanson approached the two women. "You shouldn't be doing that. It's the therapist's job to walk residents."

"Well, quite obviously," Kathy said, "the therapist has stopped doing her job."

Taylor shook her head and walked away. As she passed David in the corridor, she stared down at the floor to avoid his eyes.

David glared at Taylor as she hurried past him. He had heard every word. And those words were the sparks that set fire to the anger he had already felt the moment he turned the corner and saw her.

He turned to Kathy. Delighted to see her, his anger evaporated. "Matthew's father said he'd have Hannah home around four o'clock so you'd better leave now."

"Okay," she said. "But be careful walking Mom back to her room. She's really unstable."

Taking a firm hold on the gait belt, David took Kathy's place and kissed her goodbye. "Watch it out there. The roads are still icy."

"I'll drive five miles an hour all the way home."

He watched her stroll down the long hallway. "And be careful walking," he called out to her. "I don't want you ending up in a room next to mother's."

"Stop worrying," she said. "I'll be fine."

He kept watching her until she turned the corner and disappeared from view.

"David," Zelda said, smiling up at him.

"How's my sweetheart today?" He kissed her on the cheek.

"Tired."

"Well, look how bent over you are. If you straighten up and walk confidently, I bet you'll perk right up."

Zelda straightened her back a little.

"Okay. That's better. Let's go." They began walking together.

"That's it," he said, watching each step she took.

She hunched over again.

"No, mother. You're slouching again. Straighten up."

"Oh, dear," she said.

"Come on. Shoulders back. Boobs out."

She instantly straightened up, displaying perfect posture as she took another step.

"Now repeat after me," David said. "I am strong. I can walk well."

"I am strong. I can walk well." She began taking bold, confident steps. "I am strong. I can walk well."

They walked past one room after another. "Wonderful. You keep walking like this, and we'll have you home in no time flat."

Zelda smiled.

And when David raised his head, he caught a glimpse of Nurse Jennings, standing in the darkness of a resident's room, staring out into the hall as if in a trance. He swallowed hard.

What's she doing lurking around in there?

At six-thirty that evening, Taylor Hanson and Nina Petrovski were watching a brown spider crawl across the pale, sleeping face of an old man.

"It was funny minute ago," Nina said in broken English. "But you need kill it now."

Taylor smiled as the spider moved closer to the old man's mouth.

"Taylor, you need kill it. Kill it now."

Taylor squealed with delight. "Look, it's going right into his mouth!"

"Won't crawl in mouth. Spiders too smart. But could bite him."

The old man let out a loud snore, and the spider slipped off his lip and landed on his chin.

Taylor burst out in laughter.

Seated in a chair next to Zelda's bed, David heard the laughter. He glanced at the open doorway, and then fixed his eyes on his mother. She was sitting straight up in bed, in a cheerful mood; her mind sharper than usual.

"And while those two men were watching me paint that farm scene," she said, "Emile came over to see how I was doing. He started pointing out mistakes I had made."

Distracted by more laughter, David pursed his lips and narrowed his eyes.

Zelda went on. "He was saying things like clouds are not white. The grass there is not green, it's yellow-orange. The barn in the distance is not red. It's blue-violet."

"And then what happened?"

"That's it."

"No, there's more to that story."

"That's all I remember."

"When Mr. Gruppe walked away from you to help another student, what did one of those men say?"

"What men?"

"The two men who were watching you paint."

She laughed. "Oh, yes. I heard one man say to the other—how does a guy who's color-blind get to teach a class on painting?"

David chuckled. He got up from his chair. "Excuse me, mother. I need to close the door."

He peeked out into the hallway, looking for the source of the laughter. It was coming from a room down the hall. He hesitated for a moment, and then closed the door.

The spider circled the elderly man's mouth.

Taylor screeched, excitedly dancing in place.

Nina let out a laugh too, but quickly stifled it. "No. Should not do this. Very bad thing to do."

"I thought you hated this guy."

Nina frowned. "I do not hate him. Why would I hate him?"

"He called you a dirty slut when we were giving him a shower yesterday. And he smacked you right in the face with that wet washrag."

"He did not mean do that."

"Sure he did," Taylor said. "He's an old bastard. Has he ever said a kind word to you?"

Nina pondered the question as she stared at the old man.

The spider crawled into his mouth and disappeared.

Nina squeamishly put her hand up to her lips. "Enjoy your dessert. Old fart."

Taylor cracked up.

Nina smiled, then joined in the laughter. In stitches, they fell into each other's arms.

Zelda turned the page of a photo album and pointed at a picture. "Do you remember this day?"

David smiled at the picture. "Yep."

He was twelve years old then, waving to the camera as he trudged up a steep hill wearing a backpack so large and cumbersome that it looked like a giant insect had landed on him and wouldn't let go.

"That was the day you learned not to take all the painting equipment you own with you out into the field," Zelda said.

He slowly turned the page.

"Look here," he said, tapping on a photo. It was a twenty-year-old picture of Zelda with a blue bandana wrapped around her head. She was looking up at the sky, about to raise a pair of binoculars to her eyes. "I love this picture of you."

"Birdwatching. Oh, how I used to enjoy that."

"Me too. I remember how excited you'd get whenever you spotted a cardinal. Is that still your favorite bird?"

She nodded. "And do you know why?"

"Because of its vibrant red color?"

"No. Because cardinals appear when angels are near."

He smiled and turned the page.

"David, I'm thirsty."

He picked up a plastic water pitcher from the over-bed table and gently shook it. "It's empty. I'll go find someone to fill it."

David wandered down the hallway, looking for someone to help him. There was nobody in sight. He approached a room, glanced inside and saw an aide tending to a female resident. The aide was Nina Petrovski.

"I need take dentures out of mouth," Nina said to the resident.

"No. Leave me alone."

"Must come out before you get in bed."

Nina attempted to remove the dentures. The old woman bared her teeth and pushed her away. "No, I'll bite you!"

David decided not to bother the aide. He walked away.

Nina kept trying to remove the dentures. The old woman snapped at her, nipping her finger.

"Ouch!" Nina cried out.

Fear filled the resident's eyes. "Oh, dear. I'm sorry."

Nina glared at her.

The old woman removed her dentures and held them out to Nina as if they were a peace offering.

Nina grabbed the dentures and marched into the bathroom. She set the false teeth down beside the sink. *So sick of this shit*, she thought as she turned on the tap and waited for the water to warm up.

Noticing a smelly pair of soiled disposable underpants in the wastebasket, she snatched up the dentures, wrapped them in the filthy pants, and dropped the bundle into the wastebasket.

An evil grin filled Nina's face. Feeling a surge of power, she turned and left the bathroom.

Zelda was asleep.

David stared at the TV, but instead of seeing a broadcast station, he was focused on memories he would rather forget.

In his mind's eye, he saw himself inside the Louvre in Paris, France. Walking down one of the spectacular halls, inspecting old master paintings with his friends, Charlie Peters and Andrew Shepard.

What a selfish ass I was.

Now he saw Zelda sitting alone in her living room, drinking tea and gazing at the snow falling outside her big picture window.

Left my mother alone on her sixtieth birthday. To go to Europe. Just couldn't pass up that bargain-priced airline ticket.

The next memory popped into his mind. There he was, surrounded by the gorgeous landscape, instructing students in Rocky Mountain National Park.

That workshop class should've been canceled. It was way too close to Kathy's due date.

He imagined Kathy in her hospital room, alone, waiting. A nurse walked into the room and happily presented Kathy with her baby girl.

Missed that precious moment. What an idiot I was.

Now David was in Venice, Italy. Painting buildings along the Grand Canal at dusk with his two painting buddies.

Chose Venice with my friends over Disney World with my family.

He pictured Kathy giving a female tourist her digital camera. The tourist composed a picture of Kathy, Hannah, and Zelda standing in front of the Cinderella Castle. A click and the moment was captured.

David snapped back to reality. Filled with regret, he looked over at the sweet, peaceful face of his sleeping mother.

Nurse Jennings stood outside a resident's closed door, checking medical information printouts in a large three-ring binder on her medication cart.

Taylor walked up to the door and reached for the doorknob.

"Where are you going?" Jennings shot her a dagger look.

"Going in to turn Melissa."

"I've already done that. No need for you to go in. She's fine."

Taylor backed off and walked away.

When Taylor was out of sight, Jennings rapped twice on the door. She opened it a crack.

"Five more minutes," she said, and then quietly closed the door.

Inside the room, a homely man was grunting as he forced himself deeper into Melissa Delaney, a young woman with a beautiful saint-like face. In a drowsy, drug-induced state, too weak and dazed to fend him off, she lay there quietly, helplessly.

A few moments later, the door to Delaney's room swung open. Nurse Jennings looked up from her cart.

The homely man emerged. He pulled out a gold money clip, peeled off several bills, and tossed them down on the nurse's medication cart.

"Thank you, Doctor Ramsey."

"Doubling the dose of Xanax made a big difference," he said as he briskly walked away.

Nurse Jennings picked up the money.

"Three hundred?!"

"Merry Christmas," he said.

Jennings smiled, stuffed the cash into her pocket, and returned to the printouts in her binder.

An hour later, David was asleep in the chair beside his mother's bed. But as he slept, another resident was about to lose something he had been looking forward to for months.

A discharge from Haven.

The unfortunate man was watching television from his bed. He was slightly agitated.

"Want to see Andy and Barney. Andy and Barney," he said.

Nurse Jennings entered the room.

"Andy and Barney," the old man repeated.

Jennings walked over to the side of his bed, placed one of her arms under the man's legs and the other under his back. She moved his legs over the edge of the bed while pivoting his body, so he ended up sitting on the side of the bed.

"Can you please turn the channel to Andy and Barney?"

"Turn the channel yourself," Jennings said. Then she strolled out of the room.

The elderly man rose from the bed. His bed alarm immediately kicked in, sending out a high-pitched beeping noise. Hands trembling, legs wobbling, he tried to steady himself. Looking like a drunken sailor, he made it halfway to the TV set before he lost his balance and fell. He hit the floor with a loud thud and a crack.

David woke up to the relentless, piercing wail of the bed alarm. Accustomed to the annoying sound, he ignored it. He slipped into his coat and kissed his mother goodnight. As he moved toward the TV set to turn it off, a news topic piqued his interest. He stopped to listen to the newscaster for a few minutes and then left the room.

On his way out of the building, he saw a group of people watching a medical crew carry an injured old man through the lobby on a stretcher. The entrance doors were propped open and he could see the ambulance, its red and blue emergency lights swirling silently.

David moved closer to the group. He stood near two nurses' aides and watched as the man on the stretcher was carried outside to the ambulance. The two aides, Dawn Mitchell and Katie Weber, both stood with their arms folded, concerned looks on their faces.

"I feel so sad," Dawn said. "Hank completed his therapy and was supposed to go home on Monday."

"I know." Tears welled up in Katie's eyes. "He wanted to go home so bad. Now he'll end up right back here."

"Yeah," Dawn said, lowering her voice. "Right where management wants him."

Overhearing the conversation, David's face registered disbelief. Fear-stricken, he quickly moved past the group of people in the lobby, past the paramedics at the rear of the ambulance, and across the dark parking lot to his car. The ambulance's flashing lights added to his dread as he climbed into his Lexus and drove away.

David sat on the edge of the bed, still wearing his coat, staring down in anguish at his hands. Kathy closed the book she had been reading.

"Oh, David. I'm sure it was just an accident. Those aides are over-worked and underpaid. Who could blame them if they despise their superiors?"

"No, I'm convinced. Once Haven admits someone, they intend to keep them until the day they die." Staring into space, he began cracking his knuckles. "All they care about is money."

"Speaking of money, we're never going to get your two Visa cards paid off by paying just the monthly minimum. I need to increase the payments next month. How much should I increase them to?"

"Just keep paying the minimum and forget about it."

"Forget about it? We need to get rid of some of this credit card debt."

"Credit card debt is the least of our worries. We need to conserve our savings. Make it last as long as possible."

Kathy took a deep breath and blew it out in frustration.

"I'm sorry, okay?" David said. "Sorry I maxed out those credit cards with trips to Europe. I thought the paintings I created in France and Italy would bring in enough cash to boost our savings account. And wipe the slate clean on both those cards. It's not my fault the economy went down the tubes."

"Of course it's not your fault—"

Kathy reached out and took his hands. "I'm not blaming you. These are unfortunate times. And not just for us."

He gave her a weak smile, his mind still locked on troublesome thoughts.

CHAPTER 18

K athy strolled into David's studio, twirling her reading glasses. "Guess what?" she said.

By the sound of her voice, David felt she had good news for him. He looked up from his painting and saw the big grin on her face.

"You sold a house?"

"No, I've found a job for you."

He furrowed his eyebrows, a look of dismay spreading across his face. "A job?"

"Yes. One of my clients owns an insurance agency in Camden. It's the one who wants a home overlooking the Penobscot Bay. And she told me she's looking for sales people."

"You want me to give up my art career? To sell insurance?"

"Of course not. But this could be a good opportunity to generate income until your business picks up."

"I'm not going to sell insurance."

He turned back to his painting. He studied it for a moment, and then swept his brush across the canvas, applying a big, bold brushstroke.

She folded her arms and stared at him.

"No way am I going to waste all those weeks sitting in a classroom."

"It's not like real estate," she said. "You're not required to take any courses. Sarah told me all you have to do is study a handbook, take some online practice tests, and pass the exam. Then you can be out selling insurance in no time flat."

He stepped back to study the painting, stroking his face and chin with his right hand. Feeling Kathy's intense gaze on him, he turned and looked her straight in the eye. "I am not going to sell insurance. Not when I'm making great strides with my painting."

She smiled at him.

"Does that mean I'm off the hook?"

"No, it means you've got streaks of red paint all over your face."

"So?"

"So I can't take anything you say seriously when you look like that." She burst out laughing. "It looks like you're wearing war paint."

"Well, there will be a war if you try to force me to sell insurance."

When Kathy stopped laughing, she put an arm around his shoulder. "Okay. If you don't want to, you don't have to. However long it takes, we'll wait for the fine art market to bounce back. Even if it means bankruptcy. Even if it means keeping your mother imprisoned in that hellhole until she loses her will to live."

She kissed him on the cheek and then walked away.

He stood there, his mouth agape.

She's right. But I'll find another way to make money. I'm not selling insurance.

On Friday, November 17, 2009, David was cold calling at his desk in the office of Sarah Morgan's Insurance Agency.

"Hello, is this Edward Canfield? Oh, Hi, Edward. This is David Reid with the, uh, Sarah Morgan Insurance Agency."

David looked down at the cold calling script on his desk, crinkling the piece of paper as he frantically searched for what to say next. "The reason for my call is . . . I have a lunch appointment with a client of mine tomorrow. I saw that your business is only a couple blocks away from the diner. So I'd like to come over and introduce myself to you and buy you a cup of—"

Click.

"Hello?"

The prospect had hung up.

Someone at a personal residence cutting him off was expected. But a business owner hanging up on him was quite a jolt. He set the telephone receiver into its cradle and sat back in his chair to contemplate his next move.

After procrastinating for over a half an hour, David closed the solitaire app on his iPhone and dialed another number from the list in front of him.

"Hello, Mr. Steinberg? This is David Reid from Sarah Morgan Insurance. I know how much the economy is impacting companies like yours. And what I've found is that many employers are paying too much for their employees' health insurance."

David paused to take a breath, hoping the prospect was still on the line.

"If I could show you a way to trim your expenses by up to thirty percent, would you be interested in talking to me?"

He listened intently to the man on the other end of the line. "You wouldn't? Can I ask you why you're not interested in saving money?"

The man told David his business was declining so badly that he was going to lose it soon.

"I'm sorry to hear that," David said. "Hopefully, things will pick up for you soon." He hung up and promptly entered another number on the keypad of his cell phone.

"May I speak to Margaret Blake, please?"

He tapped a pencil against his desk as he waited. "Yes, Margaret?

Hello. This is David from Sarah Morgan Insurance. I'm calling to see if you'd be open to talking to me about—"

Surprised by an interruption, he listened to Margaret's voice. "You don't say. How long has your brother-in-law been in the insurance business?"

"Thirty-seven years? Wow. If I were him, I'd think about retiring and enjoy myself."

She told him her brother-in-law enjoys selling insurance.

He chuckled. "He does? Really?"

How could anyone enjoy doing this grunt work?

She went on about how her brother-in-law and his wife were planning to go on a cruise around the world to celebrate his sixty-fifth birthday. He kept listening to her go on and on until beads of sweat appeared on his forehead. He couldn't get a word in edgewise. Squirming around in his seat, he grew more anxious with each passing moment.

What a waste of time, he thought. *How long do I have to sit here and listen to this?*

After a few minutes, when he felt so nervous he couldn't stand it any longer, he tapped the red end button on his phone.

I hope I don't get into trouble for doing that.

Wait a minute! If she reports me, Sarah might dump Kathy and find another realtor. Oh God, why did I do that?

His heart pounded so fiercely he could hear the rapid, powerful thump in his ears.

Ok. Calm down. Everything will be fine. If she calls right back, I won't answer. If she calls later to ask why I hung up on her, I'll tell her my battery died.

He sat there and stared at his phone, waiting for it to ring. When it remained silent for several minutes, he figured Margaret was probably still talking and didn't even notice the call had ended.

I can't do this. I just can't.

I'll have a heart attack for sure if I go on with this madness.

I'd rather work as a bag boy at Shaw's Supermarket than do this. At least there I could count on a weekly paycheck.

He looked around the office; at the inspirational plaques on the walls, at the empty desks around him, at the calendar on the wall filled with days he was throwing away.

The next afternoon, David's manager handed him a small stack of white index cards. The cards contained the names of potential leads. After cold calling for over an hour, he found a prospect who agreed to meet with him.

"Would you like to get together this afternoon at one o'clock or would three-thirty be better?"

The prospect told him something that made his enthusiasm disappear. He wanted David to come over to his house at 8:30 that night. David frowned. He didn't like the idea of sacrificing an evening with his family for a business call. But he agreed and spent the rest of the day preparing for the appointment.

At 8:30 sharp he arrived at the address the prospect had given him. It was a different address than the one on the index card because the potential client had purchased a new home in August. Smiling with satisfaction, he parked his car alongside the curb and got out.

He admired the big colonial house as he walked up the sidewalk to the front door. He rang the doorbell and waited patiently for someone to answer. No one came to the door. Standing on the welcome mat, he stuffed his hands into the pockets of his black wool topcoat and stamped the snow from his Florsheim shoes. The shiny burgundy shoes were so glossy he could almost see his face in them. He rang the bell again. And waited.

He turned around to view the beautiful houses across the street; a charming cape cod, a rambling brick ranch, and a stylish, weathered saltbox that looked like it was built during the American Revolution.

Snow fell onto his hatless head; his dark hair now covered with white flakes. He turned back around and knocked on the door again. Still, no one answered. He pulled his phone from the pocket inside his overcoat and keyed in the prospect's number. The phone rang and rang. After seven rings, he hung up.

What the hell? He's not home, and he didn't even bother to call me and cancel our appointment.

As he stomped down the sidewalk toward his Lexus, he swore under his breath. One curse word after another.

I am finished with this shit. Finished!

Then he looked up and saw headlights cutting through the darkness. A car was coming his way. He stopped and waited, and to his surprise, the colonial home's garage door began to rattle and squeak as it opened. He smiled, a big grin that revealed his perfect white teeth. The car, a blue Mercedes-Benz CLS sedan, pulled into the drive and glided into the garage.

David strode up the driveway to meet the owner. He waited for the man to lock his car and step out of the garage before closing the distance between them.

"Hello, Mr. Campbell. I'm David Reid. It's a pleasure to meet you."

"Campbell?" the man said.

"Isn't this the Campbell residence?"

"No, it's not."

"But Morris Campbell gave me this address."

"I don't know any Morris Campbell. Are you a salesman?"

David nodded. "Insurance."

"Well," the man said, trying to keep from laughing, "I'm afraid someone sent you on a wild goose chase."

David swallowed hard. "You're not kidding me, are you?"

"I don't have time to play games or jerk people around. Sorry." The man turned and walked back into his garage.

"Do you happen to know of anyone who needs some life insurance?"

"I don't know anyone right now who can afford to buy anything. Other than the necessities of life. Goodbye, sir, and good luck."

David's teeth chattered in the freezing cold. His eyes glistened in the moonlight. He made his way back to his car and climbed into the driver's seat, a flood of curse words pouring from his mouth. He pounded his fists against the steering wheel until he felt a pain shoot across his collarbone. Fearing the pain could be a symptom of a heart attack, he sat back against the cold leather seat, closed his eyes, and calmly inhaled and exhaled.

No more of this. No more.

David stood in the backyard that night, gazing up at the stars.

"Are you just a myth like Santa Claus? If not, show me a sign you're up there." He crossed his arms, looking for a sign, a miracle.

If you do exist, send a shooting star across the sky. Right now. Just one little shooting star.

He waited and waited, but nothing happened.

Looks like I've been right all these years. It's just a myth. There is no God.

His nose was running. He wiped it with the sleeve of his flannel shirt. *Out here with no coat on,* he thought, scolding himself. *Do you want to catch pneumonia?*

David turned and hurried up the steps of the redwood deck. He opened the door to his studio, and as soon as he walked inside a brilliant white star shot across the sky.

Early the next morning David stood in a wheat field, surrounded by patches of melting snow. He was painting a small study of an old barn when he heard a distant bark. Then a howl. And another bark. He looked around, at the woods to the east of the barn and to the west where a small stream flowed, but he didn't see a dog. He turned back to his painting and added a thick stroke of white to the background. The slightly blurred swipe of paint resembled a distant farmhouse.

The barking grew louder, and now he saw the dog, trotting next to its master—a farmer carrying a shotgun. David bit his lower lip and decided to play it cool. He turned his attention back to the plein air painting on his easel.

"Skipper. Heel boy, heel."

David turned to see the dog racing ahead of the farmer. His heart began to pound.

Great. Coming to take a chunk out of me.

"Heel, damn it!" The farmer called out. "Get back here, you stupid moron!"

The American Foxhound stopped in its tracks. Looking back at its owner, it wagged its tail, and then glanced back at David, panting and shaking with excitement. The farmer, his gun held across his chest, caught up with the dog, scolded it, and then ambled up to David with a quiet, obedient dog at his side.

"Hope he didn't scare you," the farmer said.

"Oh, no. I'm all right," David lied, his heart pounding fiercely. He took a deep breath to slow it down and smiled at the old man.

The farmer peeked at the painting. "Nice picture."

"Thank you."

The farmer inspected it in awe. "That white streak there," he said, pointing to the distant background. "That supposed to be my house?"

"Yes."

"You created a house with one stroke of paint?"

David nodded. "Do it all the time."

"Amazing. Absolutely amazing." The farmer studied the painting as David put on the finishing touches. "Would you be interested in selling this to me?"

"Well, when I do small paintings like this for my workshop demonstrations, I usually charge between five hundred to seven hundred dollars."

"Whoa. Really?"

"Yes. But I'll sell this one to you for three hundred and ninety-five dollars."

"Sounds like a good deal. But I don't know if I can work that into my budget." The farmer stood there, still scrutinizing the painting. "Well, mister, what is your name anyhow?"

"David. David Reid." He wiped his paint-covered hand with a rag and extended his hand to the farmer.

"Johnny Johnson."

"Nice to meet you, Mr. Johnson."

"Just call me John." Johnson shook David's hand and after releasing his grip, he reached down and patted his foxhound on the head. "You're welcome to come out and paint on my property anytime you wish."

"Thank you, John. I really appreciate that."

Johnson walked away, through the brown field, his hound at his side, padding along the wet soil and weeds. But before Johnson got five yards away, he turned around and shouted at David.

"Would you take three hundred dollars for that painting?"

David smiled with delight. "Absolutely."

———

"You didn't?" Kathy said with a shocked expression.

"I did." David guided her toward a stool at the kitchen bar and they sat down. "Now before you blow a fuse, let me tell you what happened this morning."

"You quit your job," she said. "I can't believe it."

"Believe it. After what I've gone through, I have nothing but the deepest sympathy for any salesperson that has to go door-to-door to get business."

"How can you say that? I've been very successful canvassing neighborhoods for listings."

"You sell real estate. Not insurance. People love to buy homes. But they hate to spend money on insurance."

Now she was near tears. "What are we going to do for income?"

"Listen, I've stumbled onto something that should generate enough money to pay most of our monthly bills."

Then he told her how he had sold a plein air painting to the farmer. And how the farmer liked the painting of his barn so much that he commissioned him to paint one of his farmhouse.

"You quit your job just because a farmer asked you to paint a picture of his house?"

"Look, I can make more money and make it much faster by doing what I love. By going out early this morning and doing a little painting of a barn, I pulled in three hundred bucks. Tomorrow evening I'll bring in another three hundred for doing a painting of his house."

"Six *hundred* dollars? Our monthly expenses are nearly six *thousand*."

"I can create a plein air painting in two hours. If I do one a day, five days a week, and price them at three hundred, that's six thousand a month. Those big paintings that take days to do and sell for thousands of dollars are just not selling in this crummy economy."

"Is that a fact?" she said, sarcastically.

He sighed. "I can do one plein air piece a day, then spend the rest of the day working on the big paintings. I can't believe I didn't think of this before."

"How are you going to sell a painting a day?"

David thought about it for a moment. And then he cringed at the idea. "By going door-to-door?"

"There you go," she laughed, with a twinge of despair.

"How about by painting homes that you've sold?"

"Ha! Some of my buyers are underwater on their mortgages, and they're blaming me for selling them houses during the bubble."

"You warned most of them, didn't you?"

"I warned all of them. But they didn't believe it. After all, the great maestro—Federal Reserve Chairman Alan Greenspan—said there was no real estate bubble. You think they would believe me over the Fed Chief? Ha!"

"Well, you were right. That guy was just blowing smoke up—"

"So what is your plan? To go door-to-door like a homeless man begging for money? Or to ask gift shops and tourist traps to display your wares?"

"Those are all great ideas." David grew even more excited. "That's exactly what I'm going to do."

That night David headed to Stone Cliff to visit his mother. He brought her a meal from her favorite seafood restaurant and watched as she finished the plate of grilled salmon, asparagus, and white rice.

"Tastes like more," she said happily, sipping the last of her ginger ale and then rattling the half-melted ice cubes around in her empty glass.

"You really want more?"

"No, I'm full, honey." She laughed. "It was just so good I could eat it all day long."

"So do you like my idea of painting houses?"

"Inside or out?"

"Outside. En plein air."

"Plein air?" She roared with laughter. "Oh, I thought you meant painting *the walls* of houses."

CHAPTER 19

Christmas tree lights twinkled in the late afternoon light. Snow gently fell outside the large picture window while Kathy snuggled close to David on the sofa.

"I'm so glad my sellers canceled my open house. I love spending nice quiet Sundays with you."

David smiled at her. "I'll give up Sunday painting sessions if you'll give up Sunday open houses. How does that sound?"

"Impossible." Kathy laughed.

"Nothing's impossible. And when our financial situation improves, I want you to focus on your dream."

"Oh, David, I can't give up my real estate career to write books. I'm not like you. You've got extraordinary talent."

"Then why am I not selling as many of those plein air paintings as I thought I would?"

"The economy sucks, that's why. Most people would love to own one of your paintings, but they simply don't have the money. One day they'll realize they missed out on a great opportunity."

"If I could just get a one-man show at a major art museum." He leaned his head back against the sofa.

"Which museums have you been in contact with?"

"Portland. Boston. Cleveland. The Butler. Philadelphia. Carnegie."

"Maybe you're aiming too high."

"Remember that book you bought me years ago? *The Magic of Big Thinking?*"

She blushed in embarrassment. "Forget what I just said. You're on the right track. You'll get there. And thank God for your idea about doing those plein air paintings. At least now we've got some cash flowing in."

"But not enough to pay all the bills."

"But it's enough to keep our savings account from dropping like a lead balloon."

He smiled at her. "I still think you're a great writer. And you deserve the chance to finish your novel."

Kathy grew quiet as she contemplated the idea.

"If you believe in yourself, you can achieve anything you desire," David said.

"The only thing I desire is . . . you." And with that, she planted a soft kiss on his lips.

David grinned. "But you've already got me," he said as he returned the kiss.

Hannah sauntered into the family room, her shoulders sagging to emphasize her sadness. "I miss Gram. Why can't I go see her?"

"Because of the nursing home's policy," David said, winking at Kathy. "Remember? Only children twelve or older can visit residents at Haven."

"Then when can I see her again?"

"We're hoping to bring Gram home soon."

"When?"

"Very soon."

Hannah climbed onto David's lap. "Daddy, last year you said you would teach me how to paint someday. When is someday ever going to be here?"

"Well, Hannah . . . the way I see it, someday has finally arrived."

"It has?"

"Yes. Tomorrow after school your painting journey will begin."

"Oh, thank you, Daddy!" she said as she hugged him. "Matthew told me he wants to learn how to paint. Could you teach him too?"

"I would love to," David said with a big smile.

David stood before his French easel, glancing back and forth between an abandoned grist mill and a medium-sized linen panel. He painted the snow-covered roof of the mill and its red paddle, the white water cascading over the falls into a stream of clear emerald green water, and the ice that coated the bare branches of the trees surrounding the building.

Hannah and Matthew watched carefully as David applied each brushstroke to the canvas. With their hands stuffed into their coat pockets, they stomped their feet on the snow-crusted ground to keep warm.

David stepped back from his easel and scrutinized the painting. "That's it. I'm done. After dinner, I'll give you two your first lesson."

Hannah smiled at Matthew. The young boy returned the smile, and then looked up at David. "Can I carry the painting, sir?"

"You certainly can."

The evening sky cast a blanket of blue, pink, and violet colors across the winter landscape. They trudged through the snow-packed field. All of a sudden, David stopped. He held his hands out, gesturing for the children to keep quiet. "Don't make a sound," he whispered.

"Why?" Hannah asked. "What's wrong?"

"Look." David pointed to a large moose slowly clopping down a snowmobile trail, its impressive antlers bobbing up and down with each step. "We're too close. We don't want to spook it. It might feel threatened and charge."

The moose came to a halt. It raised its head and looked straight at them.

"It's so beautiful," Hannah said.

"Yeah. And that one is, too." Matthew said, pointing to another moose galloping through the snow toward the first moose. But this one was a youngster. The calf joined its mother and stood close to it for protection.

Disturbed by the intruders, the brawny moose lowered its head and raised its hackles.

"Time to move on," David said. "But don't run. Just follow me, and we'll slowly walk away."

They took a few quiet steps and then David glanced over his shoulder. He saw the moose's ears go back. It was preparing to charge.

"Stop," David said. "Don't turn around. And *do not* look at the moose." He timidly dropped his head and looked down at the ground to appear as non-threatening as possible. When he raised his eyes, he saw that the moose was still staring straight at him.

The angry moose tossed its head upward like a horse and stood on its haunches, its front hooves pawing at the air in front of it. Dropping back down on all four legs, it leapt forward, took a few steps, and then abruptly stopped.

"You're bluffing, buddy," David mumbled, sucking in a deep breath of cold air.

"Daddy." Hannah whimpered, clinging to his side. David reached out to Matthew and the three of them huddled together.

Out of the corner of his eye, David watched the moose. It stared at them. Then it nudged its calf with its nose.

David raised his head to get a better view. He watched as the moose turned and continued its trek up the snowy trail, its calf trotting close behind.

"It's okay now, kids," he said as he straightened up. "Now let's go home, have some burgers, and paint to our heart's content."

Matthew beamed with joy. "Sounds great."

"Yay!" Hannah shouted.

"Shh," Matthew said, giving her a soft punch in the arm. "That moose might come back, pick us up by the crotch, and toss us into a tree."

"You got that right, Matthew." David laughed. "Come on. Let's get out of here."

Wearing a camel-colored wool coat, Kathy entered the family room and found David on the sofa watching television. She bent down and gave him a kiss.

"How did it go?" he asked.

"I got the listing."

"Congratulations! What price did they decide on?"

"Three point seven million."

"Awesome."

"And it's worth every penny," she said, filled with excitement. "Wait until you see the indoor pool."

"That's a huge jump from the price range you've been working in for the last year."

"Yep. The meat and potatoes price range is no fun. Hopefully, the market will turn soon. We could sure use a big commission."

Dressed in her pajamas, Hannah skipped into the family room with her painting. "Look at my picture, Mommy!"

"Why aren't you sleeping?" Kathy asked.

"I couldn't wait to show you my—"

"That canvas is wet along the edges," David said. "Now look at your fingers."

Hannah examined her paint-covered fingertips. "It'll wash off." She raised the painting up so her mom could see it. "Look."

Kathy's eyebrows arched in surprise when she looked at the painting. "Very good job."

"We had so much fun, Mommy. We hiked through the snow to this old mill. Watched Daddy paint it and then—"

"You can tell me all about it in the morning. It's nearly eleven o'clock. Now put this away. Wash your hands. And go back to bed."

"But I haven't told you the most interesting part yet—"

"Hannah. To bed."

"We saw a moose and it—"

"Tomorrow," Kathy said firmly. "You can tell me everything tomorrow."

With a dejected look, Hannah lowered her head and walked away.

———

An hour later, Kathy checked on Hannah. She was pleased to see her daughter had drifted into a peaceful slumber.

So far so good, she thought.

She tiptoed to the bedroom window and looked up at the sky.

Thank you, Lord God. I know you have a hand in this. And I have faith that those terrible thoughts will no longer torment my little girl.

CHAPTER 20

I t was quiet when David entered Haven that night, carrying a small wet canvas carrier. As he walked past the empty nurses' station on the south wing, he had an eerie feeling that everyone had gone. Had abandoned the place. But then he heard the sound of a soft, beautiful voice singing *Away in the Manger*.

He followed the sound to the room where the singing was coming from. Becoming aware of his shoes clicking against the floor as if there were cleats on his heels, he took lighter steps. Walking more softly, he arrived at the room and peeked inside.

Melissa Delaney, confined to a wheelchair, sat in the front of the room, singing into a microphone. Her voice, pouring over the speaker of a Karaoke machine, was as sweet and lovely as she was.

"The stars in the bright sky looked down where He lay, the little Lord Jesus asleep on the hay—"

David spotted his mother. She was watching Melissa along with a few other residents. He quietly entered the room. There was an unoccupied seat next to Edgar. David slid into the chair.

Edgar mouthed the word "Hello" to David.

"Hi," David whispered. Then he turned his attention back to Melissa. In the front row, he could see Kevin Fitzgerald, smiling as he watched Melissa sing. It didn't look like just a friendly smile to David. It looked more like Kevin was love-struck. And no wonder. With long, wavy hair the color of burnt sienna, Melissa had a face that looked like it belonged on the cover of Glamour magazine. And not only was she beautiful, she sang like an angel.

"I love Thee, Lord Jesus, look down from the sky. And stay by my cradle til morning is nigh."

Scattered applause broke out among the residents and their visitors.

Zelda noticed David was in the room and waved joyfully to him. A handsome white-haired resident sitting next to her in a wheelchair tapped her on the arm. She turned to him, pointed at her son, and the man waved at David.

David waved back to the older man. Then he watched Kevin scurry over to Melissa to help her put away the Karaoke equipment. Melissa smiled affectionately at Kevin. She appeared to be as interested in him as he was in her.

David turned to Edgar. "Your brother seems quite smitten by that talented lady."

"Aye. He is at that."

"She's so young. How'd she end up in this place?"

"Auto accident. In here for rehab. Doing pretty well."

"Is she single?" David asked.

"Aye. As is he."

"Looks like love is starting to blossom."

"I hope so," Edgar said. "Kevin has been alone for far too long."

Feeling a hand on his shoulder, David looked up to see Dawn Mitchell smiling down at him. A white quilted parka covered most of her nurse's aide uniform.

"Well, hello stranger," David said.

"David! How are you?"

"Fine. And you?"

"Happy to be on my way home. I'm exhausted."

While David was talking to Dawn, Edgar rose from his chair and walked over to the kitchen doorway. He looked in just in time to see Nina bend over a stainless steel workbench and spit onto a slice of pecan pie. Taylor covered her mouth to contain her laughter.

"Make sure Nadine gets this plate," Nina said.

Taylor stuck her finger into her nose and flicked a booger onto the piece of pie. "That'll spice it up."

Edgar backed away from the entrance. Shocked by what he had just witnessed, he stood there for a moment, trying to figure out what to do. In a daze, he returned to his seat. Settling into his chair, he turned to see his father, Thomas Fitzgerald, sitting lopsided in his wheelchair. The old man was pale, thin, and as helpless as a newborn child.

Edgar noticed that Thomas was shivering. "There, there, Da." He reached over and pulled a plaid fleece blanket up to the old man's quivering chin. "That feel better?"

Thomas did not respond. He just stared straight ahead.

Tears welled up in Edgar's eyes. He wrapped his arm around his father's shoulders and sat there, worrying about the miserable situation his father was in; knowing there was nothing he could do about it. A tear slid down his cheek. Fearing someone would see him crying, he quickly wiped it away.

A little later that night, Kevin was sitting in the lounge with Melissa, watching the movie *It's a Wonderful Life*. A few sleepy residents in robes surrounded them. During a commercial break, Kevin turned and smiled at Melissa. Looking into her eyes felt like catching a glimpse of paradise. She was everything he had ever dreamed of.

"Have you seen this movie before?" she asked.

"Only a dozen times," he laughed. "And I hope to see it a dozen more before I buy the farm."

"You're planning to buy a farm?"

"No," he laughed again. "I meant bite the dust. You know, die."

Melissa grinned. "I knew what you meant. I was just kidding."

Out of the corner of his eye, Kevin saw a flash of blue. He turned his head and saw Katie Weber approaching them.

Katie was dressed in royal blue scrubs, the clothes Haven's aides were required to wear. She smiled at both of them. "I hate to be a party pooper. But it's time for your shower, Melissa."

Kevin walked with Melissa and Katie to the shower room, and then told them goodnight. He hated that the night had to end so soon. But when he left Melissa, he was still on cloud nine.

He strolled down the long corridor, his hands stuffed inside the pockets of his navy blue pea coat. Turning a corner, he headed toward a dark green door that led to the back of the building. He yanked open the door and sailed through the doorway, skipping down the cracked flagstone steps.

At the bottom of the steps, he pulled out a pack of Camels, tapped out a cigarette, and stuck it between his lips. Digging around in his coat pocket, he produced a vintage brass lighter, flicked the tiny metal wheel, and lit the cigarette. He inhaled deeply, watching the tip turn cherry red in the darkness. He stared up at the stars, the sky a clear dark blue.

A shooting star leapt across the sky, and Kevin's heart leapt with it. He smiled, taking it as a sign of something good about to happen between Melissa and him.

He breathed in the cool night air and noticed the sparkling icicles dangling from the roof of the carriage house. Drops of water frozen on the edges of the thin branches above his head popped and cracked as the wind gently tossed them about. He looked straight up and was amazed by how beautiful they were, like crystal droplets on a chandelier. But his face fell when he heard an ominous hoot.

He scanned the treetops; searching the limbs of the red oaks, birches, pines, and sugar maples. Hearing another loud hoot, he turned and saw a pair of huge, piercing yellow eyes with big black pupils staring down at him. Roosting on the low branch of a giant beech, the great horned owl sent a foreboding message with its sinister eyes, daring him to even look in its direction. Startled by the menacing appearance of the owl's face and its powerful talons gripping the branch, Kevin froze.

The owl seemed to be standing in a spotlight as a shaft of moonlight fell upon it. It hooted once more, and then flapped its wings, the wide wingspan sending a chill down Kevin's spine. As it struck its feet against the branch, Kevin backed away, watching the great bird, wondering if it was true that owls are harbingers of doom and death.

Then, in the blink of an eye, the owl sailed right over his head, circled around him, and flew into the woods. A cold chill swept through him. His bare hands shaking, he took one last drag from his cigarette, dropped the butt, and shredded it under the heel of his boot.

It was a quarter after eight that night. With a pair of reading glasses perched on the end of her nose, Zelda inspected a painting that David held up in front of her.

"Hannah did this?" she asked.

David nodded.

"All by herself?"

"I drew the big shapes," he said. "Then she laid in the color."

"You helped her mix the colors?"

"She did it all on her own."

"Can I hold it, please?"

"It's still wet."

David inched the painting closer to his mother. "There. Can you see it better now?"

"Yes," she said. "Oh, I love the ridges in those thick brushstrokes."

At that moment Katie entered the room with two plates of dessert. "Would you two like some pecan pie?"

"None for me, thank you," David said.

Zelda shook her head. "I'll pass too."

"No, mother. You should have some. Got to keep your weight up."

"And it'll keep your stomach from growling in the middle of the night," Katie said.

Zelda peered at Katie over the top of her glasses. "Not tonight, thank you."

"Okay." Katie took a step back.

"Katie, could you come over here, please?" Zelda gestured with her index finger. "I'd like your opinion on this."

Katie walked over to them. David turned the painting toward her, and she studied it.

Zelda eagerly waited, anticipating her reaction.

"The colors are breathtaking," Katie said. "It's beautiful. Who painted it?"

"My granddaughter," Zelda said with great pride. "She's only seven. And it's her first painting."

"Well, it looks like she's inherited your family's artistic talent. Is she planning to follow in your footsteps and become a professional painter, David?"

"To early to tell."

"Well, I think she should," Katie said. "I'll be back to tuck you in a little later, Zelda."

"Thank you, sweetie!" It was obvious that Zelda adored Katie.

Katie handed Edgar Fitzgerald a package of oatmeal raisin cookies.

"Thank you, Katie. Da loves these cookies."

"Well in that case, here you go." Katie gave Edgar another package of the cookies.

Edgar grinned at Katie. "Thanks again."

"You're very welcome. See you later."

"Yep." Edgar smiled at her. "See ya."

As she turned to leave the room, a question popped into Edgar's mind. "Say, Katie, I haven't seen Luke around here lately. Did he quit? Or get put on a different shift?"

"He died."

Edgar was floored. "What? How?"

"In a car crash."

A wave of relief swept over him. "That's awful. Do they know what caused the accident?"

"Luke was drunk. He hit a car with five people in it. Father. Mother. And three children."

"Oh God—no. Did any of them survive?"

"Everyone in that family not only survived, but each one of them walked away without a scratch. Even though their car had been split in half during the impact."

Edgar's eyes widened as he absorbed the incredible news.

Katie stared down at her hands. "Two of the patrolmen on duty said it was the strangest thing they had ever seen."

After David left his mother's room that night, he was thirsty. He headed toward the snack area inside Haven and when he arrived he saw Edgar pulling a package of cheese crackers from one of the vending machines.

"We've got to stop meeting like this," Edgar said.

David laughed. "I know. People will start talking."

"Aye. They'll think we're plotting to bring this place down. And after what I saw today, maybe we should."

"Pardon?" David said with a puzzled look on his face.

"Did you and your ma eat any of that pecan pie they served for dessert tonight?"

"No."

"Good thing you didn't. I saw two aides in the kitchen spitting on the pie and flicking boogers onto it."

David shook his head in despair. "I've got to get my mother out of here."

"Why don't you just take her home?"

"We can't. Not until she gets stronger. Last week she fell while I was walking her. Told me she was too tired to take another step. When we tried to make it to her wheelchair, she got so weak her right leg buckled under her and she collapsed. Luckily, I was holding onto her gait belt and was able to gently lower her to the floor."

"Oh my gosh."

"I had to call the nurses' station for help." David raked his hand through his hair. "I couldn't lift her. I injured my back last year. Fell while painting in the Rocky Mountains. The doctor warned me to never lift anything over thirty-five pounds."

"Couldn't your wife help with the lifting?"

"No. She's had rotator cuff surgery twice on the same shoulder. Lifting could put her at risk for another injury."

"Then why not hire an in-home nurse?"

"Because full-time nurses cost over five thousand dollars a month. No way can we afford that right now."

"Sorry to hear that," Edgar said, sadly. "I guess we're in the same boat. Would like to take Da home but me brother and me both work full-time. We have Da on the waiting lists of two other facilities, but it could be—"

"Weeks before they have an opening," David said. "I know. My mother is on several waiting lists too."

"And the sad par—" Edgar suddenly sneezed. "The sad part is, like I told you before, they're mostly all the same. All of them are bad news."

"Nothing could be as bad as this place."

"I have a friend who lives in California." Edgar sneezed again, and then wiped his nose with the back of his hand. "Sorry. My allergies flare up regardless of the season. Anyway, my friend from Fresno watched two aides put his ma in bed one night. They were in a big rush because a bunch of call lights had all gone off at once. He said they tossed her into bed as if she were a bag of trash. Her head smacked up against the wooden headboard and she cried out in pain."

David grimaced. "It's just one thing after another, isn't it?

Edgar nodded. "And to top it off his ma's on Warfarin. She could've bled to death from that blow to her head. The last time I talked to my friend about nursing homes, he said they're all—" He sneezed again. Angered by the interruption, he exploded. "They're all *fuckers*. That's what he said." Edgar wiped his nose with his handkerchief and watched as David began to pace the floor.

"Somebody's got to take a stand against these nursing homes," David said. "The only way justice will prevail is if somebody takes a stand."

"I agree. And that's exactly what the spirits want too."

"Spirits?" David said with a stunned look on his face.

"Yes, the ones who haunt this place."

David swallowed hard. "Who filled your head with that nonsense?"

"Nobody. I've seen them with my own eyes."

"You're pulling my leg, right?" David said, his voice cracking with emotion.

Edgar was stone-faced. "I am dead serious."

David locked eyes with Edgar. "What do they look like?"

"Like you and me. Only the color has left them."

"How's that?"

"They're black and white and . . ." Edgar gazed into space as he surrendered himself to his memory. "And they shimmer a little bit. Float above the floor. And when they walk they look like they're ice skating in slow motion."

Rendered speechless, David's eyes widened as he studied Edgar's stony face.

Edgar blinked once. Twice. Then snapped back to reality. "You don't believe me, do you?"

David rubbed his hand across his brow as if fending off a headache. "My daughter saw one of them. We thought it was her imagination. Or a hallucination."

"Well, these things are not figments of our imaginations," Edgar said. "Or hallucinations. They're spirits of people who died here. And they want revenge against the people who abused them."

David felt lightheaded. The room began to spin.

CHAPTER 21

The screen of David's laptop displayed an uncluttered white page. In the center, six letters spelled *Google*.

The keys of the laptop clacked softly as his fingertips rapidly typed "Ghost" into the search bar. He tapped the return key, scanned the results, and clicked on "Ghost: Wikipedia-the free encyclopedia."

A page popped up.

Scrolling down the page, he skimmed through one subtopic after another. His fingertips hovered above the silver touchpad as he read:

Descriptions of ghosts vary from wispy, translucent shapes or shadowy figures to realistic, lifelike visions.

Scrolling further down the page, he read:

Most of the Christian Church believes ghosts are beings tied to earth. They teach that ghosts linger in an interim state of full consciousness before making their journey to heaven.

David sat back in his chair, contemplating what he had just read. He closed the lid on his laptop and looked around the studio as if an answer to his dilemma existed somewhere in the room.

But there were no answers, only silence.

That night David strolled into Zelda's room carrying a small black case. Seeing that his mother was asleep, he set the slim case down on the nightstand, slipped off his coat and draped it over the back of a chair.

He padded across the floor, entered the bathroom, and inspected it in the dim light.

He looked into the mirror.

His face stared back at him.

He glanced up at the ceiling, and then stooped to check the floor beneath the sink. He slowly straightened up, using the sink for support, and stood for a moment with his back to the mirror, listening, half-expecting to be visited by the same spirit his daughter encountered.

He rebuked himself for his strange behavior.

If anyone saw me doing this, they'd think I was nuts.

But when he thought about what Edgar had said, he left the bathroom and stepped out into the dreary corridor.

It was empty. Not a soul in sight.

He made his way down the hallway. As he approached a room, he glanced into the darkened area and saw an old man sitting on the edge of his bed, staring blankly at a TV.

Continuing down the hall, he looked to his right, then to his left as he passed one darkened room after another.

He saw light spilling from a resident's room, casting a bright, yellow pattern onto the floor of the corridor. When he reached the doorway, he glanced inside.

An elderly lady, her face buried in her hands, was sitting in an armchair. Every light in her room was blazing.

He listened carefully for sounds of distress. Hearing none, he decided to mind his own business. He proceeded down the hall and turned a corner. Hearing a strange noise, he stopped and listened.

A low-pitched, eerie howling sound appeared to be coming from the far end of the hall.

He walked toward the noise.

Before he reached the end of the hall, he saw a door that led to a stairwell. He opened the door.

The howling noise grew louder.

Entering the stairwell, David looked up. The noise seemed to be coming from the top of the landing. He walked up the steps, the sound gathering strength with each step he took. At the top of the stairwell, he opened the door and entered the second floor. Before him was another dimly lit corridor. This one, too, was empty. No nurses or aides anywhere in sight.

David walked along, glancing into each dark room he passed. Flickering white light emanated from one room, the one where the howling noise was coming from. He hesitated for a moment, and then looked into the room. He saw two old men sitting in front of a television.

The howling peaked.

Then there was a bloodcurdling scream.

Awakened with a start, one of the men nearly fell out of his chair. The other man slapped his leg as he burst out in hysterical laughter. "Didn't see that one coming, did ya? Shouldn't be snoozing while the Wolfman is on the loose."

David resumed his walk down the corridor. He turned a corner and the noise from the horror film dissipated.

It was quiet for a moment, then another noise; a strange, stuttering voice. "Shh—shh—shh—"

David moved toward the room where the sound was coming from. He stood outside the room, listening.

"Shh—shh—"

He peered down the hall, then looked over his shoulder to see if anyone was behind him. Satisfied that nobody was around, he stepped into the room. He inched past an empty bed and moved toward a white curtain that divided the living space.

"Shh—shh—shh—"

He gently pulled back the curtain and saw an old woman sitting in bed, rocking back and forth.

"Shh—shh—SHIT!" she said, spitting out the last word.

David flinched, but the old woman did not even notice him. She simply resumed her chanting.

"Shh—shh—shh—"

He quietly backed away and left the room.

Fluorescent light tubes buzzed and crackled high above his head as he moved toward the end of the hallway. One tube flickered, popped, and darkness spread, adding to the depressing gloom. Maintaining his stride, he arrived at another stairwell, yanked open the door, and walked inside.

When he reached the top of the stairs, he saw a sign posted next to an arched Gothic-style double door.

LEVEL 3 - CLOSED TO PUBLIC
EMPLOYEES ONLY

Leaning his shoulder into one of the heavy doors, he pushed hard, and it creaked open, allowing him access to the third floor.

Now enveloped in complete darkness, David pulled out his smart phone and clicked on the flashlight. Scanning the stone walls with the narrow beam of light, he spotted an old push-button light switch. He pushed the top button and a row of iron sconces on the right-side of the wall lit up.

Slipping the phone into his pocket, he surveyed the scene.

Directly ahead was a stone corridor that looked as if it had not been used for a century. Cobwebs hung from the wrought iron lamps, and dust-covered busts on pedestals lined the passage.

As David walked down the corridor, he saw a black spider scurry across the floor and climb a water-stained column toward the arched ceiling. He passed a suit of armor, its gold and black striping and intricately engraved details coated with dust and grime. He stared at the helmet, trying to imagine the face of a medieval knight lurking behind the visor. In his mind's eye, a man's face appeared, his eyebrows furrowed, his intense eyes filled with hatred. A chill ran up David's spine. He backed away from the daunting figure and walked down the passageway until he came to a doorway with a sign posted next to it.

ENTERTAINMENT HALL
DEDICATED - AUGUST 25, 1897
SAMUEL LYON

David entered the dark hall. Moonlight spilled down from a few square medieval windows near the ceiling. Locating a light switch, he activated it. Three of the five vintage chandeliers came to life. Even though the light was inadequate and subdued, it still made the golden hardwood floor glisten.

He glanced about, taking it all in.

It was an imposing hall with granite block walls and a ceiling that towered thirty feet above his head. He studied the gymnasium floor around him, scuffed in spots but mostly smooth and still glossy. Then he focused on the stage. Dark blue drapes concealed most of the back-stage area.

He walked toward the stage. Then he stopped.

Did those drapes just move?

He shook his head and walked closer to the stage. The curtains moved slightly. He froze, eyes widening with fear.

"Is anyone there?" he said.

He stepped closer to the stage, his eyes glued to the drapes. Then a clatter echoed throughout the enormous hall as something dropped to the floor.

David spun around.

That sounded like a mop. Or a broom handle.

He saw nothing. Unrelenting, he moved toward the stage and climbed the steps. Parting the curtains, he saw a mop lying on the floor, its handle partially obscured by the long, billowy drapes.

He walked around the stage, searching for some sign of life. A mouse scurried past his shoes and vanished. He smiled, left the stage, and went back into the corridor. He noticed warm light emanating from a room down the hall. He strode across the stone floor toward the chamber. He looked inside and saw that it was a sitting room.

Golden light streamed into the room from a row of five arched, double lancet windows. Enticed by a comfortable-looking armchair near one window, he walked in and sat down. On the wall across from him, he saw an intricate three-dimensional framed carving of the Virgin Mary seated on a golden throne. She was staring down at baby Jesus, comfortably resting on her lap.

David studied the incredible piece of art. Then he gazed through the window beside him.

Several old-style street lamps spread their light across the vast space between the street and the grounds that belonged to Haven.

David's gaze turned upward, and he took in the intricate carvings in the dark mahogany ceiling. Scooting down deeper into the comfortable chair, he stretched his legs out and closed his eyes.

A shape behind his chair struggled to manifest itself, vacillating in and out as it tried to break through an invisible portal. A tattered slipper touched the carpeted floor, and the colorless shape of a hunched-over elderly man appeared for a brief instant and then disappeared in a burst of crackling steam.

David heard the hissing noise. He opened his eyes and looked around. He saw a cast-iron radiator enclosure with a dark marble top standing at the far end of the room.

Assuming the hissing steam came from the radiator, he leaned back and glanced out the window.

The view had changed.

Warm sunlight streamed past the golden leaves and thin branches of a huge oak tree. The light penetrated the glass window panes as it spilled into the room. A few neat piles of leaves were spread out across the lush green lawn. A rake was lying beside an empty, straw-colored basket. Perched on the edge of the basket, a bright red cardinal flapped its wings and flew away.

Shocked by the scene, David rubbed his eyes. When he took another look, he saw the original scene.

Street lamps glowing brightly, their light sparkling on the snow-covered ground.

Dazed by the incident, David stared out the window with his hands on his cheeks. Then he got a grip on himself.

For God's sake. I was half-asleep.

He took a deep breath and blew it out.

It was just a dream.

Pushing himself up from the chair, he left the room. As he made his way down the corridor, he realized something that made him stop in his tracks.

A cardinal? Of all the birds. Why a cardinal?

───────

Zelda was sitting up in bed. She flashed David a big smile when he walked into her room.

"Oh, goody!" she said. "Turn on the TV. Let's watch a movie."

David grabbed his black case, unzipped it, and pulled out an iPad. He held it up. "How about this instead?"

Zelda frowned. "No. I don't want that thing."

David turned on the iPad, pulled up a solitaire game and gave the device to her. "Look. It's solitaire. Your favorite game."

"I don't like it anymore."

"It's important to keep your mind active. Come on. I want to watch you play. Okay?"

Zelda nodded, but the frown remained. She looked down at the touchscreen tablet and saw seven playing cards, face up, lined up in a row. Above them was a deck of cards and four empty spaces.

She tapped the deck and a six of hearts appeared. She stared at it in confusion. Then she slid the six of hearts down the screen and placed it on a seven of diamonds. The six of hearts snapped back to its original position at the top of the screen.

David was silent for a moment, stunned that his mother had forgotten how to play her favorite game.

"Mother, that was good. You tried to put a six on top of a seven.

That's very good. However, a red card needs to go on top of a black card. Now try again."

Zelda brought the six of hearts down again and placed it on the seven of clubs.

"Perfect. Now tap on the deck again."

A king popped up. She stared at it.

"There's no available spot for it," he said. "Tap the deck again."

Zelda tapped the deck. A three of spades appeared. She placed it on the four of clubs. The card sailed back to the top of the screen.

"Black on red. Red on black. That's all you need to remember."

"I don't want to play. I don't like this game anymore."

"Come on. Don't give up. I know you can do it."

She tapped the deck again.

"That card doesn't go anywhere. Tap the deck again. And remember—black on red, red on black."

She tapped the deck. A jack of hearts flipped over. She placed the card on top of a ten of spades. The jack snapped back to the top of the screen.

"I'm not playing anymore. Take it away."

"But you—"

"Take it away."

"Mother, you're doing very—"

"Take it away!" she screamed. "Take it away, or I'll throw the damn thing across the room!" She lifted the iPad above her head.

David snatched it away from her. As he picked up the tablet's case, Zelda suddenly went into a wild fit of laughter. He looked up with a jolt.

His mother had turned her attention to the television, to a scene from the Andy Griffith show. Barney Fife, his head in a strange contraption, was hanging inside a closet, calmly reading a newspaper.

David stared at his mother as she laughed like someone who had lost their mind. Then he sadly slid the tablet back into its leather case.

CHAPTER 22

The art school was in Camden, Maine. It was a gray rustic-looking building with long, thin icicles clinging to the roof. A small red fishing trawler skimmed over the water near the school. A sign attached to the building read "Coastal Maine Art Workshops".

In one classroom David was drawing on a green chalkboard; the simple outline of a house with a tree connected to it. "By combining two adjacent shapes into one larger, better shape," he said, "you'll create a more interesting, interlocking pattern." Brushing the white chalk dust from his hands, he turned to his group of students. "One that will look like a puzzle piece. This is a design theory you should incorporate into your paintings."

He watched as students copied the chalkboard drawing and wrote notes next to their sketches just as he had done on the chalkboard.

David cleared his throat. "I want you to know I'm cutting back on my workshops. Instead of meeting on Mondays and Wednesdays, classes will be held on Wednesdays only, twice a month."

There were groans from some of the students.

"I've also canceled all out-of-state workshops for the time being."

A male student spoke up. "So no workshop in Jackson Hole this August?"

"I'm afraid not," David said.

The student lowered his head in disappointment.

A young woman, clearly dismayed, ran her hand through her long, dark hair. "Are you okay, Mr. Reid?"

"Yes, yes, of course. I just need to take some time to be with my family. I've been a workaholic for too many years." And then, with a grin, he said, "Instead of painting roses, it's time for me to stop and smell them."

On the screen of the MacBook Pro was a stunning image of Venice, Italy, at dusk. Deep blue-violet clouds hovered above vibrant pastel-colored buildings along the canal. Gondoliers, wearing straw boater hats and striped shirts, propelled their gondolas through the blue water and the golden reflections from the vintage lamp posts.

With his cell phone pressed against his ear, David drummed his fingers on his desk as he stared at the image on the screen. "I just can't go this time, Andrew. But you and Charlie can."

He swiveled around in his studio chair, putting the dream-like image behind him.

"Yeah. Go. Have fun. Send me a postcard. Hopefully, the three of us can make the trip in a couple years." He paused, listened for a moment, and then laughed. "Venice is not going to be completely submerged by then."

He heard a beep. "Hey, I've got another call. Omigosh, Boston Museum is calling? Gotta go, Andrew! Catch you later."

A half hour later, Kathy was scrolling through property listings on her computer. She clicked on the image of a beautiful luxury home, then looked up as David entered the room. He stood there, arms crossed with a smug grin on his face.

"What's going on?" she asked.

"The door has finally opened."

"What door?"

"The door to the Boston Museum of Fine Arts. Another artist had to cancel an exhibition due to illness and they've selected me to replace him."

Kathy's jaw dropped. "Oh. My. God."

CHAPTER 23

I t was late afternoon, and the pink light was disappearing from the sky. A large U-Haul truck cruised down Interstate 95 in busy traffic, passing high snowbanks alongside the road.

David sipped from a Dunkin' Donuts cup while keeping his other hand on the steering wheel. He glanced down at the wrinkled map in Charlie's lap and smiled.

Why does he have that out? We all know the way.

He looked over at Andrew, who was sleeping, his head resting against the window of the passenger door.

Charlie spotted a green highway sign. "There it is. Exit for ninety-three."

David steered the truck into the exit lane, and they headed for Interstate 93, moving south toward Boston.

"Toss this in that bag, will you?" David handed his empty cup to Charlie.

Charlie took the cup and discarded it.

"Have you and Liz decided about what to do with her mother?" David asked.

Charlie frowned. "Looks like we're going to have to put her in a home."

David shook his head. There was sadness in his eyes.

"Can't be helped. We both have to work full-time. Got no money for in-home care."

They quietly rode down the freeway. Each man plugged into his own thoughts. The truck struck a pothole and bounced, bringing Charlie out of his trance. "Say, what was the name of that high-risk drug they gave your mom?" Charlie asked. "The one that's not approved for elderly people with dementia?"

"Lyzapine," David said.

"So by giving her that drug, they increased her risk for death by stroke . . . and what else?"

"Heart failure. Pneumonia. Diabetes."

"Dang! It's hard to believe the board of health let them get away with that."

"Well, you know, it's common practice among many doctors to give that drug to their elderly patients. So that makes it A-Okay."

"Common practice," Charlie said. "Bullshit. If it were common practice to give elderly patients a thimble-full of Liquid Plumber every night to clean out their digestive track, would your mom's doctor have given her that?"

"More than likely."

They arrived at the Boston Museum of Fine Arts that evening. David turned onto the long circular driveway that led to the front entrance, pulled the truck over to the curb and cut the engine. The three painters emerged from the truck's cab and stared at the majestic neoclassical granite building in awe.

The gargantuan museum, which featured a 500-foot facade of granite and a grand rotunda, stood tall against the dark blue evening sky. A bronze statue of a Sioux chief on horseback, his arms spread wide, perpetually appealing to the great spirits above, stood in front of the museum.

A huge gibbous moon loomed overhead, glowing brightly, fighting for dominance over the impressive structure.

"What a gorgeous sight," Charlie said.

Andrew glanced over at David and found him standing there in sheer mind-numbing awe. "How many times have you been here before, David?"

"More times than I can remember."

"You look like you're just seeing it for the first time."

"I am, Andrew. I am."

Filled with wonder, David wandered through a magnificent hall inside the museum, taking it all in. Charlie and Andrew lagged behind, carefully inspecting the paintings that lined the walls.

When David finished viewing the paintings in that area, he wandered back in search of his friends. He found Charlie studying a huge oil painting by Paolo Veronese, *The Dead Christ Supported by Angels*. Sensing David's presence, Charlie glanced at him. David was surprised to see that his eyes were misty.

"So sad," Charlie said softly. He turned back to the painting and stared as if he were paying his respects at a funeral.

David focused on Christ's face. The closed eyes. The harsh physical reality of death that Veronese captured. Cool light intensified the paleness of Christ's skin and contrasted with the glowing hands of an angel who was clutching his upper arm and wrist.

A fashionably-dressed, sophisticated young woman walked up to David. She touched the sleeve of his jacket. "Mr. Reid?"

"Yes?"

"I'm Allison Lombardi," she said, extending her hand. "Director of the museum."

They shook hands. "It's so nice to meet you," David said. "Thanks again for this wonderful opportunity."

"It's our pleasure to have you here. If you'll come along with me now, I'll take you to the crew of workers who'll help you unload your paintings and hang them in the exhibition hall."

David beamed with joy. He had died and gone to heaven.

The next day was a dream come true for David Reid.

With one arm folded and a hand touching his chin, he strolled past a row of his elegantly-framed oil paintings, carefully inspecting them. The room was crowded with people, whispering among themselves as they scrutinized the paintings.

"Mr. Reid, is this painting still available?" a senior patron asked.

David walked up to the distinguished-looking man who was admiring a painting of a seascape David painted in Rockport Harbor.

"I'm afraid not, sir."

"Which of these paintings are still available?"

"The last one just sold a few moments ago."

The elderly patron raised a hand to his face. "Oh, my—" As his disappointment vanished, he extended his hand to David. "Well, in that case, congratulations are in order."

David grasped the man's hand and patted him on the shoulder. "Thank you so much, Mr.—?"

"Branson. Anthony Branson." The man took another look at the painting beside him and gestured toward it. "Any chance you have more of these beauties in your studio?"

David smiled. "I sure do."

"Splendid." The gentleman was elated. "I have your brochure. I'll be in touch."

"Wonderful. I look forward to hearing from you, Mr. Branson."

As Branson walked away, a hand came down on David's shoulder. David turned to see his mentor, Yuri Zykov.

"Yuri, I'm so glad you could make it."

Zykov gave David a big bear hug. "Hey, buddy. I wouldn't have missed it for the world. I'm very proud of you."

David was delighted. "Well, the only reason I'm standing here now, in this place, is because of your mentoring. I owe you so—"

"Daddy, Daddy!" Hannah raced ahead of Kathy as they made their way through the crowd toward David. David crouched down on his heels to greet Hannah.

She jumped into his arms. "Daddy, you're the best artist in the whole wide world!"

Filled with joy, David embraced his daughter.

***

"This is the swankiest place I've ever been in," Charlie said. "And I've been in some swanky places." He winked at Hannah.

Advertised as Boston's most romantic restaurant, The Top of The Hub was spectacular. And what made it most dramatic was its skyline views of the city, harbor, and the Atlantic Ocean. David was glad he chose the restaurant to celebrate his successful show. Pleased with himself, he peeked over his menu at the elegantly-dressed people that surrounded their table.

"Is that the ocean?" Hannah asked, staring out the window. "Way out there?"

"Yep," Charlie said. "And what do you think of all those skyscrapers?"

It was dusk. The skyscrapers stood like an army of giants, tinged in hues of dark red and gold. Above the reddish-orange horizon, a cloudy, blue-gray sky warned of the possibility of snow.

"Awesome." Hannah smiled, filled with enthusiasm. "They're prettier than our Christmas tree."

"Can you see the ships in the harbor?" Andrew said, leaning in close to her.

Hannah searched for the boats. "You mean those tiny white specks in the water?"

"Yes, honey," Kathy said. "They're covered with snow." She took David's hand in hers and squeezed it.

"Whoa, David," Charlie said as he examined the prices of the meals. "Are you sure you want to treat us to dinner tonight?"

"Quite sure." David smiled. He felt prosperous. A feeling he hadn't felt in a long time.

"I can't let you pay for my meal," Andrew said. "A New York strip steak is forty-eight dollars."

"Nonsense." David laughed. "Every one of my paintings sold. Do you know what that means?"

"You priced them too low?" Charlie said.

Kathy smiled. "David earned enough money today to pay our household expenses for two years—and that includes in-home care for his mother."

"So stop worrying about money." David took a sip of wine. "We're here to celebrate."

Andrew raised his wine glass. "A toast."

"Here, here," Charlie said, lifting his glass. "A toast to one of the greatest American impressionists of this decade."

"I don't know about that," David said. "But I sure do like the sound of it."

They all clinked glasses. And it was a first for Hannah, who laughed with delight as she bumped glasses with everyone.

A moment later, Andrew raised his eyebrows as he watched an elegant woman walk past their table. "Oh, my God. That was Catherine Zeta-Jones."

Charlie craned his neck to get a look at her. "Where? Where?"

David watched the woman sit down at a table not far from where they sat. "Is that Michael Douglas with her?"

"Can't see the man's face. But it better be." Andrew stared at the couple.

"Don't stare," David said, glancing down at his menu. Then he lifted his head and took another look. He blushed when he saw Catherine Zeta-Jones staring straight into his eyes.

"Oh, shit," he whispered. He watched as she scooted back her chair and approached their table. "She's coming over here. To give us hell. Told you guys not to stare at them."

She strolled over to the table and bent down next to David, who was pretending to study his menu.

"Excuse me," she said.

"Yes?" David looked up.

The woman was breathtakingly beautiful. But she was not Catherine Zeta-Jones.

"Are you David Reid, the landscape painter?"

"Yes."

"My husband and I missed seeing you at your exhibition. We arrived late, loved what we saw, and learned your show was a sellout." She held out her hand. "Congratulations."

David took her hand, and they shook. "Thank you."

"We're interested in buying a couple of your oil paintings," she said. "Do you have any others available?"

———

While David was celebrating with friends and family at The Top of the Hub, Zelda was all alone.

"I'm hungry," she cried out from the darkness of her room. "I'm hungry!"

Taylor walked into the room. "Quiet down, will you?"

"I'm hungry," Zelda murmured.

"That's too bad. You had your chance to eat at dinner. But you chose not to."

"I wasn't hungry then."

"Well, your dinner is gone now. Scraped your plate into the trash can."

"May I have a snack? Just two cookies."

"It's nearly ten o'clock. We're done passing out snacks. Go to sleep."

Zelda sank back into her pillow. "I can't wait to get out of this horrible place. Out of here and into my own bed at home."

"This is your home now."

"Now. But not for long."

"Where did you ever get that idea?"

"What idea?"

"Lady, you're dying. And you're never going to leave this place."

Zelda was stunned. "Liar."

Taylor shook her head, a smug look on her face.

"Yes, you're a liar. Wait till I tell my son how badly you've treated me."

Taylor moved closer to Zelda. So close she was inches away from her face. "You say anything bad about me to anyone . . . and I'll kill you. I swear I will."

Zelda frowned. She bit her lower lip, her eyes glistening with tears.

"One word," Taylor said. She raised her index finger. "One. And you'll be a distant memory."

Taylor turned and headed toward the door.

"You're still a liar. I am not dying."

"Yes, you are." Taylor spun around. "You have Alzheimer's. Your brain is dying. You're finished."

Tears flowed from Zelda's eyes. "But my son told me he's planning to take me home soon."

"He's just appeasing you. The doctor will never release you. You'll never leave Haven."

Taylor left the room, closing the door behind her.

"Please open the door," Zelda cried. "Please. It's too dark in here."

Taylor opened the door a crack and peeked in. "It'll be darker in your casket when they close the lid." She pulled the doorknob slowly so the door would creak before shutting.

The door closed.

"No. Please," Zelda whispered. "Help me, Mary. Please help me."

———

After she left Zelda's room, Taylor Hanson walked into the lounge. There was no nurse or aide at the nurses' station, so she plopped down on the sofa. She had a splitting headache. And no wonder. Earlier that night, she made the biggest mistake of her life.

She killed one of the residents at Haven.

What am I going to do when they find out she's dead? If I act nervous, they'll be suspicious.

She was sweating yet her hands were cold and clammy. She shivered.

God, stop acting so nervous! They'll think the woman died in her sleep. At least that's what they'll tell her family.

It all started during lunch that afternoon. Since it was Saturday, she was able to meet her friends for a leisurely lunch of burgers and beer at the Rockland Bar and Grill.

This is all Holton's fault. Why did he have to suggest they play "Truth or Dare"?

"You're next, Taylor," Holton said. "Come on. Tell us. What's the worst thing you ever did?"

"Yeah, Taylor." Amy Sinclair pushed up the sleeves of her red turtleneck sweater. "I dare you."

Taylor shot them a mischievous grin. "Well, let's see. One night I spray-painted cuss words all over the walls and the front door of the First Presbyterian Church. The next day was Sunday. But when I drove past the church during service, I was surprised to see all the graffiti was gone."

"Oh, my God," Holton said, laughing along with Amy and Richard.

"But that wasn't the worst thing." Taylor grinned. "Let me think. Oh, yeah. I emptied a jar of blackberry jam onto the white leather seats of a Jaguar XKE."

Richard and Holton cracked up.

Amy was disgusted. "Taylor, that's terrible. How would you like it if someone did that to your car?"

Taylor was glad that Richard and Holton thought it was a funny thing to do. She wanted to hear more laughter from them. "No, wait a minute. I forgot about this one. When I was fifteen, I got this idea while watching my next door neighbor mow his lawn. Eddie was two years younger than me. Thirteen. Anyway, I told him my idea. He frowned at first. But after I called him a "sissy" he decided to join me."

Taylor took a sip of her beer.

"So what'd you do?" Amy said.

"We buried three cats up to their necks in dirt and then ran over their heads with the lawn mower."

Holton stared at Taylor, his mouth wide open.

Richard shook his head and swiveled around in his chair to face the mirror behind the bar.

Amy glared at her. "You killed those innocent cats?"

Taylor began to sweat.

Oh, no. I went too far.

"That's the meanest thing I've ever heard," Amy said. "You know, Taylor, you are evil. I don't want to ever see—" She got choked up and her nose started to run. "Those poor cats." She shook her head, glowering at Taylor. "Don't ever contact me again. I'm outta here." Amy grabbed her purse, slid off the bar stool, and marched away.

"That is the worst fuckin' thing I've ever heard, Taylor," Holton said as he stood up. He pulled out his wallet and threw some bills onto the bar.

"Yeah, Taylor," Richard said, taking a place next to Holton. "Stay away from me. You need help."

"What?" Tears welled up in Taylor's eyes. "But guys, I was so young then. And stupid. Please . . ."

Richard spun around. "You were fifteen. You knew right from wrong. A prank that can be undone is just a prank. But to kill an innocent animal . . . you need to see a shrink," he said, and then he walked away.

Taylor ran outside, skidding in the gravel as she followed them to their cars.

"Amy, they were just cats. When my dad lived on a farm—when he was a kid—his father used to stuff kittens into a burlap sack and drop them into a lake to get rid of them."

"*Just* cats?" Amy said. "What were you thinking about all the times you held my cat in your arms? Were you thinking you'd like to wring its neck?"

"If you want to talk about killing innocent animals," Taylor said, "what about all the deer hunters?"

All three cars drove away, leaving Taylor standing alone in the center of the lot. She ambled over to her car, a rusty Buick, and climbed in. She sat for a minute, staring into space, and then she broke down in tears.

Fuck you. Fuck you all.

I don't need you.

Strings of snot dripped onto her steering wheel. She smacked the wheel with the heel of her hand so hard that she moaned in pain.

I don't need you.

I don't need anybody.

A light snapped on in the lounge, bringing Taylor back to the present moment.

"What's wrong with you?" Betty stood over Taylor, her balled-up fists resting on her waist.

Sprawled across the couch, Taylor shielded her eyes from the brilliant light and peered up at the sour-faced, dowdy nurse.

Is this bitch for real? Taylor thought.

Wearing those starched white scrubs and that ridiculous 1960s nurse's cap she bought on eBay.

Taylor sat up, both hands pressed against her forehead. "I've got a killer migraine."

"Well, speaking of killers . . . the grim reaper took one of our residents tonight," Betty said, a feigned look of sadness on her face.

"What?" Taylor said. "Who?"

"Shirley Fischer."

Taylor faked a look of horror. "What happened? Heart attack?"

"Most likely," Betty said, "because the look on her face doesn't indicate that she died peacefully in her sleep."

Taylor sat there, her mouth twitching as she fought off a smile.

"Well, don't just sit there," Betty snapped. "I need you to get the body cleaned up. The funeral home's hearse will be here within an hour."

Taylor crossed the threshold into Shirley's room and came to an abrupt halt. The sight of the woman's body on the bed made her heart thump against her ribs like a bird beating its wings against the bars of a cage. The old woman's face was blue. And the room already reeked with the smell of death.

Taylor recalled the last time she entered this room. It was about four hours ago. She had just put the man across the hall to bed, and while she was removing his soiled underwear, he passed gas. She watched in despair as green diarrhea poured out onto the clean bed pad. The stench was so bad she backed away from the bed, clapping a hand over her nose and mouth to keep from puking.

I am so sick of this shit.

As she stood there gaping at the mess on the bed, the incessant moaning coming from Shirley Fischer's room made her anger flare up. She ran out into the corridor.

When will that woman ever stop groaning? I am so sick of her—

"Ahh—ohh, I'm thirsty," Shirley said. "Water. I want a drink of water."

Taylor walked back into the man's room.

"Water, ohh! I need a drink of water!"

Taylor whirled around and bolted into Shirley's room.

"When are you going to give us a break and stop all this fucking moaning?" Taylor said.

"Want a drink of water."

Taylor reached for the glass of thickened water on the bedside table and handed it to Shirley.

The old woman glared at Taylor. "Not that crap. I'm thirsty. I want real water."

"You're not supposed to drink anything unless it's thickened."

"I want real water."

"You'll choke if you drink—"

"I don't care. Give me a glass of water!"

Taylor marched into the bathroom, filled a glass with water, and held it out to the old lady.

Shirley grabbed the glass and took a sip. "Oh, this is so good," she said. She took one more sip and then held out the glass to Taylor.

Taylor stood there, her arms folded across her chest. "That's all you're going to drink?"

"Yes." Shirley extended her arm and jiggled the glass. "Here. I'm through. Take this."

"If it's so good, why not drink some more?"

Shirley frowned. "Take this glass, you evil witch."

That does it, Taylor thought.

Taylor strutted over to the door and glanced up and down the hall-way. Satisfied that nobody was around, she quietly closed the door.

"Take this glas—"

Taylor snatched the glass away from Shirley and pressed it up to her mouth. Pushing her head back, she poured the liquid down the old woman's throat.

Shirley began choking, frantically gasping for air. She pushed the glass away.

Taylor stepped back and watched her.

"Help me," she said, in a raspy voice. Clutching her throat, Shirley wheezed and gagged. She fought for breath, clawing at the air around her, her eyes bulging in fear.

Taylor grinned.

It was the same evil grin she wore the day she seized that pull string, gave it a hard yank, and listened to the push mower roar to life.

I guess this tops running a lawn mower over those cats' heads.

Amy, Richard, and Holton—my fair-weather friends.

You're next.

I'll make you pay for hurting me.

CHAPTER 24

I t was a crisp winter day. Snow covered the ground. Sunshine reflected off the sparkling glass windows of the Reid's log home.

Inside the family room Sven Olsson, a quiet young man who was built like an NFL linebacker, ran his fingertips over a smooth piece of river rock as he inspected the floor-to-ceiling fireplace.

David walked into the room, carrying two cups of steaming coffee. He handed one to Sven. "So what day can you start?"

"As soon as I get back from Cleveland."

"Right after Christmas?"

"Well, my parents would like to have me there for New Year's Eve, too. So how does the second of January sound?"

"Perfect."

"Great. I'll do my best to help you with your mom."

"I have a good feeling about this arrangement." David gestured toward the sofa. "Have a seat."

Sven sat down on the sofa and David took a seat in a chair across from him.

"So what made you decide to become a nurse?"

"My mother was a nurse—"

"*Was?* She passed away?"

"No. She quit her job at the Cleveland Clinic after her father died in a nursing home."

"Why would she do that?"

"She was devastated by all the things that led up to my grandfather's death. He went in for rehab after he broke his leg. And instead of getting better, he rapidly declined. The staff neglected to do things my mother asked them to do. It got so bad it was like Mom had two jobs. One tending to the patients at the hospital. And the other tending to her father."

"Why didn't she move him into a better nursing facility?"

"Because none of them were any better. Her friends told her they experienced the same problems with the other nursing homes in the area. They were all the same. Miserable places. So Mom gave up nursing and formed The Cleveland Advocates for Nursing Home Reform with a group of her friends."

David's eyebrows arched up. "*Really?*"

That night David slept better than he had since his mother's accident. He closed his eyes and slipped into a vivid dream. A dream where he received a call from Haven.

The nurse on duty, a very pleasant one, told him it was time for him to make arrangements to pick up his mother and all of her things. He panicked at first, thinking she had died. But the nurse calmed him down.

"No, no. Your mother is fine. She's up and walking around. And without the aid of her walker. She's talking to everyone. In a very happy mood."

"Is this a joke?"

"No joke. Wait'll you see her. She's fully recovered. Making everyone laugh. It's a miracle."

As soon as he heard the word "miracle" David floated up and out of the dream. He opened his eyes.

A dream.
Why couldn't it be for real?

CHAPTER 25

Lying on her back with her knees flexed and her legs spread apart, Zelda struggled with Nurse Jennings and two aides as Jennings tried to insert a catheter into her.

"Leave me alone!" Zelda screamed. "Get away from me!"

David walked into the room, his arms filled with bags of pretzels, cheese puffs, and potato chips.

"Ooh. She nearly bit me." Taylor cried out.

Jennings glared at Nina. "Hold her down, or this catheter will wind up in her vagina instead of the urethra."

Shocked by what he saw, David stared in disbelief.

"Ouch! That's cold. It hurts. Mama . . ." Zelda sobbed. "I want my mama."

Tears filled David's eyes. He left the room. With his back pressed to the wall in the corridor and bags of his mother's favorite snacks held against his chest, he squeezed his eyes shut.

I can't believe this.

My poor mother.

Crying for her mama.

A few minutes later Nurse Jennings came out of the room and hurried down the long hallway toward the nurses' station.

David trotted after her. "Nurse, what was that procedure you were conducting on my mother?"

She stopped and turned. "We were catheterizing her."

"Why?"

"Because she's been agitated. And agitation is a symptom of a UTI."

"UTI?"

"Urinary tract infection."

"Oh," he said, but he was still confused. "I don't understand why she's so much worse since she broke her hip. I've never heard of a broken bone leading to a change in personality."

"It's her age. When an elderly person breaks their hip, they go downhill. Didn't your mother's surgeon explain that to you?"

"No. He came into the waiting room after surgery. Said mother was doing very well. Showed us an x-ray of the rod and pin he attached to her femur. And then he rushed out of the room."

Nurse Jennings shook her head and smirked. "Like a frightened little mouse."

"Pardon me?"

"Who was your mother's surgeon?"

"Dr. Fontaine."

"Really? He's one of the best surgeons in Maine. I'm surprised he didn't explain the future outlook to you."

"What are you talking about?"

"Well, Mr. Reid, most people your mother's age usually pass within six months after a hip fracture."

David's eyes widened. His mind began to race.

"And that's why Dr. Fontaine got the hell out of that room as fast as he could."

He felt faint.

We're going to lose Mother? In six months or less?

"Any more questions?" Jennings said, boldly crossing her arms over her chest.

In an unresponsive stupor, David just stood there.

"I didn't think so." Nurse Jennings turned and walked away.

At ten-thirty that night, Zelda was sound asleep. David sat in the chair next to her bed, arms folded, legs stretched out. He was deep in thought, his expression a mixture of anger and sadness.

Nurse Jennings sauntered into the room. "Need to give your mother a pill."

David nodded his head and sat up in the chair. He watched as Jennings shook Zelda's shoulder. Zelda stirred, and her eyelids fluttered open. "What?"

"Time for your pill," Jennings said.

Zelda began to whine. "No. Let me sleep."

"Come on, Miss Zelda. The sooner you take your medication, the sooner you can go back to sleep."

Jennings pressed a button. The motorized bed hummed as the head of the mattress rose, bringing Zelda up to a full ninety degree sitting position. The nurse popped a pill into Zelda's mouth, put a cup of water up to her lips, and watched as she drank. Satisfied that she had swallowed the pill, Jennings turned to David.

"Your mother needs to remain in a fully erect sitting position for at least thirty minutes. Were you planning on staying here for a little while longer?"

"I can if you need me to."

"I would appreciate that. We're short of help tonight." And with that, Jennings strode confidently toward the door.

"By the way, what kind of pill did you just give her?"

"A sleeping pill," Jennings said as she disappeared from view.

David put a hand up to his forehead.

Madness. It's sheer madness.

Nurse Jennings passed one of the shower rooms and a linen closet on her way down the corridor, and then she entered another resident's room. Inside the somber, unpleasant room, she grabbed the handle on a plastic pitcher and poured water into a glass. Moving over to the bed, she shook the arm of an old man until he opened his eyes.

"What is it?" The old man scowled at Jennings.

"It's your Ativan." She held the pill in front of his mouth.

He turned his head. "No. Take it away!"

"You've got to take this pill."

"Stick it up your ass!" he shouted.

"Okay." She said, giving up without a fight.

On the way out of his room, she popped the pill into her mouth and swallowed it. Pleased with herself for duping the man out of his medication, she began to sing "The Caissons Go Rolling Along".

Over hill, over dale. As we hit the dusty trail . . .

Thirty minutes later, Zelda was snoring softly.

David lowered the head of her mattress to a thirty-five degree angle and slipped into his leather bomber jacket.

On his way out of the room, he passed by the bathroom. He turned around and entered it. He raised the toilet seat, dragged down his zipper, and listened as his urine splashed into the toilet bowl.

When he finished relieving himself, he zipped up, turned around, and came face-to-face with—*a ghost; the wavering, shimmering, colorless face of a sad old man.*

Scared out of his wits, David gasped for air as he stared at the ghostly shape before him.

This was the spirit of Fabian. Tears streamed down his wrinkled, craggy cheeks. "Help me," he said with a weak voice.

David swiftly moved to his right in an attempt to squeeze past Fabian, but the ghost blocked his move. David moved to his left. Again he was blocked by Fabian.

"You know you could walk right through me if you wish."

David's teeth were chattering. "Who—who are you? What do you want?"

"Don't you recognize me, David?"

David gazed into Fabian's eyes, and then shook his head. His whole body was quivering with fear.

"I'm Fabian Macchiavelli. I attended one of your painting workshops. In the Rocky Mountains. I saw you fall. You hurt your back."

"Fabian . . . the hound dog man?"

"Yes, yes—that's what you called me during the entire workshop."

The trembling didn't stop. David had difficulty getting the words out. "What happened . . . to you?"

"I died. Last year. In this horrible place."

David was about to keel over. "Can you please step aside? Give me some room to breathe? Please. My heart is pounding so hard."

Fabian backed away in one smooth, fluid motion as if on roller skates.

Like a drowning man, David gulped in air as he stepped out of the bathroom. He put his hands over his face for a moment and then dropped his arms. He turned and saw Fabian, hovering a couple of inches above the floor.

Beads of sweat dripped from David's forehead as he stared at the frightening figure before him.

"Please help me, David. Help me escape from this ghastly place."

"I can't possibly help you—"

"Yes, you can," Fabian said, his voice cracked, and a sob escaped from his throat.

"How? How can I help . . . you?"

"Agree to help lead us out of this place."

David placed a trembling hand over his heart. He gasped for air, swayed, and looked as if he were going to pass out.

"I suffered unspeakable horrors in this place when I was alive." Fabian burst into tears. "The staff here is cruel—so cruel and evil. I don't understand why I'm still here. What did I do to deserve this?"

"I'm sorry."

"I want to move on," Fabian lowered his head as he wept. "I want to go home, to the Kingdom of God, so I can join my mom and dad . . .

and my sisters. All of my family and friends who left this earth before me."

David jammed his sweaty palms into his armpits. He took a step back to put more space between them. "I wish I could help you. But I can't."

"Yes, you can."

"No, I can't."

Fabian's gray face turned brilliant red with anger. Steam hissed as it rose from his ears.

David expected his heart to fail at any moment. "Please leave me alone. I can't help you—"

Fabian blew his top. "YES, YOU CAN!"

David shrank back in horror, shielding his head with his arm. "I don't know what to do—I don't know what to do!"

Fabian relaxed, and the color vanished from his face. "You and two other people have been chosen to help lead us out of this dreadful place."

"Chosen? Chosen by who?"

"Our leader, Professor Graber."

David trembled so badly he nearly lost his balance. He grabbed the door jamb for support "I can't—" And then he ducked out of the room and quickly headed down the dreary corridor.

Fabian floated out into the hallway. "You can walk away from me. But you won't be able to walk away from Professor Graber."

David's pace picked up until he was running. He raced out of the building and stood in the cold night air with his hands on his knees, gasping for breath. He looked in every direction, seeking a way out of this nightmare. Suddenly alarmed by a thought, he gritted his teeth and darted back into the facility.

He sprinted down the corridor and bolted into his mother's room. Abruptly stopping, he looked around.

Fabian was gone.

Everything was fine.

He took a deep breath and quietly moved toward his mother's bed. He looked down to see Zelda, sleeping soundly.

Relieved, he managed to crack a smile.

Stirring in her sleep, Zelda peeked up at him. "There's my sweetheart," she said, the corners of her mouth turning up in a smile. "I love you, David. I'll love you forever and ever and ever."

Then she closed her eyes.

David kissed her cheek. "I love you too, Mother. Forever and ever."

CHAPTER 26

It was a bleak, foggy afternoon at Rockport Harbor. Everything was gray. The sky. The snow-covered ground. The boats.

Throngs of people bustled about in a flurry of activity.

With his hands stuffed into the pockets of his black trench coat, David searched the lobster wharf, scanning the faces of the workers. He spotted the person he was looking for. Dressed in orange clipper bibs, Edgar looked up from handling a large lobster. "Hey there, what're you—"

"I saw one," David said.

Edgar's expression turned solemn as he realized what David meant.

Minutes later the two men were seated at a table in a seaside restaurant.

Edgar downed a swig of beer. He watched David take a sip of gin and tonic, a slice of lime swirling around with the tiny bubbles and ice cubes inside his glass.

"Do you know of any other Haven visitors who've seen one of these—these spirits?" David asked.

"No. No one."

"Then why were we able to come in contact with them?"

"Because they chose us."

"But why us?"

Edgar shrugged. "I don't know. But I do know this much—there's a reason behind everything that happens on this earth."

David stared at Edgar, considering what he had just said.

Edgar took another big gulp of beer, and then wiped his mouth with the back of his hand. "So will you join me and me brother?"

"Following your plan will land us all in jail."

"You will not end up in jail."

"Oh, really? How can I possibly avoid that?"

"By having faith. By trusting that everything will work out for the best."

David laughed and shook his head. "You want me to get involved with abducting people? No way. We'll all end up in prison."

"We're just going to lock the staff in a room, call the press, and tell them why we did it so we can shed some light on this situation. Make the public wake up."

"No way."

Edgar stared at David. "Somebody needs to take a stand. That's what you told me, David. And you were right. Nothing will change unless someone takes a stand. And we're the ones who need to do it."

"But not like this. There has to be another way."

"There is no other way. You know it. And I know it."

David stared down at his glass, and then locked eyes with Edgar. "Let me think this through. I'll get back to you in a couple of days."

"Don't take too long. The natives are restless." Edgar scooted back his chair, tossed a handful of bills onto the table, and walked away.

At the entrance to Macy's in the Bangor Mall, Santa Claus stood next to The Salvation Army's red kettle, ringing a brass bell. As David, Kathy, and Hannah approached the jolly old man, he stopped ringing the bell, winked at Hannah, and began singing "Jingle Bells".

Hannah yanked on David's sleeve. He pulled out a big handful of change and dropped it into her palms. She smiled at Santa as she tossed the coins into the kettle.

"Ho, Ho, Ho—and a Merry Christmas to you!" Santa chuckled, his red cheeks glowing. He continued singing where he had left off.

The Reid family walked past LensCrafters, Victoria's Secret, and The Children's Place before coming to the Sleep Number Store.

David steered them into the store.

"Why are we going in here?" Hannah asked. "We've got enough beds."

"We're looking for an adjustable bed for Gram," David said. "To make it easier to get her in and out of bed."

"Gram's coming home?" Hannah shouted with delight. "When?"

"Very soon," David said.

A salesman showed them two twin-sized automatic beds, but before he could demonstrate the benefits of his third selection, Hannah started pulling on her mother's hand.

"Mommy, let's go look at the beds for kids."

Kathy excused herself and allowed Hannah to lead her across the store.

"Sorry about that," David said.

"No need to apologize." The salesman pushed a button on a remote control and the head of the mattress began to rise. "I've got three kids of my own."

After the salesman had shown him how to operate the bed, David made his decision. He selected the best twin-sized adjustable bed in the store. When the salesman left to get a purchase form, David walked around the bed, continuing to scrutinize it. He pulled a mint out of his pocket, unwrapped it, and slipped it into his mouth. Then he strolled over to check out another bed.

Seconds later the sound of squeaky old springs startled David. He turned and saw a ghost in a reclining position with his hands behind his head, floating a few inches above the bed that David had chosen.

"Hmm. Good choice, David. This is very comfortable." The ghost winked and then disappeared.

"Daddy, did you see that?"

David spun around. When he saw Hannah, his face registered alarm.

Oh my gosh! Did she see that ghost?

"See what?" he asked.

"That little elf who just walked by us."

David turned to see a dwarf, dressed as an elf in green attire, trying to talk to a timid little boy who fearfully clung to his mother's arm.

David put his hand over his heart. It was thumping like a sledgehammer.

Was that Fabian?

If so, how could he be here in Bangor? If he can't escape from Haven, how could he appear anywhere else?

Then he smiled as he reassured himself.

Because there was no ghost, David.

It was a delusion.

Up your dose of Paxil. At least until your mother gets out of that hellhole.

CHAPTER 27

Kevin Fitzgerald watched as Dawn Mitchell wheeled his father out of the bathroom. Thomas's hair, still slightly wet, was combed back neatly and his face looked fresh and clean, but Kevin was bothered by the raggy pajamas his da was wearing.

"He looks so nice and refreshed," Kevin said, "but those pajamas belong in the trash."

"Want me to change him into another pair?" Dawn asked.

"Yes, please. I'll grab one of his nightshirts," he said as he walked over to his father's dresser, opened the top drawer, and looked inside. "Is this all he has left?" He pulled a tattered, gray nightshirt from the drawer and held it up in front of him.

Dawn was surprised. "Nothing else in the drawer?"

"This is it."

"How many did he originally have?"

"I believe he had four nightshirts. And two pairs of pajamas."

"Maybe laundry has them."

"Five of them all at once? Aren't clothes washed here every day?"

Dawn took a deep breath and then blew it out. "Sometimes things go missing."

"Yeah, so we've noticed. Clothing, candy, cans of Pepsi Cola—"

"I can go get him one of the facility's nightgowns."

"You mean one with the opening in the back?"

She nodded.

"Where his bare butt will stick out?"

"Lots of the residents wear them."

"Well, not my da."

"No one will see his butt," she laughed. "I promise."

"No. My da's not a pauper. He deserves the best. And that's what he's going to get." Kevin walked over to his father, bent down, and looked into his eyes. He noticed the pale blue color seemed to be fading more every day and the cloudy white ring around the iris was getting more pronounced. "Da, I'm going to run out to the store and pick you up some new pajamas. Would you like that?"

Thomas squeezed out a smile. "Yeah." Tears twinkled in the old man's eyes.

An hour later Kevin was browsing through the men's pajamas at Harbor's Department store in Rockland. Finding a pair he liked, he carefully pulled the pajama top out of its transparent plastic bag, inspected it, and then ran his hand over the soft flannel.

Red and black plaid. The same color and pattern as his favorite shirt. He'll love this.

With a smile on his face, Kevin made his way toward the registers at the front of the huge store. He stood in line, patiently looking out the big, wide windows as cars cruised through the parking lot, their headlights cutting through the darkness.

When I get paid on Friday, I'll come back and buy Da two more pairs of pajamas and a couple of nightshirts.

Now it was his turn. Kevin stepped forward and gave the pajamas to the cashier, a gangly, pale-faced young man wearing black horn-rimmed glasses. The clerk passed the plastic-wrapped package over the barcode scanner and rang up the sale.

"That'll be thirty-one dollars and sixty cents," he said.

Kevin pulled a twenty dollar bill from his wallet and handed it to the cashier. Then he counted out nine ones. Surprised to see that was the last of his bills, he stuffed his hand into the pocket of his jeans. He wiggled his fingers, and loose change jangled. "Hold on," he said, smiling at the cashier. "I've got lots of change in here."

The cashier did not smile back. He straightened his glasses, his fingers touching the dirty, white adhesive tape that held one temple to the frame.

Kevin pulled out a handful of coins and poked them around in his palm. He placed three shiny quarters on the counter next to the glass scanner, and then added four dimes, two nickels, and three pennies.

The cashier plucked up the coins and counted them. "You still need a dollar thirty-two."

"I know," Kevin said as he searched his coat pockets for change. He found another quarter and gave it to the cashier. Digging deeper into both coat pockets, he searched for more money.

"You need one dollar and seven cents more." The cashier impatiently shifted his weight onto one foot and glanced at the line of customers waiting behind Kevin.

Kevin shrugged his shoulders. "That's all I have."

The cashier frowned. "Well, you'll have to come back when you have enough to pay for this."

"Would it be possible for you to lend me the money?"

The cashier shook his head.

"I'll pay you back tomorrow."

"Against store policy."

"I'll pay you double the amount tomorrow," Kevin said, panic setting in as a female voice announced that the store would close in five minutes.

"I won't be here tomorrow. And what you're asking me to do is outrageous."

"You don't understand. I need these pajamas tonight. My da's in a nursing home and I promised I'd be back tonight with a new pair of—"

"Please step aside," the cashier said, "so I can take care of the man behind you." His black brows furrowed into one straight line above his nose as he straightened his glasses again.

"Kevin glanced over his shoulder at the short, stocky man standing behind him.

The man glared at Kevin.

"Sir, could you please lend me a dollar and seven cents?"

"Are you kidding?" The man chortled. "What do I look like? Santa Claus?"

"Mister, please do not bother the other customers," the cashier said to Kevin.

A lady behind the stocky man waved a dollar bill above her head. "Here, son. I'll help you out."

Kevin's eyes lit up. He tried to move back to the lady, but the stocky man blocked his path. The man scowled at the woman. "You crazy? Encouraging this kind of behavior? The guy's a bum."

Now confused, the lady let her hand drop to her side. She timidly took a step back.

"Mister, you need to leave this store now." The cashier glowered at Kevin. "Do you understand me?"

Desperate, Kevin removed his driver's license from his wallet and handed it to the cashier. "Here, take my license as security for the debt. I'll come back in tomorrow morning and leave six dollars and seven cents with your customer service department. They can give the money to you on your next shift. That's a five dollar profit for helping me."

"Hey, what's the holdup?" A man in the back of the line called out.

The cashier gave the license back to Kevin. "No way."

"Why not?" Kevin pleaded.

"Step out of the line," the cashier said.

"But, I told you—"

"Step out of this line so I can wait on the next customer."

"You don't understand—"

"Get out!" The cashier said as he whipped out his cellphone. "Or I'll call the police and have you arrested."

"Arrested?" Kevin said, rubbing his forehead. "For what?" Then he threw his hands up in the air and stomped out of the store.

Once outside Harbor's, he smacked his fist into the palm of his left hand. He stood there for a moment as rage built up inside him. He looked back inside the store and watched the lanky cashier fold a pair of slacks and slide them into a bag. Then he turned away from the big window and jogged through the parking lot toward his car.

Inside the car, he gripped the steering wheel so tight his knuckles turned white. He lowered his head as if to cry.

This is such a screwed-up world. Why are people so damn mean?

He tried to contain his anger but he couldn't. He turned on the ignition, shifted into gear, and with one foot on the brake, slammed into the accelerator. The tires squealed as they searched for traction. The Camaro peeled out, its rear end swaying back and forth, the entire car spinning around like it was on solid ice. In a plume of gray smoke, the car sped out of the parking lot.

Kevin returned to his father's room empty-handed.

"Sorry, Da. I didn't have—" He cleared his throat. "I didn't find anything good enough. But I'll get you some real nice PJ's tomorrow."

"Thanks, son," his dad said, his weak, gravelly voice filled with love. Thomas reached out for Kevin's hand.

Kevin took his dad's hand in his, biting his lip to fend off tears.

CHAPTER 28

It was a gloomy, depressing day. Haven looked darker and more sinister than ever. Like a prison in a cold wasteland, its chimneys belched black smoke into the gray sky.

Edgar walked down a hallway in the south wing, a pastry box tucked under his arm. He took a bite of a powdered donut, and when he came to his father's room, he straightened the crooked name card in the slot next to the door. Finishing off the donut, he licked the sweet white powder from his fingertips, and strolled into the room.

He stopped in his tracks when he saw a young nurse jabbing a needle into his father's abdomen.

"What are you doing?" he said.

The nurse pushed the plunger all the way in, and then pulled the needle out. She turned to Edgar. "Just giving your father his insulin."

"Insulin? My da doesn't have diabetes."

Fear crept into the young nurse's face. "He doesn't?" She quickly scanned the chart in her hands. "This is room one hundred and three, isn't it?"

"No, it's one hundred and eight."

"Oh, my—" The nurse spun around, and rushed out of the room.

"Where are you going?" Edgar called out. "Will that stuff make him sick?"

Twenty minutes later, Kevin was walking down the hallway in the south wing of Haven.

Edgar was asleep when I got home last night. And gone when I woke up. But now I can get the money I need from him. Then I'll go get those pajamas.

He paused when he saw a group of nurses' aides gathered around the entrance to his father's room. He sprinted toward them. "What's going on?"

Taylor turned to him. "Your dad thinks there's a crocodile underneath his bed."

"What?"

"He's been screaming and yelling," Taylor said. "Having all kinds of hallucinations."

Kevin pushed past the aides and went into his father's room. Joining Edgar at the side of the bed, he looked down and saw his father squirming around in pain, sweat dripping from his flushed red face.

Kevin glanced at his brother. Edgar's brows were drawn together and his teeth were digging into his lower lip.

"Get me out of this phone booth!" Thomas screamed. Raging like a lunatic, he kicked off his bedcovers. "Get me out of here!"

Kevin stared in disbelief. "What's wrong with—?"

"Stupid nurse gave him a shot of insulin by mistake," Edgar said.

Thomas was panting, trying to suck in some air. "I'm so hot. Turn off the heat. Turn it off," he screamed. "Get me out of this phone booth—I'll smash this fucking glass wall to pieces!" Thomas frantically kicked at an imaginary wall and then screamed even louder. "Out—out! I want out of here. God, get me out."

Kevin turned to Edgar and saw a tear roll down his cheek.

"Bloody hell. I'll kill somebody if he doesn't snap out of this," Kevin said, tears welling up in his eyes.

"Ambulance should've been here by now," Edgar said. "What'd they do? Stop off for a cup of coffee?"

Kevin left the room to confront the group of aides in the hall. "Where's that damn ambulance?"

Dawn glanced at Kevin. Her eyes were wet. "It'll be here any minute."

"Yeah. Just calm down," Taylor said.

Kevin glared at Taylor. If looks could kill, this one would do her in. "Shut your yap, you rotten bitch."

Kevin returned to his father's bedside. "Jennings did this on purpose. She's getting back at us for the complaints we filed against this place a few months ago."

"It wasn't Jennings," Edgar said. "It was that new nurse."

"Then it was a set-up. Jennings is behind this. You can bet your ass she is."

Now Thomas was panting wildly, like an animal. Suddenly his entire body stiffened, and his arms and legs jerked spasmodically.

Consumed by his emotions, Kevin clapped his hand over his nose and mouth to trap his sobs. He glanced at Edgar who stared helplessly at his father.

Forty-five minutes later, David drove into Haven's parking lot and saw Edgar and Kevin standing beside an ambulance. He parked his car, flung open the door, and ran toward the ambulance.

Edgar and Kevin stared silently as the paramedics pushed a stretcher containing a shrouded body into the back of the vehicle.

Seeing the despair on their faces, David cautiously approached the Fitzgerald brothers.

"What's happened?" David asked.

"Our da is dead," Edgar said, staring blankly.

David lowered his head in sadness. "I'm so sorry, Edgar."

"The bastards killed him," Kevin said, wiping his nose on his shirt sleeve. "And they're gonna pay for this!"

Kevin followed Edgar home, tears streaming down his face, his Camaro right behind Edgar's pickup truck the entire way.

Da can't be dead. He just can't be.

Dear Lord, I wanted him to come back home and live with us.

The pickup truck turned into the gravel driveway of their rural home in Rockland. Kevin parked his car off to the side of the house and cut the engine. He watched Edgar climb the steps of the side porch and unlock the door. Stepping inside the kitchen, he stood there, waiting for Kevin to get out of the car.

Kevin rolled down his window and shouted. "I'm going for a ride. Be back soon."

Edgar said nothing. He waved to his brother and closed the door.

Kevin twisted the ignition key forward, and the Camaro's engine roared to life. He backed the car out of the driveway and slowly drove away.

A few moments later, while traveling down Maverick Street in Rockland, he found himself in a trance-like state. Blinking his eyes, he looked around. He felt lost, like he had no idea how he had arrived at his current location. Feeling drowsy, he wound down his window and took a deep breath of fresh air. Cold, misty rain sprayed against his face, and it felt good. Leaving the window half-way open, he continued down the street until he caught sight of the sign.

The sign that read "Harbor's Department Store".

Kevin slammed on the brakes. He sat there, staring up at the sign. A horn honked behind him. He lifted his shoe from the brake, hit the gas, and turned into Harbor's parking lot. Seeing a space near the front entrance, he guided his car into it and parked.

He was in a daze when he entered Harbor's. Traumatized by the death of his father, he wandered up and down the aisles like a zombie. He passed by the greeting cards, the toy department, sporting goods, and electronics before he found what he was looking for—the men's department. He walked down the aisle toward the pajamas and robes.

Digging through a neatly displayed stack of men's pajamas, he found the pair he tried to buy the night before. He slid the package out from under several other sealed bags and stared down at the red-and-black plaid pajamas. Then he began to weep.

Bastards, he thought as he sobbed.

A saleswoman confronted him. "Do you need any help, sir?"

Startled, he glared at her. "I needed help last night, but no one would help me," he said, wiping away his tears.

"Is there anything I can do?"

He tore open the package, slowly but savagely, as if beginning a ritual he wanted to relish. "Yes. You can get the fuck away from me," he said, a steely shine in his bloodshot eyes.

He yanked the pajamas out of the bag and let the torn plastic-wrap slip from his fingers and fall to the floor. He held the flannel top in front of his eyes and stared at it for a second, then ripped off a button and dropped it. The black button bounced a couple of times on the cream-colored vinyl floor, whirled around like a top, and finally came to rest.

"What do you think you're doing?"

Kevin glanced over and saw the saleswoman watching him in wide-eyed disbelief. "Why are you still here?" he asked as he seized another button and tore it off.

"You're going to have to pay for that."

He turned the pajama top upside down and ripped it in half. "Go mind your own fuckin' business," he shouted.

The saleswoman made a hasty retreat.

He watched her go, then walked up to a round clothing rack. He pulled a hanger from the chrome bar. Removing a blue button-down shirt from the hanger, he stood there like a sleepwalker, staring at it in a daze. And then he tore the shirt in half.

"Mommy, why's that man ripping up that shirt?" a little boy said, clutching onto a young woman's hand.

The woman slowed her pace and took in the sight of Kevin tearing the shirt into ragged strips. Without a word, she briskly walked away, her son in tow, his head turned, straining over his shoulder to get another look at the crazy man.

"I'm hurting like hell, too," Edgar said. "But still, Kevin, how could you do such a thing?"

"Because, now that da's dead, I don't care about anything anymore."

They pushed open the doors of the police station and walked outside into the damp night air.

"You're just lucky the store manager was sympathetic and only made you pay for the merchandise you destroyed," Edgar said as he trudged down the wet concrete steps. "You could have been sent to prison."

Kevin slid a cigarette between his lips and lit it. "Like I said, I don't care about anything anymore." He snapped the lid shut on the lighter, and they walked in silence toward Edgar's pickup truck.

The next night, Edgar was slouched down in an armchair in Haven's lobby with his fingers steepled, staring up at the ceiling. The sound of footsteps on the marble floor made him sit up straight. He glanced over his shoulder and saw David walking across the lobby, looking down at his cell phone.

Edgar pushed himself up out of the chair. "David."

The two men met in the center of the room.

"The time has come for us to make a stand," Edgar said. "Have you decided to join us?"

"I'm sorry, Edgar. I—I just can't."

"You want to see things change, don't you?"

"Of course I do."

"Then help us."

"I can't. Things are just starting to turn around for me. And I'm not going to jeopardize my family's future by taking the law into my own hands."

"It could have been your mother who got that fatal dose of insulin,"

Edgar said. "Would you be joining us now if she was the one who died because of Haven's negligence?"

David looked into Edgar's eyes. He didn't know what to say.

"You know, as well as I do, that justice is rarely achieved through our court system," Edgar said. "We've got to pursue it on our own."

"Then we've got to find another way."

"There is no other way."

David shook his head. "Sorry. Count me out."

Edgar pulled out a piece of paper and handed it to David. "Here's my phone number. Call me when you change your mind."

"I'm not going to change my mind," David said firmly.

"Yes, you will." Edgar turned and walked away.

CHAPTER 29

D avid parked his Lexus in front of a spectacular multi-million dollar home with a Hoffman Properties for sale sign planted in the yard. Two sign riders hung on chains below the large professional sign. One with Kathy Reid's name and phone number, and one that read:

Open Today: 2 to 5 p.m.

David got out of his car and headed for the elegant portico entrance, smiling proudly at the sight of Kathy's sign. He tried the door. It was locked.

I'm glad she's taking safety precautions.

He rang the doorbell.

After a moment, Kathy opened the door, and he stepped inside the impressive foyer.

"Got time to give me the grand tour?"

"I'm in the middle of showing a couple through right now. Wife's the chief of staff at Waldo County Hospital."

"They interested?"

Kathy gave him a broad grin. "So far. So good."

"I'll just take a quick look around. Which way is this fabulous pool?"

Kathy gave him a sheet of paper. "Here's a copy of the floor plan. Go down this hall," she said, pointing to the east end of the house. "Turn right. You'll pass a billiards room."

"Okay. Cool."

"Then, at the indoor gardens, make another right and—"

"I see," David said as he studied the floor plan. "And then I'll come to the pool."

Two minutes later David walked into the room. Light poured through a row of towering arched windows, filling the area with ambient light. Translucent images of tall windows, potted plants, and chic pool furniture reflected off the turquoise water of a magnificent pool.

David was impressed by the beauty of his surroundings. "Oh, my gosh. This *is* a fabulous pool." He strolled alongside the pool, enjoying the peaceful ambiance.

Then, out of nowhere, he heard a voice. "Help! Help me!"

David spun around. He saw a man in the pool splashing around, struggling to stay above the water.

The man went under, popped back up, coughing and spitting up water. He was frantic. "Please, help me!"

David dove into the pool and swam underwater toward the drowning man. Beneath the surface, he saw the man's legs kicking. As he submerged again, he thrashed about, then gave up and began a slow descent to the bottom.

Moving his arms forcefully, downward and outward, David swam toward him.

But now the drowning man had disappeared.

David rose to the surface, gasping for air. He treaded water as he looked around for the man. After making a partial sweep of the area, he turned and came face-to-face with Kathy and her two prospects. They were standing at the edge of the pool, staring at him in surprise. He swam over to them and climbed out, streams of water dripping from his clothes onto the pool deck.

Kathy led the couple out of the area, and then quickly returned to find David squeezing water out of his socks. "David, what in the world are you doing?"

"There was a man in the pool."

"*What?*"

"I was trying to save a man. He was drowning."

Kathy stared at David as if he had lost his mind.

"Don't look at me like that. There was a man in the pool. I jumped in to help him. He must have gotten out and taken off. A nut case or something. Some bum who walked into your open house and—"

"Just listen to you—"

"I'm telling you—"

"I don't see any wet footprints except for yours. Explain that."

David looked around the pool, then back at Kathy. "Either I'm losing my mind or—"

"Or what?"

"Or this place is haunted."

Her eyes blazed with anger. "I've got to get back to my customers." She promptly left.

He sat there on the concrete deck, a pensive look on his face, his legs dangling in the pool's sparkling water.

She thinks I'm nuts. And who could blame her?

He picked up one of his shoes, turned it upside down, and watched the water dribble into the pool.

David entered his house from the garage and staggered into the kitchen. Tiny bits of ice clung to dark strands of his hair. He stopped shivering for a moment to let out a loud sneeze. Then he pulled off his coat and let it drop to the floor. On his way to the family room, he began peeling off his wet clothes.

As he walked into the family room, he was stunned to see that the room was empty. No furniture. No area rugs. Nothing.

His face registered panic.

He walked into the dining room. No table. No chairs. No china hutch. Nothing.

He raced into the master bedroom. Empty.

Hannah's room. Empty.

His mother's room. Empty.

Reaching into the pocket of his slacks, he pulled out his cell phone, selected a number and waited as it rang.

"Kathy, we've been robbed," he said, breathlessly. "I'm at home. There's nothing here. Not one stick of furniture. Nothing."

David paced back and forth across the kitchen floor. Hearing the grinding gears of the garage door as it opened, he rushed out to greet his wife.

A white Cadillac XTS Sedan pulled into the garage.

He opened the driver's door and Kathy climbed out.

"Wait'll you see this. There's nothing left."

He took her by the hand and led her into the kitchen. Kathy slipped and nearly fell on the wet tile floor as he pulled her through the kitchen and into the family room.

David came to an abrupt stop. He couldn't believe his eyes. He glanced all around the beautifully furnished room.

Everything was in its place. Furniture. Lamps. TV. Paintings. Plants. It was all there.

Kathy's gaze traveled around the room. Bewildered, she looked at David. "What kind of a joke is this?" she snapped.

"I don't understand. There was nothing in this room a few minutes ago."

She shook her head. "There is something seriously wrong with you."

"There is nothing wrong with—"

"David, you need to see a doctor."

"I'm not sick. I don't need a—"

"Get some dry clothes on. I'm taking you to the emergency room."

"I am not going to the hospital."

"Yes, you are."

"No, I'm not."

"You will go with me to the hospital right now, or you can leave this house and find another place to stay tonight."

David's mouth opened, but he didn't speak.

"Hannah will be home soon. I don't want her exposed to whatever you're going through right now."

"You have got to be kidding . . ."

"First the pool. Now this. No, I'm not kidding."

David stomped out of the room and into his studio. Slamming the door shut, he sank into the chair at his desk and began massaging his forehead.

"What is going on?" he said out loud. "Why is this happening to me?"

"It's happening to you for one reason, David. You're a coward."

David reeled around and saw a spirit; a bold, dignified entity with a booming voice.

"And I'm going to haunt you for the rest of your life if you don't help us break the chains that keep us tied to Haven." The professor stood there with his arms folded across his chest like a genie that had just popped out of a bottle, his image wavering like a mirage on a hot blacktop road.

"Are you Professor Graber?" David asked. "The spirit Fabian told me about?

The professor nodded.

Trembling with fear, David took a step back and collided with a stool that crashed to the floor. "Why me? Of all the people you could choose, why me? I've got a life most people would kill for. And you want me to risk it all by committing a crime that will put me behind bars for the rest of my life?"

"If you don't help us, you'll risk losing the most valuable thing you possess."

"My life?"

"Your soul."

Now David trembled so bad that his knees buckled under him and he sank to the floor.

"Your goal has always been to achieve immortality through your painting," the professor said. "You think that if your paintings hang in great museums, then you will live on forever through your achievements. Although that is a noble act, it is a selfish one in some cases. In your case, it is far more important to go down in history for doing an unselfish act—by being the David that fights the Goliath's of this world—the David who brings about change that will help millions of people."

"How can your plan possibly save my soul? Bring me honor and respect?"

"We ask only one thing of you, David. To have faith and trust in the great power who wants this task accomplished."

"And I ask only one thing of you. Leave me the hell alone!" David shouted. "Be gone, you evil spirit."

Professor Graber glared at David, and then vanished.

Distraught, David gasped for breath. He placed his finger against his neck and checked his pulse, then he lay down on the maple-planked floor and closed his eyes. He felt a moment of peace.

Then his eyes popped open.

He touched the back of his head. Startled, he recoiled and looked up at his hand. Water was dripping from it. He sat bolt upright. His eyes widened as he discovered he was surrounded by water about an inch deep. David jumped to his feet. He grabbed a large painting on the floor that was propped up against a wall. Seeking a safe place for it, he laid it down on his workbench.

Now the water was up to his knees. He looked around for the source of the water. There was none. He took a step. Now the water was up to his waist.

As he stared at the water in utter shock, he heard a crash. Now water gushed through a broken window, cascading into the studio like a mini-waterfall. The other windows burst, exploded. More water came gushing in.

At that point, the water was up to David's neck, a virtual lake inside his studio. He dove underwater, searching for a way out. He swam among paint tubes, canvases, and brushes that were floating through the water. He swam toward the door that led into the hallway, took hold of the doorknob, and pulled on it. It wouldn't budge. He tried again but it was no use.

Quickly rising to the surface for air, David bumped his head against the ceiling. Panicked by the realization that the water was only a few inches away from the ceiling, he turned his head sideways in a desperate attempt to take in air. "Okay, you win. I'll do it," he said, sputtering and choking on the water. "I'll do it!"

The water splashed up against the ceiling.

David swam down to one of the windows that imploded, but the force of the rushing, oncoming water prevented him from escaping. He swam toward another door. The one that led outside. He grabbed the doorknob, frantically twisting it back and forth. He tried to pull it open using such great force that the knob popped off. He released it and watched as it gracefully sunk to the bottom of the room. He closed his eyes and gave up, floating lifelessly among all the artistic paraphernalia in his studio.

It was nine-thirty that night when David woke up on the floor of his studio. Completely dry, he staggered to his feet and looked around.

Everything was in its place. Nothing damaged.

Looking like he had single-handedly done battle with an army of soldiers, he faltered out of the room.

***

The only time David had ever been to his father's gravesite was during his funeral. His mother visited the grave often, but he refused to go. He wanted to forget, not be constantly reminded of that tragic day when his father died. But now he was on his way to the cemetery where he was buried, walking through the fog that blanketed the entire landscape.

"To be, or not to be, that is the question," he said as he moved through the thick, white clouds in front of him. "Whether 'tis nobler in the mind to suffer the slings and arrows of outrageous fortune, or to take arms against a sea of troubles and by opposing, end them."

He stopped when the top of a tall gray headstone emerged from the fog. As he drew closer, he saw the corner pillars of the gate that led into the cemetery. Misty clouds swirled around the black wrought-iron gate. He looked up and waited until the bold black letters slowly appeared; the letters that arced across the top of the lofty iron gate. The letters that spelled out the name "Resurrection Cemetery".

He stood there, staring at the words.

"To die; to sleep, no more," he said with a shudder.

He gulped in some air, swallowed it, and then pushed the gate open. He looked at the ground before him as if it were quicksand, a trap that would swallow him up if he dared enter the graveyard.

He marched onward, through the gateway, watching as the peaks of tall headstones pierced through the dense fog.

He searched for his father's grave as if in a blinding storm, tripping over tree roots and stumbling over dips in the ground. Feeling like he was walking in circles, he began to panic. He had no idea where the gravesite was until he noticed a landmark headstone, a huge one that towered above all the others. It was the one of Jesus Christ hanging on the cross. The one he fixed his attention on while they were lowering his father's coffin into the ground.

He walked toward the large monument, moving through patches of mud and dirty gray snow. As he moved closer to the shrine, he saw a group of people gathered around a shiny white coffin and an open plot. From that point, he got his bearings. He turned and saw the sandstone and mortar wall that stood behind a long row of graves.

He moved toward the wall, the fence that enclosed the entire cemetery, and scanned the grave sites; some marked with big stones in the shape of hearts or benches, others marked by tall pointed headstones of black granite.

Then he saw it. The headstone he had been searching for.

The mere sight of it brought forth a feeling of utter despair. It shook him like an old, frail tree standing alone in a windstorm. Feeling ashamed, he edged over to his father's grave.

Tears ran freely as David studied the big statue; a figure of a weeping angel. The angel was kneeling as if in prayer, her head resting on one arm, her other arm drooping gracefully in front of an exquisitely-crafted marble base, her pale gray, delicate wings nearly touching the ground.

The sight of the grieving figure was so heart-wrenching that David let out a loud sob. He dropped to his knees in front of the headstone and bowed his head.

I'm sorry, father.

I am so sorry for not coming here sooner.

He looked up at the angel again, wiping his wet face with his hands. Then, through bleary eyes, he stared down at the names on the front of the headstone:

JOSEPH L. REID

AUGUST 28, 1924

NOVEMBER 24, 1970

ZELDA M. REID

JANUARY 10, 1925

Then he read the two sentences engraved below his parents' names:

I'LL BE WAITING FOR YOU.

SOMEWHERE VERY NEAR,

JUST AROUND THE CORNER.

David raked a hand through his hair. *Oh, if only that could be true,* he thought. His gaze traveled back up to Joseph's name.

Something strange is happening to me, father.

I'm losing my mind.

I'm seeing ghosts. And they want me to do something very bad.

I'm sorry if you're angry with me for denying God all these years.

But I just can't believe a merciful God would let you die such a tragic death. And why would He punish mother and me so harshly when we loved Him so much?

Just then a little boy skipped by, holding a small bouquet of red and white carnations.

"Through despair and hope, through faith and love," the little boy sang. "Till we find our place on the path unwinding in the circle. The circle of life."

David watched the child.

The boy waved the bouquet at his mother. "I found it, Momma! Uncle Bill's grave is right over there." He gestured with the fistful of flowers to a gravesite a few yards from Joseph's grave.

David turned his attention back to the statue. He stood up, the knees of his trousers soiled and wet, and stared down at the ground in front of the headstone. He found it hard to imagine his father lying in a casket beneath that snow and mud, beneath the bits of brown grass.

He shut his eyes and sent his thoughts to his father.

Mother still believes in God.

I wish I could too.

When he opened his eyes, he studied the grieving angel for another moment, then he turned and walked away.

As David made his way through the lingering fog, he caught a glimpse of a man standing in front of a small mausoleum. David kept his head lowered, not wanting the man to see his tear-stained face. But as he passed the man, he glanced up, only briefly, but long enough to look into the eyes of Jesus Christ.

Taken aback, he turned around and walked up to the man.

"Something I can help you with?" the man asked as he flicked a cigarette butt through the air.

David stepped back.

"Sorry. I thought you were someone else."

David walked away.

Now I'm seeing Jesus.

And that man looks nothing like him.

Oh, please— father, help me.

CHAPTER 30

Having a restless night's sleep inside a hotel room, David rolled over on his side, his face damp with perspiration. He was in the grip of a nightmare. Tightly grasping the bars of a jail cell, he peered through the space between two slender iron rods. "Please. I can't stand this anymore. I want my life back," he said.

A guard strolled past his cell.

David reached through the bars. "Guard, help me get out of here. I didn't want to be involved. They forced me into it."

"That's what they all say," the guard said as he walked away, twirling a black police baton.

"No, please! Don't leave me here to die," he begged. "Help me get out of this place!"

David bolted upright in bed. He glanced around the unfamiliar room. Then, realizing where he was, he let out a sigh of relief, settled back into his pillow, and stared hopelessly at the ceiling.

Later that morning, David watched as Edgar emptied freshly caught lobsters into a big bin. "So you've encountered Professor Graber?"

Edgar nodded. "On more than one occasion."

"Did he torture you the way he's been torturing me?"

"I wouldn't call it torture. He talked. I listened."

"Was he a college professor when he was alive?"

"Yes. A professor of religious studies at Boston University. And he claims he's got connections with the most powerful force in the universe."

"Do you believe him?"

"It's pretty hard not to."

"What if that powerful force is evil?"

"It can't be. Otherwise, I . . ."

"What?" David asked.

"I wouldn't feel so at peace with the plan."

"Well, I don't feel at peace with it. I want out."

David walked into the kitchen and startled Kathy as she was pulling a roast out of the oven. "Oh, you scared me half to death," she said, putting a hand up to her breast.

"I'm fine now, sweetheart," he said, raising his palms.

"What do you mean—you're fine?"

"I mean I believe I've got a handle on what's been happening to me," he said, placing both hands down on the granite surface of the center island.

"Have you seen a doctor?"

"No."

"Then you're not welcome here until you get evaluated by a doctor."

"Not welcome in my own home?"

"Right. Not until you get help."

He frowned. "More medical bills. Is that what you want? To give every cent we've just earned to doctors and hospitals?"

"I don't care about the money," she said. "I care about our daughter. And I don't want her exposed to anymore strange, frightening situations." She folded her arms over her chest. "I think you should see a psychiatrist. The one who treated Hannah did a good job."

He sighed in resignation. "Okay. If it'll make you feel better, I'll go see him. What was that guy's name?"

She opened a drawer next to the refrigerator and pulled out a business card. "Dr. Benjamin Graber," she said as she handed him the card.

He glanced down at the card. "I'll call his office right now." But upon closer inspection, the doctor's name seemed to leap off the card.

Graber?

David froze.

Dr. Benjamin Graber.

"What's wrong?" Kathy asked.

He slowly looked up. "Nothing. I'll call him right now and make an appointment." He reached into the pocket of his trousers and pulled out his phone.

Could there be a link between this doctor and that spirit?

David dialed the number on the business card. A receptionist picked up and put him on hold.

"I need to put some clothes in the dryer," Kathy said, adjusting the heat on one of the range's burners. "Can you keep an eye on this pot?"

"Sure."

After she left the kitchen, David picked up a piece of celery and munched on it while he waited. Ten minutes later, he had an appointment with Dr. Graber.

"It's all set," he said when Kathy came back into the kitchen.

"For when?"

"Friday morning."

"Today's Tuesday." Fretting, she wrung her hands.

"I know. But don't worry. I didn't check out of the hotel."

"You didn't?" She pursed her lips and gazed into his eyes.

He knew that look all too well. "Why don't you just lock me in my studio?"

"Don't joke about this."

"I'm not joking. I practically live in that studio anyway."

She pondered the idea. "And the sofa in there is as comfortable as a bed."

"So is the recliner. Look, all we have to do is put some distance between Hannah and me. Keep her as busy as possible. Tell her I'm working on an important commissioned painting and can't be disturbed. Take her away every day after school. Out to dinner. Shopping. The library. To visit friends."

"Sounds like a good plan." She walked up to him, wrapped her arms around his neck and hugged him. "I'm sorry I kicked you out of here."

"Don't apologize," he said. "You did the right thing."

<hr>

On Thursday afternoon, David stopped by Haven to visit his mother. As he approached her room, Katie Weber met him in the hall and told him Zelda was taking a nap.

"But we'll be getting her up in about thirty minutes."

"That's fine. I'll take a walk out back until then."

"Okay." Katie smiled sweetly. "We'll see you later."

As David turned and headed for a door that led to the rear grounds, he felt a rush of happiness.

That Katie is so sweet. Always a cheerful look on her face. I feel so much better when I know she's looking after Mother. And Dawn is excellent, too. They're the only good things about this place.

When he opened the door, the bright light made him squint. After his eyes adjusted, he scanned the rear grounds. The snow-covered gardens and sculptures. The once naked trees, their bare limbs now covered in a jacket of white. The abandoned greenhouse. The roaring sea.

Yes, Katie and Dawn—and this enchanting area—are the only good things about Haven.

David sauntered down the concrete steps. Deciding to take

another look at the greenhouse, he walked down a path toward it, snow crunching beneath his shoes. Allured by its magical charm, the way it was able to thrive on its own even in its dilapidated state, made him eager to see if he could get inside the building.

Clumps of snow covering the glass panes fell upon him when he pushed in on the door. He brushed the snow from his hair and shoulders and tried the door again. It creaked and then popped open with a loud crack.

He stepped inside and looked around in amazement at the ice-crystal blossoms on the glass walls, the snow-covered plants and tables, and the long icicles hanging from broken panes of glass on the ceiling.

"Ha, ha." An eerie voice laughed. "Good luck in there!"

David whirled around, searching for the source of the voice. He saw nothing.

"I think I'll join you."

Frantically, David looked all around. Through one of the glass windows, he saw something peculiar, a shadowy form materializing out of thin air.

Professor Graber appeared. He passed through the glass wall, his blurry black-and-white shape wavering like a flag in a light breeze.

David backed away, bumping into a big tree as he did. The professor moved closer to him. Panic-stricken, David whirled around and scurried up the tree. As he made his way toward a jagged hole in the ceiling where the tree had pierced through the glass, he glanced down.

The professor was nowhere in sight.

Then, out of the corner of his eye, David noticed a strange flickering. He turned his head and there he was—Professor Graber, floating in the air right beside him.

"You can't get away from me!"

David crawled up the tree, up through the hole in the glass. As he stuck one foot out to lower himself onto the roof, the tree began to tremble violently. With a sudden spurt of energy it shot up into the sky, growing taller and taller like Jack's beanstalk.

David hugged the trunk, his eyes wide with panic.

The tree broke through the low-hanging clouds. And day turned into night.

A flock of wild geese flew past David, their wings flapping leisurely in the night sky. He held on for dear life, his arms wrapped around the trunk and his teeth chattering, as the tree sped toward the stars and the big yellow moon.

Extreme fear took his breath away. *This isn't real. It can't be happening,* he thought.

The tree came to an abrupt stop.

David looked down at the clouds and the earth below. When he saw how high he was, he clung tighter to the tree, using his knees, feet, and both arms.

The spirit of Professor Graber flew up to greet him.

"Had enough?"

"You can do whatever you want to me, but I'll never help you."

The professor spat on his hands and pulled out an ax. "Are you sure about that?" he said, running his hand over the shiny silver blade.

David swallowed hard. "Yes, I'm sure."

"Okay, then . . . TIMBER!" The professor swung the ax handle back and thrust its blade into the bark just below David's feet.

"I'm not a criminal," David said. "Please, go find someone else and leave me alone."

The professor drove the blade into the tree, again and again, wood splinters flying as he chipped away. The top of the tree creaked, leaned sideways, and split in two, sending David tumbling through the sky towards the earth.

David woke up in the greenhouse, his head and clothes covered with ice and snow. He wiped his face and sat up. His nose and cheeks were bright red. Tiny icicles clung to his hair.

He looked around at his eerie surroundings.

The stillness inside the greenhouse nearly stopped his heart. He climbed to his feet, struggling as if he had been half-buried in a snow-covered ditch. He stood there, wobbling, as he brushed the snow from his coat and pants. Unsure of what time or day it was, he checked his watch.

I've only been in here for five minutes? That can't be.

CHAPTER 31

D r. Benjamin Graber sat and listened to David explain the strange events: how he had been visited by a ghost at Haven, how he had made a fool of himself at Kathy's open house, how everything in his house had vanished and then reappeared, how he nearly drowned in his studio, and how a spirit tormented him inside Haven's greenhouse.

"You said you've had patients who've claimed to have seen ghosts. Have you ever had one who's been haunted as badly as I've been?" David asked.

Dr. Graber shook his head. "Never."

"Do you believe my experiences are real or imagined?"

"Imagined."

"Do you believe they're hallucinations caused by anxiety?"

Graber nodded.

"You do?"

"*Intense* anxiety."

"Okay, then, I've got one more question. Do you know a Professor Graber?"

Astounded, Dr. Graber leaned forward in his chair. His eyes probed David's.

"He was my father. Why?"

Was? So he passed away?"

"Yes, but what does this have to do with—"

"Where did he die?"

"At the same place—" Graber's voice caught, and he coughed to clear his throat. "The same place where your mother is right now. Haven."

"Then it's the spirit of your father who's been haunting me."

Graber stared at David in disbelief. He tried to speak again, but no words came. He coughed again, and then took a drink of water from a glass on his desk.

David sat back, digging his fingers into the fabric on the arms of a wingback chair. "Tell me about your father."

Graber sat there, spellbound, studying David's face. "He was a professor of religious studies. At Boston University. And he—I'm sorry. I'm having a difficult time processing all this. You're telling me you were visited by the ghost of my father?"

"Yes."

"He spoke to you?"

"Yes."

"About what? What did he want?"

Well, so much for hallucinations, David thought. "He wants to get the hell out of Haven."

"So that place is holding him captive? It wasn't enough that he suffered every day he was there. Now that he's dead, it still won't let go of him? Is that what you're saying?"

David nodded. "Your father and many others who died at Haven need help from us to escape and move on to where they were meant to go."

"How can we help them?"

"Not you, Dr. Graber. Me. And two other men."

"Can you take me to my father?" Graber asked, his eyes moist with tears. "I would give anything to see him again."

David smiled and shook his head. "I'm amazed."

"Amazed?"

"Yes. Amazed that you believe me, and that you haven't called the men in white coats to come and take me away."

"Well, then maybe you'll find this fact interesting," the doctor said, pausing for a moment, uncertain of whether to go on. Then he made the decision to share his secret.

"I saw a ghost at Haven a month before my father died."

David's jaw dropped.

"Just a glimpse of one. A ghostly figure moving down the corridor outside my father's room. It vanished the moment I realized what I was seeing."

"You knew all along that Hannah really did see a ghost? But then why—"

"How could I tell anyone I'd seen a ghost? Especially the family of a patient."

David stared intently at Graber. He could not believe what he was hearing.

Mortified by his confession, the doctor blushed. "If I had mentioned that to anyone—anyone other than someone like you—someone who's had the same experience, I'd more than likely be at Mount Auburn in Cambridge right now."

The room was silent.

"I was told your father is the leader of this group of spirits. Do you have any idea why he would've been chosen for that role?"

Graber swallowed hard. He tugged on his left ear lobe and shifted his body in his chair.

"More than likely because of his strong religious beliefs. Several times he told me he felt a powerful connection to God."

"How so? Did he claim that he talked to God?"

"No. He said God spoke through him."

"Spoke through him? What do you mean?"

"One evening father invited me to have dinner with him and his colleagues. You know, other professors from the college. Father was asked to say the prayer. And while he was praying, he started speaking in tongues."

"Really?"

Dr. Graber nodded. "And when the Holy Spirit left him, as we say, and he finished the prayer, one of the other professors, a man named Kaito Higashi spoke up. Higashi told my father he didn't know he was fluent in his native language. Father gave Higashi a puzzled look and told him he didn't know how to speak Japanese."

"Then how could he—"

"But my father *was* speaking *perfect Japanese* according to Higashi. And then Higashi interpreted the words for us."

"What did he say?"

"The gates of heaven are starting to close."

David felt a tingling sensation in his chest. His hands felt cold and began to tremble.

"Everyone at that table sat there in shock."

"So do you believe God was speaking through him?" David asked, digging his fingernails deeper into the fabric covering the arms of the chair.

"If you had been sitting at that table, what would you think?"

"I would think that . . ." David avoided Benjamin's eyes. He focused, instead, on the thin black frame of a watercolor painting that hung on the wall behind the doctor. "That he *did know* how to speak Japanese. And his goal was to gain power over the other men."

"Trust me. My father did not know how to speak any Asian language."

David ran a hand through his hair. He focused on the painting again. "Who painted that watercolor behind you?"

"Forget about the painting."

David stared down at his hands.

"My father believed there is one god for all mankind. One god who created this earth and everything on it. And that god is the God of the Holy Bible. The Heavenly Father of Jesus Christ."

"That god couldn't possibly exist," David said.

"Why not?"

"Because of all the horrible tragedies that happen in this world. If that god was real, why hasn't he put an end to wars, hunger, and disease? Why does he continue to let us suffer?"

"Have you ever read the Bible?"

"Some of it."

"Then I guess you missed the part that taught how Satan is the reason the earth is in a state of constant turmoil. Remember Adam and Eve? And the apple?"

"That's just a story."

"Yes, it's a story. But it's not fiction. All of our suffering, including death itself, is a result of man's rebellion against God."

"I know, I know," David said. "I've heard it all before. God provided a rescue by sacrificing his own son, Jesus Christ."

"And that's why Jesus died on the cross. Why he rose from the dead. To save us."

David frowned. "I hope you're not charging me for all this talk about God."

Stunned by the comment, Benjamin Graber rolled his chair back from his desk.

David stared at him. "Look, I didn't come here to listen to a sermon. I came here for help with a problem. But it sounds like you've got bigger issues than I do."

"You're right. I do. And that's why I want you to take me to him."

"You want to go see your dead father?"

"Yes."

"It's not an easy task to locate him. He appears when he feels like it. And if we do meet up with your father, I'm afraid you'll be sorely disappointed in him."

"Why?"

"Because he's a very wicked spirit. A kind, loving soul wouldn't threaten people and scare the hell out of them."

Tears welled up in Benjamin's eyes. "Please, David. Will you go to Haven with me and help me search for him?"

Dr. Benjamin Graber met David at Haven that night, and they began their search for Ben's father. The first place they looked was an empty room, the one where Professor Graber had died. Benjamin sank into a chair. He wanted to sit alone in the room for a while, hoping his father would pay him a visit.

"Take your time," David said. "My mother is in room one-o-seven. I'll be in there with her."

Ben nodded.

David left the room.

Ben sat silent for a while and then paced around the room. He searched the bathroom and the closets. Then he checked the nightstand and dresser, opening and closing every single drawer. Finally he stopped his maddening search. Peering through the window at the silhouettes of the trees, he patiently waited, his hands crossed behind his back.

"Father, I've come to see you," Ben said, turning away from the window to face the room. "If your spirit is anchored to this evil place, then I want to know what I can do to help you."

Ben sat again. And waited. Quietly, with bated breath.

"Dad, I would give anything to see you again. To be with you for just one more minute."

The minutes ticked by and, feeling foolish, he scolded himself. Then he stood up and left the room.

While Benjamin was walking toward Zelda's room, he heard a man's voice. It sounded like his father. He spun around in expectation. But all he saw was a middle-aged man walking down the hall with a teenage girl. He watched them stroll into a resident's room.

David smiled as Ben entered his mother's room.

"Here he is, Mother," David said as he stood up to greet Benjamin. "This is my friend, Benjamin Graber."

Ben smiled at David. *My friend,* he thought. *How kind. Not my doctor, but my friend.*

Ben took a step toward Zelda and extended his hand. "Pleased to meet you, Mrs. Reid."

"It's my pleasure," Zelda said. She grasped his hand with both of hers. She seemed thrilled to meet him and beamed with joy as if she had just been introduced to a king.

After an unsuccessful search of all three floors at the facility, Ben approached one last door. It was a dark mahogany door with iron jail-cell grillwork and a rounded top.

At first, the door wouldn't budge. But after a few attempts, it finally burst open. He looked inside. It was too dark to see anything. The stench of mold stung his nostrils. Pinching his nose, he felt around for a light switch. His fingers found a metal button, and he pushed it. A dim bulb overhead cast its light upon a winding staircase.

He turned and saw David studying the ceiling in the corridor, searching for signs of supernatural activity.

"Looks like this leads up to a turret," Ben said.

David walked over and glanced into the little room. He saw the staircase, spiraling upwards toward the roof. "I've never been up there. Never even noticed this door before."

"Well, let's have a look see, shall we?" Ben gestured toward the first step. "After you."

David began to climb the narrow staircase. "I don't know. It's freezing in here." He turned to see Ben coming up behind him.

"My father always liked the cold. Winter was his favorite season."

"But your father's no longer alive. He's a spirit. He wouldn't need to hide up here. He just pops up wherever he chooses."

"Well, maybe he's chosen to appear before us right up there." Ben raised his eyebrows.

When they reached the top of the staircase, they stepped into a round room. Orange wallpaper with a pattern of flower swirls covered the walls in between three tall windows. Each window had a pair of gold velvet drapes that curled onto the hardwood floor.

Ben looked up. In the center of the circular wood-planked ceiling was a crystal chandelier with bulbs in the shape of candles. Only three bulbs were lit.

Four royal blue parlor chairs surrounded a small white marble-topped coffee table. David had already sat down in one of the velvet upholstered chairs. He was inspecting the carved lion head arm supports that were gilded with gold.

"Strange. It's not chilly up here." Ben sat in a chair across from David. "Feels as warm as if we were sitting in front of a cozy fire."

"And it doesn't smell moldy," David said.

"No, it smells like—" Ben drew in a deep breath. "Jasmine on a warm summer day." He glanced around the room, his nerves tense, waiting to hear the sound of footsteps or knocking or better yet, his father's voice.

They sat quietly in the peaceful turret room for several moments. And then the two men began talking about their fathers. Ben started the conversation by recalling memories of his father; what a sincere man he was, a devoted father and husband, and a great inspiration to Ben.

David told Ben about all the good things his father did not only for their family but for others as well; neighbors, the community, visiting kids in hospitals at Christmas time and Easter.

"Is your father still alive?"

"He died when I was nine."

"Of natural causes?"

David shook his head.

"What happened to him?"

"I'd rather not talk about it."

Ben gazed at David with concern. "David, have you ever shared your feelings about the loss of your father with *anyone?*"

"No."

"Not even your wife?"

"No one."

"Well, I'm your psychiatrist. And I'd like to help you get past that pain."

David stared at the posh oriental carpet that covered the center of the hardwood floor.

"Was your father killed in a motor vehicle accident?"

David shook his head.

"Did he drown?"

"What difference does it make how he died? He's dead. And that's the end of it."

Ben straightened up in his chair. "There's a reason you won't talk about it. And I think I know what that reason is. He committed suicide, didn't he?"

The insinuation filled David with rage. "Absolutely not. My father would *never* do such a thing."

"So what happened to him?"

David could no longer hold his temper. He exploded.

"He was killed in a hunting accident. Two days before Thanksgiving. Shot in the head by a stray bullet. And I was there. Walking right behind him. In the woods."

Ben closed his eyes and shook his head. "I'm so sorry, David."

David's eyes glazed over as he traveled back in time to that day.

"We were hunting pheasant. My mother was with us. And our foxhound, Gabriel, trotting along beside me. I remember hearing the honking of geese flying overhead. I looked up but couldn't see them through the thick tangle of branches. And then a sharp gunshot rang out."

David clasped his hands together to stop them from shaking.

"It startled me so bad I nearly dropped my shotgun. And then—it was like slow motion—my father collapsing onto the wet leaves and wilted grass in front of me."

"Oh, God." Ben put his palms together and pressed the tips of his fingers against his lips.

"The images still haunt me. The startled look on Father's face. Blood streaming into his eyes from the hole in his forehead. Mother frantically wiping blood from his face with her scarf. Gabriel resting his head on father's chest, gently pawing at him to get up.

"But the sounds that haunt me are even worse than the images. Mother weeping. Gabriel baying and whining as if he were the one who had been shot. But the worst sound, the worst sound of all was my father's frightened voice. The one inside my head. Telling us he didn't want to lose us. Telling us how much he loved us. Telling us he would—" David sobbed. "Would never *ever* leave us."

On their way out of Haven, they passed the receptionist's station. David noticed there were no nurses or aides anywhere in sight. He eyed the large blackboard where the schedules for the aides were listed, glanced at it just long enough to catch a flicker of movement as he and Ben walked past the station. David stopped, glanced over his shoulder and saw that the blackboard had been wiped clean.

"Did you see that?" David said, turning to Ben.

"What?"

"The blackboard. A few seconds ago it was filled with writing. Now it's blank."

Ben looked at the blackboard. There were no words or marks on the black surface; only cloudy remnants of chalk that hadn't been rubbed out completely.

"Are you sure?" Ben said, turning back to David.

The squeal of chalk scraping across the board caused Ben to clap his hands over his ears. They both saw the stick of white chalk, moving on its own as it drew a large capital "B".

Ben's body trembled as he watched the chalk complete the first few letters of his name:

B-E-N-J-A

He slapped his right hand over his heart and sucked in some air.

The chalk kept moving, screeching across the hard black surface, scrawling out crooked words, capitalizing every letter. Then the stick of chalk fell to the floor after completing the exclamation point at the end of its message:

BENJAMIN, GO HOME. STAY OUT OF THIS!

Ben's eyes closed as he lost consciousness. He fell straight back as if someone had laid both hands on his shoulders and pushed him over.

David kneeled beside Benjamin and patted his face. When he didn't respond, David slid his arms under Ben's legs and raised them above heart level. The sound of footsteps caused David to look up.

Katie Weber was walking down the corridor toward the receptionist's station. When she saw David kneeling on the floor, she raced to his side.

"Oh, my! What happened?" Katie asked, alarmed by the sight of Ben lying on the floor.

"Fainted," David said. He looked up at her and then glanced over at the blackboard.

The message on the chalkboard was gone. It now contained the schedules for the nurses' aides.

It was very late the next night. Determined to speak to Professor Graber, David walked along the third-floor corridor, searching for him. He looked into room after room before coming to an abandoned physical therapy room. Golden light from the vintage street lamps streamed through the window panes, creating a mysterious, dreamlike atmosphere.

David stepped inside the spacious room. He looked around and saw nothing but a chest pulley weight system attached to one wall and a wheelchair sitting in the center of the room. He walked across the green and white checkered linoleum floor and sat in the wheelchair. "Okay, Professor Graber. I'm tired of playing hide and seek. I've got a bone to pick with you."

Professor Graber appeared directly behind the wheelchair. He put his mouth close to David's ear and whispered, "I hope you're here for a friendly visit."

David jumped up from his seat, but Professor Graber grabbed him by the shoulders and slammed him back down into the chair.

"I am not going through with your plan," David said. "Find someone else."

The professor pointed his index finger skyward and made a twirling motion with it.

The wheelchair began spinning in circles. David grasped the arms of the chair as it jerked around like a bucking bronco, spinning around, stopping abruptly, moving backward and forward. Then the chair sped around the room like it was a car in the Indianapolis 500. David hung on for dear life until the chair abruptly screeched to a halt, sending him flying from the seat. He landed face first on the floor.

David slowly rolled over. He sat up and opened his eyes. The room was spinning. He squeezed his eyes shut and puked. Then he looked up and saw Professor Graber hovering above him, arms folded over his chest.

"Had enough?" Professor Graber chuckled.

"Go to hell."

Graber's boisterous laugh echoed throughout the room. "Since you're such a tough nut to crack, I'm going to let you off the hook. But be prepared, David. You'll be spending plenty of time in mental wards —visiting your wife and daughter."

The professor vanished.

Fear slammed its mighty fist into David's chest. He felt his heart flutter. He gasped for air. And then he passed out.

CHAPTER 32

To David's dismay, Christmas Eve had arrived. He lingered around the house, helping Kathy and Hannah bake one last batch of Christmas cookies. He had to avoid their line of vision to keep them from seeing the tears in his eyes.

This is the end of the road for me. It'll be years before I'll get to spend time with my family again. Ten to twenty years.

And Edgar thinks we won't have to spend any time in prison for abducting Haven's staff and locking them up. He thinks we'll get off scot free for kidnapping.

It's ridiculous.

He slipped on an oven mitt and pulled a sheet pan out of the stove. The intense heat made him step back and wave the quilted glove in front of his face. The brown, butter-based cookies, loaded with caramel and red sprinkles, made his mouth water. He set the tray on top of the range to cool.

Move the residents to the lobby. Then call the press.

What good will that do?

It's the dumbest idea I've ever heard. Yet, if I don't go through with it, I'll lose—

"Daddy, look at this," Hannah said, pulling on his sleeve.

He looked at a shopping bag Hannah was holding. She glanced around, making sure her mother was nowhere in sight, then opened the black plastic bag and pulled out an elegant, blue-and-white silk scarf.

"Wow," he said. "Hannah, that's beautiful."

"Do you think Mommy will like it?" She heard him sniff and looked up into his eyes. "Are you okay, Daddy?"

He wiped his nose with the back of his hand. "Must be getting a cold."

Edgar placed the big red container on the floor next to the wall. Stepping back, he stood in the darkness, staring at the gas can, lost in thoughts of how that container and the others like it planted throughout Haven were going to change his life forever. The long, drawn-out howl of a wolf brought him out of his daze. He turned his head toward the room's only window and looked outside.

A thin veil of clouds passed over the moon. Stars peeked out as the clouds journeyed across the dark sky. Patches of snow on the frozen ground glistened in the crisp, clear moonlight.

Edgar knew tonight would bring an end to such beauty for him. But he hoped his sacrifice would be worth it. He hoped and prayed that what they were doing tonight would open the eyes of the public and cause enough unrest that justice would finally prevail.

He moved away from the window and looked down at the red container again. He thought about how easy it was for Kevin and him to bring in all the gas cans. Haven was always so deserted. Especially at night. How many times had he searched the abandoned halls for an aide or nurse to help him with his da? At times it seemed as if they had all gone home. But this was the only time he could see where being understaffed was an advantage. For once, he could thank those greedy corporate executives.

His mind reeled with thoughts about the negligent staff. Where were they when you needed them? Out back, smoking a cigarette. Sitting in the lunch room, drinking coffee. Watching TV in a chair beside a sleeping resident, an excellent hiding place where they could take a nap without being seen. And then there was the texting. Always texting. As they walked along the corridors, their heads down, serious looks on their faces as if they were doctors and had to react to every message with great urgency. A matter of life and death. Yes. That was the way they were.

But then he shrugged.

That's the way everyone is with these cell phones.

And our government loves it. A population addicted to something that will keep them dumbed-down, out of the way of the scheming bureaucrats.

He pondered the gasoline can for a few more seconds and then left the room. In the corridor, he found two wheelchairs and pushed them toward the elevator lift. He pressed a button and waited as the elevator door opened with a shrill, teeth-gnashing squeal. Stepping inside the jittery cage, he hit another button. The elevator lurched, then began its descent, shimmying as if it were about to fall apart.

When he reached the first floor lobby, he rolled the two wheelchairs out and parked them next to the winding marble staircase near the elevator.

He spotted Kevin and approached him.

"You done planting your cans?"

Kevin nodded.

Edgar checked his watch. "David should be here in an hour and a half. Let's go heat up the carriage house."

They walked through the lobby and out the front door. They walked in silence, passing the massive north wing before cutting across the cold, brittle lawn. They found the gravel path in the moonlight and moved closer to the carriage house, their shoes crunching over ice-encrusted pebbles.

Edgar walked up to the wooden door and slid the rusty old latch to the side. The door creaked as he pulled it open. It was pitch dark inside. He moved his hand across the wall, searching for the light switch.

Kevin pulled out his cell phone and selected his flashlight. He pointed the light at the gray, cobweb-covered wall.

"Where is it?" Edgar said.

Kevin moved the beam of light across the wall. "There it is." He walked inside and flicked on the light switch.

"What the hell?" Edgar's jaw went slack.

Kevin spun around as if they had just walked into a dangerous situation. He was pleasantly surprised by what he saw.

"Wow! Would you look at that."

A shiny red 1957 Corvette sat in the center of the big, shabby room, its gleaming white-wall tires resting on the dirty wood-plank floor.

Kevin strutted over to the Corvette. He tucked his hands into the pockets of his jeans and examined the classic car. "If I could have any car in the world, it would be this one."

Edgar approached the car with caution as if it were a booby-trap.

"Man, this car looks like it just left the assembly line," Kevin said, running his hand over the silky-smooth rear fender, its red finish gleaming.

As they inspected the Corvette, Edgar noticed a white envelope lying on the console between the red vinyl seats. Reaching into the car, he picked up the envelope. It was sealed, but that didn't stop Edgar from tearing it open. He slid out a Christmas card and read it to himself. Then he looked up at Kevin who was eyeing the car like a kid eager to rip open a Christmas present he knows contains the thing he wanted most. "Listen to this."

"What?" Kevin strolled up to his brother.

Edgar held up the card.

"Christmas card. Found it on the front seat. It's from the Governor of Maine. Gerald A. Simmons. To the Administrator of Haven. Robert Shapiro: *Bob, thanks for all you've done for us this year. We hope you'll enjoy this gift. Merry Christmas!*"

Edgar looked up to gauge Kevin's reaction. "Linda was right about this."

"Right about what?" Kevin stood there, looking puzzled.

"Remember what she told us about hospice?"

Kevin stared into Edgar's eyes. Suddenly all the pieces came together. "About how the government gives huge incentives to nursing homes if they put people into hospice who are not dying?"

Edgar nodded. "Palliative care."

"Then they hold back proper care. Deprive them of medicine they need. Starve them. Give them morphine. Tell them they'd be better off dead."

"Yes," Edgar said. "All in the name of the almighty dollar. They murder elderly and disabled people so they can save money—no, steal money. Just look at the cost savings. Someone in a nursing home dies. No more social security checks. No more payments from Medicare or Medicaid."

Kevin spied a row of garden tools hanging on the wall behind his brother. He walked over to the tools, selected a pickaxe, and showed it to Edgar.

"Think this will do the trick?"

"Splendid choice," Edgar said with a sad smile.

Kevin walked up to the Corvette.

"Sorry, old gal . . . but everyone has to die sometime."

Raising the pickaxe above his head, he brought the rusty pointed end down and smashed it into the hood, shattering the gleaming red fiberglass.

"Wow. Look at that hole."

Kevin touched the jagged hole in the fiberglass. And then he held out the axe to Edgar. "You wanna take a swing before I bust this thing up into an unrecognizable piece of junk?"

Edgar accepted the heavy iron tool, his usual calm demeanor gone for a moment as he took a position next to the driver's side of the car. "Here's to one dirty bastard who's going to be very disappointed with his Christmas present."

Edgar swung back the pickaxe and rammed it into the car, wedging the sharp iron head deep inside the door. He gave the axe a quick twist, and then yanked it out of the splintered fiberglass body.

Edgar turned to Kevin and held out the axe to him. "Here. Beat this baby into oblivion."

Kevin took the axe and jumped up onto the hood of the car.

"Step back. And shield your eyes, brother."

He spat into his hands, rubbed them together, and delivered a powerful blow to the windshield. The axe broke through the glass, creating a sound like gunfire, and leaving spiderweb-like cracks in the shattered windshield.

Kevin pulled the pickaxe from the hole, leapt off the car, and landed on the floor like a super hero.

"I've been working on the railroad, all the live-long day." Kevin sang as he strolled around the Corvette, looking for the next sweet spot to hammer into. "I've been working on the railroad, just to pass the time away."

He swung back the axe and struck the left rear tire. The tire hissed, air escaping from it like a punctured balloon.

"How sweet it is!" Kevin said, jumping onto the passenger's seat.

With his mouth curved into a smile, he drove the pickaxe into the driver's seat. Ripping the axe out of the classic vinyl upholstery, he flipped the handle around and inserted the blunt side of the axe into the seat. He pried it back and forth a few times and then jerked it out. Reaching down into the hole he had dug, Kevin pulled out a big chunk of torn yellow foam and tossed it over his shoulder. He threw back his head and hooted with laughter.

He went on singing as he walked around the mangled car, studying the damage he had done with a gleaming smile on his face.

CHAPTER 33

A full moon cast an eerie glow as David walked toward the monstrous building that was Haven. He stopped and gazed up at the towering structure like a dwarf standing before a mighty giant.

David entered the lobby and joined the Fitzgerald brothers in the center of the room.

Edgar handed him a tiny flash memory card.

"What's this?" David asked.

"Just a little something I want you to have."

David gave Edgar a puzzled look, and then slipped the card into the small pocket inside the right front pocket of his blue jeans.

"Now let's get down to business," Edgar said. "First off, it's a good thing we're doing this on Christmas Eve. Quite a few of the residents are home with their families. And just before you arrived, David, I checked each room while Kevin stood guard outside. Right now there are no visitors in here. And we don't expect any to show up this late."

Sweat dripped from Kevin's brow. "Let's nab Jennings first—"

"I'll take care of Jennings," Edgar said, as calm and cool as an army general. "We've already got some of the staff locked up in the laundry room, David."

"So you got a jump on me?"

"Yes."

A wave of relief swept over David. "Glad to hear that."

"There's one aide up on the second floor right now. Two on the first. So you guys take care of them," Edgar said. "And since the laundry room's nearly full, take *two* of the aides out to the carriage house." He gave Kevin a knowing look. "Got that, Kevin?"

"Got it." Kevin winked at his brother.

David raised his eyebrows. "The carriage house?"

"Yes. It should be nice and warm in there by now."

David clenched his jaw. *I hope there are no more surprises.*

"Once the staff is out of our way, we'll evacuate the residents."

"So we're taking the residents from their rooms to the main lobby?" David asked.

"Right," Edgar said. "And once all the residents have been gathered in the lobby, we'll call reporters from the newspapers and the TV stations. After the phone calls are made, we'll begin evacuating the residents to the sidewalk in front of the building."

"Outside?" Alarm registered on David's face. "It's freezing out there. We can't take these frail old people outside."

"Bundle them up well," Edgar said. "They'll be fine."

"No they won't—"

Edgar frowned at David. "These are Professor Graber's instructions. Would you like to file a complaint with him?"

"But—"

"Listen, David," Edgar said, taking a deep breath to calm down. "To make a forceful stand, we need to create vivid images for the public to see. Images that will fill them with outrage."

David locked eyes with Edgar.

"Do you understand?" Edgar asked.

David nodded.

Edgar checked his wristwatch. "Okay, we all know what we've got to do—so go to it."

They went off in different directions.

Taylor struggled to break loose from David's grip. They were on the first floor of the north wing, next to a stairwell.

"What are you doing?" Taylor yelled. "Have you gone insane?"

David yanked her hands behind her back but before he could tape them together, she bit him, broke loose, and scrambled down the corridor.

He raced after her and caught her. She slugged him so hard he stumbled backward and fell. She took off again and as she rounded a corner, she ran straight into Kevin.

Kevin latched onto her. She screamed as he dug his fingernails into her arms. "Let me go, you maniac!"

David bolted around the corner and skidded to a halt.

"I'm working on this one, Kevin. You're free to pursue the other two." David took hold of Taylor's arm.

Kevin pushed him away. "No, you're supposed to go after the other two aides. Katie and Dawn."

David stood there, puzzled. "What's the difference who I—abduct?"

"There's a big difference. So just do what you're told."

David watched Kevin drag Taylor down the corridor. *That's not the way to the rear entrance.*

"Aren't you taking her to the carriage house?" David shouted.

"This one goes in the laundry room."

"Why?"

"Just follow your instructions. Go find Katie and Dawn."

David looked inside a resident's room and saw Katie. She was busy putting a nightgown on an old woman. He waited for her to complete the chore, then snuck up behind her.

Katie turned around and was startled by his presence. "Oh my God!" she said. Then, realizing it was only David; she smiled and took a deep breath. "David. What can I do for you?"

"I want you to get your coat and come with me."

"What?"

"You can walk along with me. It'll be easier for both of us. Or I'll have to tie you up and wheel you out."

"What are you talking about?"

"We're taking this place down tonight."

"What?" Horrified, Katie stepped away from him.

"We don't want you to be harmed."

"Harmed? How—what's going on?"

David held out his hand for her to take. "Please, come quietly."

"Stay away from me," she said. "If you touch me, I'll scream."

Katie reached into the pocket of her smock and pulled out her phone. "Better yet, I'll call nine-one-one."

He seized the phone and slipped it into his coat pocket.

Her mouth agape, Katie stared at him.

David moved closer to her and slipped his hand over her mouth.

David wheeled Katie down the gravel pathway to the carriage house. He unlocked the door and pushed the wheelchair inside. Katie's eyes widened when she saw Dawn sitting in a wheelchair by the fire, gagged and bound, trying to squirm her way loose.

"As you can see, Katie," David said, "Dawn didn't want to cooperate either."

Katie stared at Dawn. Then she glanced over at the fire blazing in the old stone fireplace. Her gaze finally settled on the unsightly mess that was once a Corvette. She shuddered with fear when she thought of the rage that caused the damage to the car.

David walked over to the fire to warm his hands. "I know this is a deplorable act. But it was the only way. After this night is over, I hope you'll both realize that we did this for you. And for the residents here at Haven."

David cleared his throat. He turned to face the two women. "We did it for every underpaid, overworked nurse's aide—and for every neglected and abused nursing home resident in this country."

He stared at them with a plea for mercy in his eyes, and then walked over to a stack of firewood. He picked up a log, carried it over to the fireplace, and dropped it into the grate.

Sparks flew. The fire hissed; snapping, crackling, and popping as if it were complaining about being disturbed. He watched the flickering flames, and then turned back to Dawn and Katie.

"I may not get a chance to speak to you two again. So I want to take this moment to thank you. Thank you both so much for being so kind to my mother and me." David's voice cracked at the thought of his mother. His eyes misted over and sparkled in the firelight.

Katie was confused. And surprised. She glanced at Dawn and could see she was filled with the same emotions.

"Katie. Dawn. You're both angels. This world needs more people like you." He tried to smile but couldn't. He abruptly turned and left the carriage house.

Outside the building, David slid the latch into place and tugged on the handle to make sure the door was securely locked. He blew warm air into his cold, chapped hands and rubbed them together. Then he looked up at the dark sky.

"If you do exist, God, please forgive me for all the wrong I've done. Forgive me for getting my mother into this mess."

And with that, he made his way across the frozen ground and up the path toward the rear entrance of the nursing home.

Inside the laundry room, Nina and Taylor were bound and gagged. They sat on the floor with their backs to a large commercial-sized dryer, watching Kevin tie a nurse's feet together. The nurse was Betty Gerhart. Her face, usually bright red, was now a pale, sickly color. As she struggled, her gag came loose and fell onto her lap.

"Oh please, don't," she screamed. "I wanna go home. Please let me go home!"

Kevin stared into her eyes. "How many residents here *begged you* to help them get home?"

"I tried to help them," she said with pleading eyes. "I tried to help everyone."

"Like hell you did." Kevin picked up the gag, stuffed it back into her mouth, and tied it as tight as he could, ignoring her muffled grunts.

Edgar walked through the south wing of the facility, wondering how much grief Nurse Jennings had brought to the residents of Haven throughout the years.

The nurses' station came into view. He strolled up to it with a smile on his face.

Nurse Jennings looked up from her computer.

"Merry Christmas, Nurse Jennings," he said, sarcastically.

Jennings was surprised to see Edgar. To cover up her uneasiness, she gave him a smug look, and then glanced back down at her computer keyboard.

He took a bold step forward and entered the nurses' station.

"What are you doing?" Jennings said. "You're not permitted to enter this area."

"If you think you can stop me, try."

Jennings picked up the handset from her desktop telephone. Edgar ripped it out of her hand and smashed it into the side of her head. She fell off the chair and hit the floor.

He lifted Jennings up and carried her down the corridor toward the laundry room, moving slowly like Frankenstein carrying his bride.

Kevin raced around a corner and stopped in front of Melissa's room. He opened the door and saw Melissa. She was lying flat on her back; her nightgown pushed up around her neck, sheets strewn all about her. In a coma-like state, she stared into space as Dr. Ramsey sat on the edge of her bed, pulling his trousers up over his skinny knees.

In a state of confusion, Kevin took a step back. Did he enter the wrong room? He focused on Melissa's beautiful, innocent face. Rage build up inside him as his eyes met with those of Dr. Ramsey's.

Ramsey yanked his pants up around his waist and stumbled toward his shoes.

Kevin bounded across the room, tackled the doctor, and sent him crashing into a nightstand. The doctor cried out in pain as Kevin sent a flurry of powerful punches into his face.

Battered and spitting blood, Dr. Ramsey passed out. Kevin grabbed his legs and dragged him out into the hallway.

The doctor regained consciousness as Kevin hauled him into the laundry room.

"Where . . . am I?" Dr. Ramsey asked.

Kevin propped the doctor up against a dryer and, like a football player aiming for the goal post, gave him a powerful kick in the mouth.

The doctor wailed in pain. Then spat out a few bloody teeth.

The rest of the staff, bound, gagged, and seated all around the room, watched in horror as Kevin delivered one kick after another into the doctor's groin.

Nurse Jennings winced as Edgar jerked on her gag so hard that it caused blood to ooze from her lower lip. Her eyes bulged when she realized it was her friend, Dr. Ramsey, who was getting beaten to a pulp.

Kevin turned to Edgar. "Tie this pervert up, will ya?" Then he darted out of the room.

David woke up his mother and told her she was going home. She was groggy, still half-asleep as he dressed her in a warm sweater and corduroy slacks. He helped her into her wheelchair and put on her socks and shoes.

When she saw him pull her winter coat out of the closet, her eyes lit up. "You mean I'm going home *right now*?"

David nodded.

"Yes, Mother. You're going home right now."

"Oh, my goodness," she said. She perked up, eager to leave, her eyes swimming with tears. "Thank the Lord."

"Now stand up. Need to put your coat on."

With his help, she stood.

He carefully worked her arms into the sleeves of her heavy winter coat, bundling her up in its warmth. And when he wrapped a wool scarf around her neck, she kissed his hand.

Melissa, dressed in her nightgown, sat in her wheelchair. Her eyes were open, but she was in a deep fog.

Kevin slipped on her coat and draped a blanket over her lap. He wheeled her out of her room, pushed her down the corridor and into the lobby. Near the massive oak doors at the front entrance, he set the brakes on her wheelchair. He walked around the chair and gazed mournfully into her vacant, expressionless eyes.

"Help . . . get him off me." Melissa groaned. "Get him off me." Even though Kevin was right in front of her, she did not see him. She stared blankly into the space directly in front of her.

Consumed with rage, Kevin raced out of the room and back down the corridor toward the laundry room. He entered the room again, huffing and puffing, his heart pounding in his ears, his eyes taking on the appearance of a madman. Exasperated, he looked around, blinking his eyes, watching as people twisted and squirmed as they tried to free themselves.

Kevin walked up to Dr. Ramsey, and with all the power he could muster, booted the doctor several more times in the groin.

Edgar helped Harvey into his coat. He pulled a cap down snugly on the old man's head and wrapped a scarf around his neck.

Harvey was silent. He watched Edgar gently ease his crippled old hands into his mittens.

Then Harvey spoke. "Am I going to heaven now?"

"Not now, Harvey. Someday. But not now."

Harvey gave Edgar a warm, appreciative smile.

Edgar returned the smile and then wheeled him out of his room.

CHAPTER 34

Sweat dripped from Kevin's face as he opened the door of the commercial-sized dryer. With trembling hands, he reached inside and pulled out a large red gasoline can. He twisted off the black cap and tipped the container.

As the gas splashed onto the linoleum, the helpless staff members reacted in sheer terror, weeping as they floundered, making desperate but futile attempts to get free.

Kevin placed the container on the floor. He pulled a matchbox from his coat pocket, selected a blue-tipped match and dragged it across the striker on the side of the box. The match head burst into flame.

Glaring at Dr. Ramsey, he held the tiny flickering flame in front of his face. "Burn in hell."

Shaking uncontrollably, Dr. Ramsey glanced all around as if there had to be a way to escape.

Taylor looked at Kevin with pleading eyes, her tear-stained face as red as a beet, her cries for help muffled by her gag.

Kevin gave Taylor a black look. He dropped the match into the trail of gas and watched as the dancing flame began its journey to the plastic gasoline container.

Turning on his heel, Kevin raced out of the room and bolted down the corridor. He saw David in front of him, wheeling his mother down the hall. A second later, the gas can exploded. Kevin glanced over his shoulder and saw a great red ball of fire burst through the walls of the laundry room and shoot across the hallway.

David instinctively ducked, then spun around to see Kevin racing toward him. Behind Kevin, bright orange flames roared, hungrily devouring the wall across from the laundry room.

"Killing people wasn't part of the plan," David shouted.

"Well, things changed last week," Kevin said. "When my father was murdered."

"That wasn't *murder*! It was negligence resulting in wrongful death."

"They killed him," Kevin said. "That's murder in my book." He turned, took one last look at the fire, and then dashed down the corridor toward a stairwell.

Edgar was with Melissa, Zelda, and Harvey when the explosion rocked the lobby. He twirled around, whipped out his cell phone, and hit a number.

"Kevin, what the hell are you doing?! We have nearly fifty more people to prepare for evacuation!"

Kevin threw open the door to the stairwell and climbed the stairs, taking two steps at a time. "Can't stop now," he said, breathing heavily. "Firefighters will be here soon."

Rapidly pacing back and forth in the lobby, Edgar screamed into his phone. "Don't you dare set off those other cans!"

"Too late. Can't stop now!" Kevin jammed the phone into his shirt pocket and swung open the door to the second floor. As he raced down the hall, the shock of seeing a resident in one of the rooms made him grind to an abrupt halt.

Oh, my God. What have I done?

He stared at the elderly woman watching TV. Putting his hands on top of his head, he whirled around, groaning in agony. In the room he was now facing, a resident was asleep in bed.

No! No!

He darted down the corridor, looking into each room. He found two old men, sitting in their wheelchairs, playing checkers.

What am I going to do?

I can't undo what I've done.

I've got to keep moving or it's all for nothing.

He hurried down the corridor, looking for more people. Every room he passed was empty.

Thank God. All these residents must be spending Christmas with their families.

Entering a storage room, he reached behind some cleaning supplies and pulled out a gas can. He ran into an unoccupied room, poured a trail of gas, and set the bulky container down in the middle of the floor. Then he lit a match.

"You can't do this," he said, scolding himself. "You'll never be able to get those people out." He lifted the match to his lips and blew out the flame. Then he dialed Edgar and told him he was sending some people down on the elevator.

Kevin returned to the room where the old woman was watching television. He grabbed the handles on her wheelchair and pushed her out of the room so fast she nearly fell out of the chair.

"Whee!" The old woman squealed with delight as they raced down the corridor. "Where we going in such a hurry?"

"The lobby."

"Where?"

"The lobby."

"Did you say Bobby? Who's Bobby?"

"*Lobby!*"

He looked in at the men playing checkers. "Follow me to the elevator," he shouted. "Quickly now. Hurry!"

"We felt an earthquake," one of the men said, looking up from the checkerboard. "A real bad one."

"You evacuating us?" the other man asked.

"Yes," Kevin said, in a panic. "Hurry up. Follow me."

"What's happening?" the old woman asked. "Where we going?"

Kevin looked exasperated. "I've told you three times."

"Don't bother trying to tell her anything," the first man said. "She's as deaf as an old white cat."

Kevin sent the three elderly residents downstairs and then got the last resident out of bed. He wrapped her in a blanket, lifted her up, and placed her into her wheelchair. After he had sent her down to Edgar, he went back to the vacant room near the storage chamber and threw a lit match into the trail of gas that led to the canister.

Edgar had just stepped into the elevator when the powerful blast erupted, shaking the lift and rattling its cage. He seized the handles on the last wheelchair and quickly pushed the old woman out into the lobby.

As the explosion sent blazing furniture flying into the hallway, Kevin searched for gas containers in the rooms at the other end of the corridor.

Edgar said he'd placed them near the walls. But in plain sight.

None in this room.

None in here.

He hurried from room to room, snapping on lights and scanning the rooms.

There's one.

He grabbed the can in room 208, uncapped it, and poured gasoline from the center of the room to the hallway. He lit a match, tossed it into the foul-smelling liquid at the edge of the threshold, and sprinted away.

Edgar dashed up the sweeping staircase to the second floor. He looked down the corridor and saw flames shooting out of a room, attacking the opposite wall, blocking his way.

He found a stairwell and scrambled up the steps to the third-floor landing. Yanking open the heavy door, he moved into the third-floor corridor and spotted Kevin going into the entertainment hall.

Edgar tore down the hallway in pursuit of his brother. He entered the entertainment hall and watched Kevin jump up onto the stage, push back the curtains, and grab another gas container.

"Kevin, stop!" Edgar screamed. "Innocent people are going to die!"

Kevin spun around to face his older brother. "We're out of time," he said. "We need to destroy this place before the firefighters arrive." With that, he tipped the can. Gas splashed onto the floor as he created a long trail across the stage. He placed the plastic container at the end of the trail and struck a match. A yellow flame leapt up from the dark match head.

Edgar bolted for the stage and jumped onto it. "Kevin, don't!"

Edgar hurled his body into Kevin, knocking him down and sending the lit match flying through the air. The match landed in a puddle of gasoline, the tiny flame bursting into a bright flame that began crawling toward the gas can.

Kevin jumped to his feet and leapt off the stage.

Edgar tried to stand but fell. Wincing in pain, he cried out, "Help me, Kevin! I think I broke my ankle."

Kevin whirled around.

He saw Edgar, petrified with fear, his hand stretched out for help. Behind Edgar, the sizzling flame moved closer to the gas can.

Experiencing gut-wrenching agony and indecision, Kevin ran his hand through his hair, looking from the stage to the door and back to the stage. He bolted toward Edgar. Leaping back onto the stage, Kevin scooped Edgar up in his arms, raced to the edge of the stage, and jumped.

But it was too late.

As the two men were in mid-air, the can exploded. And the massive blast of swirling red flames engulfed the Fitzgerald brothers.

CHAPTER 35

Three people in wheelchairs were lined up on the front sidewalk. Two of them, Zelda and Harvey, watched as flames leapt from the windows. Melissa, tilting forward in her wheelchair with her head drooping, was oblivious to her surroundings.

David raced down the sidewalk, pushing a wheelchair with another elderly resident in it. He whirled the chair around and lined it up with the other wheelchairs. As the residents stared up at the fire, a high-pitched siren wailed in the distance.

David sprinted up the sidewalk toward the entrance. He opened one of the doors. Thick clouds of gray smoke rolled out of the building. He coughed, covered his nose and mouth with his hand, and went back inside.

Blinded by the smoke, he pulled off his coat and draped it over his head. He walked through the wall of billowing smoke, wheezing and choking, his hands stretched out before him.

I can't see.

No walls. No floor. Nothing but smoke.

He gasped for breath. Sweat mingled with tears and streamed down his face.

I can't do this.

He turned around and groped his way through the smoke. He felt something in front of him. A wall. He stepped back and moved in what he hoped was the right direction. He stumbled into something and nearly fell. Like a blind man, he moved his hands over the object and realized it was a chair.

I'm lost.

Oh, please. Don't let me be lost.

He wheezed uncontrollably.

Then he turned.

The entrance is this way.

He moved in the direction he thought would lead him to the huge double doors. It was like swimming through black clouds. Clouds that were strangling the life out of him. His hands touched a ridged wooden object. It was a shuttered window. He felt his way along the familiar wall, looking for the doors he envisioned in his memory.

Plaster.

Plaster.

More plaster.

Now wood.

He found the metal handle on one of the doors, pulled it open, and staggered outside, wiping black soot from his face. Through his red, watery eyes he saw misty halos around the street lights, and the blurry images of people sitting in a cloud of white fog.

Suddenly an earthshaking roar resounded.

Then came the eerie sound of trumpets. But the shrill blast of sound was like nothing he had ever heard before. It commanded allegiance.

As his vision cleared, David saw dozens of wheelchairs lined up along the sidewalk in front of the building. Some of the residents were asleep, others were in a daze. But those who were staring at the blazing fire, stared without fear. A shared sense of relief seemed to prevail. A few of them were even smiling.

At that moment David caught a glimpse of a phantom.

It quickly disappeared.

Another ghost appeared out of the corner of his eye.

It vanished.

And then his eyes widened in shock when he saw phantoms appearing behind the residents, their ghostly hands clutching the push handles on the wheelchairs.

David raced to his mother's side, looking around in disbelief. The ghosts were just standing there, calmly watching the roaring flames climb high above the south side of the building.

The residents, many dressed in just nightgowns and bathrobes, did not appear to be cold. But David felt a chill. He pulled up his coat collar and checked his cell phone. The current temperature was twenty-one degrees.

He looked up from his phone and saw what appeared to be another phantom. But this one was no ghost.

It was an angel.

David looked around. They were surrounded by angels, radiant white angels with their wings arched up toward the sky.

"Mary! Mary!" Zelda called out, happily.

David glanced down at his mother, then into the direction where she was looking.

And then he saw her.

The Virgin Mary.

Flanked by two angels, Mary hovered about fifteen feet above the ground. Wearing a crown of stars and the most radiant smile he had ever seen, she nodded at them. And then she disappeared.

David beamed with joy as each angel joined one of the lost souls. The angels unfurled their wings and began their ascent with the elated spirits in their arms.

David rubbed his eyes. He tilted his head back and looked up.

Yep, those white figures are angels.

Angels. Rising higher and higher into the night sky.

Mary Ann Arbus hummed along as "Jingle Bells" played on the stereo in her new Grand Cherokee. Cruising down South Shore Drive, she glanced up at the moon. She was surprised to see how huge it was, looming in the sky high above the steeple of the Stone Cliff Baptist Church.

How beautiful. What a grand night this is.

Since there were no cars on the road, Mary Ann tapped the brake to slow down. Thrilled by the gorgeous sight, she pulled her Jeep over to the side of the road to get a better view.

And that's when she saw it.

Peaks of reddish-orange flames in the distance swirling above the treetops.

Her heart thumped against her ribs.

Oh, no. A fire. The Anderson's live over that way. Please God, don't let it be their home.

And then another sight made her heart thump much harder.

Luminous white shapes were rising into the sky near the fire.

Looks like shooting stars.

But instead of falling, they're rising into the sky. And they're moving so slowly. What are they?

That's when Mary Ann Arbus picked up her phone and dialed 911.

About a mile from Haven, Roy Metzger stood on a ladder replacing a few burned out bulbs on a strand of Christmas lights.

Damn lights. Every time I turn around, there's always a problem to deal with.

The ladder wobbled. Roy grabbed onto the rain gutter, trying to steady himself.

Shit! I'm gonna break my damn neck.

As he held onto the gutter, he noticed a few shingles curling and buckling near the edge of the roof. Granules had crumbled off the shingles. He touched one of them with his fingertips.

Jesus. What next?

An explosion startled him. He held on tight as his ladder shuddered.

Damn kids. The fourth of July isn't enough for them. Now they have to set off fireworks on every single holiday.

Then he saw a white shape rising above the top of the pines that bordered his backyard. He blinked and squinted, trying to focus more clearly.

A balloon?

No, it looked like a figure. With a ring of light floating above its head.

What the hell?

His eyes widened.

"*Oh, my God!*"

The sight of the angel struck fear into Roy Metzger's heart. His whole body trembled, and the ladder teetered under his feet.

Henry Lang lived in a mansion on Sea Pines Drive just down the road from Haven. The widowed, seventy-year-old man was sound asleep, sawing logs in a deep forest when one of the explosions finally jolted him awake. He sat up in bed and glanced around the room. Shocked to see that his white drapes were now orange, he sprang from his bed and hobbled over to the window. Brushing aside the curtains, he saw the vibrant flames dancing in the sky to the south of his property.

That fire's over by the nursing home.

Then he caught a glimpse of the white figures rising into the sky. He could see that the figures had wings, wings that were flapping back and forth, propelling them higher into the sky.

Am I going crazy? Those look like angels.

He wiped his eyelids with his index finger and thumb and then peered through the glass pane again.

The angels were moving higher and higher.

Impossible. It can't be.

Then he chided himself.

How can you say such a thing? You believe in Jesus. You read the Holy Bible every night. It's a miracle, you old fool.

He watched as the white figures ascended. And then he started dancing around his bedroom.

"Oh, Janet. We *will* be together again!"

He skipped over to his stereo CD player, tapped a button, and selected a song. "Someday, We'll Be Together" by Dianna Ross and The Supremes began playing.

It was their song. Henry and Janet's favorite song. The one playing on the jukebox the day their eyes first met.

Henry Lang danced more joyfully than he had ever danced before. Snapping his fingers. Gyrating his hips. Waving his hands.

And he sang along with great joy.

"I long for you—every, every night . . ."

Dr. Graber sat alone in his den, staring sadly at an old snapshot of his dad and him. Feeling a hand on his shoulder, he looked up and saw his father. His eyes brightened. There was no fear now.

"Dad."

"We'll be together again soon, my son," the professor said, already fading away as he rose toward the ceiling.

"No, Dad. Don't go!"

The professor waved to his son as his spiritual body passed through the ceiling and vanished.

Approaching sirens emitted piercing wails. Fire trucks, police cars, and ambulances turned onto the street that led to Haven.

A fire engine was the first vehicle to pull into the parking lot. A firefighter jumped out of the cab. He looked up at the inferno, at the deep red flames leaping out of the windows. And when he caught sight of the angels, his ax fell out of his hand and dropped onto the frozen pavement.

"Hey, Steve," the fireman said. "Do you see that?"

His friend joined him, craning his neck back to watch. "Whoa."

"What's it look like to you?"

"It looks like—like an angel."

The two men, jaws wide open, watched as the angel rose into the moonlit sky.

Zelda took David's hand and squeezed it as they watched the last angel rise above Stone Cliff.

"Son, I know you've been blaming yourself for my fall. But that accident was all a part of God's plan." She released his hand. "A plan for us to be a part of all this," she said with her hands spread wide.

His eyes brimmed with tears. He bit his knuckle to hold back the emotions churning within him.

As police officers hurried out of their vehicles and firefighters pulled axes and hoses from their trucks, a blinding storm of fresh white snow spilled down from the sky.

With the angels and spirits now out of sight, David turned his attention to the firefighters and watched as they quickly attacked the burning building with powerful torrents of water.

He stood there, tears running down his cheeks, thinking about how ignorant he had been for losing his faith in God. Hoping he would be forgiven. *Praying* he would be forgiven.

Charlie and Andrew immediately responded to David's call for help. They arrived at Haven, astounded by all the mayhem. An explosion on the north side of the building caused a turret to crumble and fall to the ground in a flaming heap.

The entire building was now engulfed in flames.

Charlie spotted David and Zelda. They were among a throng of people who had gathered at the scene. A crowd that was mesmerized by the fire. He raced up to them.

"Are you two okay?

"Charlie," David said, seizing his friend by the arm. He looked at Charlie like he hadn't seen him in ages. "We're fine."

Andrew joined them. "I can't believe this fire. Do you know what caused it?"

"I'll explain everything later at my house. Now please, you guys, I want you to take my mother home. Help me get her into your car."

"Are you going to follow us?" Charlie asked.

"No, I'll meet you at my house in an hour or so. There's something I have to do first."

―――――――――

The old door creaked as David entered the carriage house.

Dawn and Katie were still struggling to get free from the rope that bound them to the wheelchairs. They glanced over at him and their eyes widened in fear.

"It's okay now. It's all over." He moved toward them and removed their gags. "You'll be free to go in a few minutes."

"We heard the explosions," Dawn said, giving him a dark, untrusting look. "And the sirens."

She'll never help me, David thought.

Neither one of them will. And I can't blame them.

"Before I untie you, I want you to know why I did this to you. And why I now need your help."

―――――――――

When Dawn got home that night, she found her husband sitting across from the Christmas tree, drinking a beer.

Mike looked up. "Honey, what's wrong?"

She rushed into his arms. "Haven's gone."

"Gone? What're you talking about?"

"It burned down." She burst into tears. "And he *saved my life.*"

"Who?" Mike asked. "Who saved you?"

"David Reid."

Dawn explained what happened.

"And now I've got to help him," she said.

"By taking care of his mother?"

"Yes. I know it's Christmas Eve, but he's asked me and I've just got to help him. If I help them out tonight, maybe Katie can help for a while tomorrow. And then I'll take over again until his mother's in-home nurse becomes available."

"When will that be?"

"The day after New Year's. He's in Cleveland now, spending the holidays with his parents."

Mike nodded his approval. Dawn had told him before how Zelda was her favorite resident at Haven. And how much she admired her son.

"I'm all for it, babe. And if there's anything I can do, count me in."

Ryan Weber stared at David's business card, and then looked up at Katie. "Do you think Dawn will help this guy?"

"Knowing how much she loves his mother, I believe she will." Katie looked more relieved than unhinged. "Especially if I tell her I want to help them too. We've always gotten along so well. Dawn is special. She's been a real friend to me."

After all she had just been through, Ryan was amazed by how calm his wife was.

"Do you think I should?"

"What?" He was in a daze. *I can't believe this. Katie could've been killed in that fire tonight. She could be dead right now.*

"Should I help them?"

"Yes. Of course. Help them," he said, handing the business card back to Katie. "Whatever it takes. You've got to be there for them."

David unlocked the front door and walked into the foyer. He heard Johnny Mathis singing "O Holy Night" over the stereo system.

"Daddy—Daddy, Gram's home," Hannah said as she raced up to him. "Gram's home!"

David stooped down, took his daughter into his arms and squeezed her tight. He felt a hand on his shoulder and looked up to see Kathy, smiling at him with deep affection.

"This is the best Christmas Eve ever," Hannah said, cupping her father's face in her hands. David carried his daughter into the living room. He was thrilled to see his mother sitting on the sofa between Andrew and Charlie.

"There he is," Zelda said, bursting with pride. "My David."

David sat down in a chair next to the couch. Hannah was on his lap, her arms wrapped around his neck.

"Mommy, can I give Gram her present now? The one I made for her?"

"Yes. Of course."

Hannah darted over to the Christmas tree and searched for the gift.

David smiled. He folded his arms and watched her dig through the presents, looking for the box that contained the watercolor painting. The one she painted of a calico cat sitting near a rosebush.

The doorbell rang, and Kathy left to answer it. A moment later she reappeared, ushering Dawn and her husband into the living room.

David choked up when he saw Dawn. Seeing her and hearing the words *Fall on your knees, O hear the angel voices* was more than he could take. He dug his fingernails into his arms to fight back tears.

"The answer is *yes*, David," Dawn said. "I would love to help you take care of your mother."

"My favorite aide," Zelda said. "Hannah, look who's here. It's my sweetheart. My friend!"

Dawn's phone dinged. She lifted it up to her ear.

"Yes, Katie." She paused as she listened. "I've made a decision. My husband and I are with the Reids right now."

CHAPTER 36

The Haven Nursing Center looked like an ice palace in the bright early morning light. Dark gray clouds of smoke filled the sky as firemen, their helmets caked with ice, continued to shoot jets of water at the building.

One of the firemen turned to a police officer who was standing beside him. "Can't say I'm sorry to see this place go," he said. "My dad died here. They treated him like shit. And there was nothing we could do about it."

Early that morning David and Kathy found Hannah asleep, curled up next to the Christmas tree with a beagle pup in her arms.

"Gotta get a picture of this," Kathy whispered. She tiptoed away.

Hannah stirred and woke up. "Daddy."

"Too late," David called out. "She's awake."

Hannah sat up, the little dog giving nonstop licks to her face.

"I never dreamed I'd get a puppy. Thank you so much." She leaned close to her father and kissed him on the cheek.

"Mommy picked her out. She sure is cute, isn't she?"

Hannah nodded. "I love her." She hugged the little dog with great joy and it snuggled up against her neck.

Kathy hurried back in with her camera. "Hold it. That's a great shot."

Hannah looked up with sleepy eyes. She smiled as her mother snapped the picture. "Thank you, Mommy, for the sweet puppy."

"You're welcome, darling. What're you going to name her?"

Hannah thought about it for a moment. "Mary," she said, cuddling the puppy. "Her name will be Mary."

David gave her a puzzled look. "Why Mary?"

"Because it's Christmas Day. And I want to name her after Jesus's mother." Hannah giggled as the puppy licked her nose. "Do you think Gram will like Mary?"

"She'll *love* Mary," David said.

Morning sunlight poured into the kitchen dining area. The Reid family and Katie Weber were gathered around the big table, feasting on blueberry pancakes, crispy bacon, scrambled eggs, sausage, and hashed brown potatoes.

A parade was moving across the screen of a TV mounted beneath one of the kitchen cabinets. It was The Disney Parks Christmas Day Parade, and a choir was singing *Hark! The Herald Angels Sing*.

Delighted to be home, Zelda lifted a fork to her mouth and took a bite of sausage. "Oh, Kathy, this is the best sausage I've ever tasted."

"It sure is," Hannah said, licking her lips.

David winked at Kathy. "Yes. Best ever."

"It's the same sausage I've been buying for years," Kathy said with a grin.

Katie picked up a forkful of scrambled eggs. "So, Hannah, I'll bet I can guess what your favorite Christmas present is."

"I'll bet you can't," Hannah said, taking a sip of orange juice.

Katie laughed. "Oh, come on now. It's Mary, isn't it?"

"No."

"No?" Katie said, surprised.

"My favorite present is the one that Jesus gave me."

Now Katie was puzzled. *"Jesus* gave you a Christmas present?"

"Yes. He brought my gram back to me."

Zelda's face lit up. "I love you, Hannah. You'll always be my little sweetheart."

"I love you too, Gram. I'll love you forever and ever."

Touched by Hannah's love for her grandmother, David smiled at his child. Love and pride filled his heart. But then he heard the sound of a siren wailing in the distance. He froze as the howling noise came closer and closer. He felt certain the vehicle was coming to their house. For a split second it was upon them, right in front of the house. But then it roared past, speeding on to another location.

Exhaling the pent up air inside him, David relaxed. "Mother, in two weeks we're planning to go to Boston. To the museum. I have a surprise for you."

"I thought your exhibition was over," Zelda said.

"It is, but the museum has—" A news bulletin on the kitchen TV caught his attention. He grabbed the remote to increase the volume.

A news commentator appeared. "We've just received video footage from the arsonist who set fire to the Haven Nursing Center in Stone Cliff last night. The nursing home was completely destroyed. At this point, we do not know how many people died in the fire. We hope to have this footage ready to broadcast within the hour. So stay tuned to ABC."

David reached into the small pocket on the right side of his jeans, pulled out the tiny flash memory card Edgar had given him, and stared at it.

Inside his studio, David sat in front of his laptop, watching the footage Edgar video-taped.

Edgar was speaking with a confident, defiant look on his face.

"And I want to make it crystal clear that David Reid is innocent of any wrong-doing. I forced him at gunpoint to help us. Threatened to kill his wife and daughter. I believe the two gracious aides he was assigned to rescue, Dawn Mitchell and Katie Weber, will attest to his innocence. David's only other task was to help evacuate the residents."

David slouched back in his chair and breathed a sigh of relief.

Now Edgar was getting nervous. He began wringing his hands.

"Why did me brother and me destroy Haven? Because our legal system and the United States Government forced our hand. Forced our hand by protecting the corporate criminals here in America, the greedy scum who believe huge profits are more important than the care our elderly citizens receive."

Edgar squirmed around in his seat. He looked as though his mind was racing with thoughts.

"Just try to file a complaint against a corporate-owned nursing home with your state's health department. You will lose every time. I promise you that. They will waive the complaint and tell you the facility did nothing wrong. Even if they overdosed your ma to a near-coma state so she'd be easier to manage. Or caused your da to get bedsores by letting him lie in bed twenty-four hours a day."

Edgar coughed to clear his throat.

"We had to take a stand against these people. Because, obviously, nobody else was willing to."

Edgar wiped his sweaty palms on his trousers.

"The neglect, abuse, and sheer stupidity of the people working in some of these facilities is mind-boggling."

Edgar paused for a moment, a recent memory threatening to tear him apart before he could finish making the video.

"Me da . . . died," he said, his voice cracking. "Last week at Haven Nursing Center. After a nurse injected him with a large dose of insulin. He was *not* a diabetic and he—"

Edgar struggled to overcome his grief. He coughed a few times, and then wiped tears from his face with his shirt sleeve.

"Before me da's death, me brother and me had filed several complaints against Haven with the Maine Department of Health. The health services supervisor sided with Haven on every single complaint."

He cleared his throat again.

"Was our da's death an accident or was it a way of getting back at us for making waves? We'll never know for sure. But what we do know is that nursing home reform needs to begin *now*. And you," Edgar said, pointing his finger at the camera.

"*All of you* are responsible for taking the action required to reach that goal. And if you don't get up off your lazy, complacent asses and do something about this mess soon, then someday you may find yourself spending *your* golden years sitting in some shit hole that's worse than state prison."

Edgar stood up, walked over to the camera, and turned it off.

Touched by the speech, David gently closed the lid on his laptop.

David returned to the kitchen to finish his breakfast. Everyone else had retreated to the family room where Hannah was passing out gifts she had gathered up from under the tree.

Over the kitchen television, the parade was interrupted again by the news commentator.

"And now for more news about the tragedy at the Haven Nursing Home in Stone Cliff, Maine." The newsman glanced down at his notes.

"Several people reported strange sightings near the nursing home last night. Some claimed to have seen white fireworks slowly moving up into the sky. Others described the phenomena as a small group of shooting stars, streaks of light that, instead of falling, were rising from the earth. Others insist they saw," he said, taking a second glance to make sure he was reading the correct word. "*Angels*. Angels rising up into heaven."

Filled with skepticism, the news broadcaster shook his head and grinned.

"However, leading experts have already contacted our station, providing us with information that tragedies like this can lead to not only tremendous anxiety and panic, but to mass delusions as well."

David frowned.

In other words, let's hide the truth from the public.

"Another expert we consulted said that since it was Christmas Eve, people were just seeing what they wanted to see." The announcer smiled at the camera. "Merry Christmas everyone from ABC news. Stay tuned for *Miracle on 34th Street* starring Maureen O'Hara, John Paine, and Natalie Wood."

After breakfast David watched Katie, Hannah, and Zelda play with the new pup.

"Do you have any pets, Katie?" David asked.

"Two cats and three dogs," she said, laughing as Mary danced around in circles, begging for the treat Hannah was holding up.

David smiled. "That's a handful. Ever thought of becoming a vet?"

"All the time."

"Why don't you do it?"

"I've tried to find a job as a veterinary assistant. But there are never any openings."

"That's a shame," David said, and then he excused himself. He went into his studio and called Charlie.

"Merry Christmas, Charles!"

David laughed at Charlie's response. "Say, did your assistant decide whether she's going to retire and move to Florida? She did? Have you replaced her yet?"

David strutted back into the family room.

What a wonderful life! It just keeps getting better.

Hannah and Katie were still on the floor playing with Mary.

"Katie, I've got something for you." He handed her a piece of paper with Charlie's name and number on it.

Katie looked at the paper and then back up at him. "Who's this?"

"My friend. He's a vet. His assistant just retired and is moving to Sarasota. He'd like to interview you for the job—"

"Oh my God," Katie jumped up and hugged David.

"Now, wait a minute. It's not a sure thing. He's got a few people on his waiting list."

"That's okay. I understand." She hugged him again. "I'm just so happy that I have a chance!"

The news of the destruction of Haven was broadcast throughout the world on Christmas Day.

Edgar Fitzgerald's speech ignited shock and outrage in millions of people. And a call for nursing home reform spread across the United States just as the Fitzgerald brothers had hoped it would.

The day after Christmas, Kathy walked into David's studio with the daily newspaper. "Take a look at this." Kathy showed him the headline in USA Today's newspaper:

NATIONWIDE CALL
FOR NURSING HOME REFORM

The destruction of the Haven Nursing Center in Stone Cliff, Maine has led to a nationwide call for nursing home reform. All across the country, angry people are . . .

David read the article. He felt a rush of great happiness sweep over him. But then he remembered the sacrifice made by the Fitzgerald brothers, and sadness filled his heart.

CHAPTER 37

A week before David took his family to the Museum of Fine Arts in Boston, he called Dawn to invite her to go with them. She was thrilled by the invitation but had to decline because she was scheduled to work that weekend. She told him she was now working at the local hospital, Pen Bay Medical Center.

"You are?"

"Yep. Got a job there as a nurse's aide."

In his mind's eye, David could see that vivacious look on her face. "That's wonderful. Did you know Katie's now a veterinary assistant at the Camden Hospital for Animals?"

"Yes." Dawn laughed that cheerful, heartwarming laugh of hers. "She called me the day she was hired. She is ecstatic. That's always been her dream job. And she told me how you helped her get it."

They talked for a few more minutes. When they finished their conversation, David felt elated.

Dawn and Katie deserve the best. I'm so happy for both of them.

The Reids spent the next Saturday afternoon at the Boston Museum of Fine Arts with Zelda's nurse, Sven.

David showed Hannah the painting *Rue de la Barole, Honfleur* by Claude Monet. He told her how Monet and the French Impressionists changed the world of art. And how his own paintings were based on impressionism.

"I've never seen a place like that before," Hannah said.

"It's in Europe. France."

"Gram told me her father was French."

"Yes. And your great grandmother was German."

"I'd like to step into that painting and explore that cute little village."

"You would?" David said with a smile.

Hannah nodded.

"How would you like to visit that place for real?"

"You mean go to France?"

"Yes."

"Can we really?"

"Of course we can."

"And can Gram go with us?"

"Absolutely."

Hannah smiled, and then she followed David into another one of the great halls. He stopped before a painting of angels. With his hands behind his back, he stood there, studying their faces. A few moments passed, and he felt a tug on his sleeve.

"Daddy," Hannah said.

"Yes?"

She motioned for him to bend down, and then she whispered in his ear. "I believe in angels."

David's eyes glistened. "I do too."

A half hour later, David wheeled his mother into one of the most magnificent halls in the museum. Nervous energy and excitement stirred within him. He glanced over his shoulder, looking for Kathy, Hannah, and Sven but they were nowhere in sight.

Most likely still in the Italian Renaissance Gallery, he thought.

He pushed the wheelchair to the center of the great hall and scanned the empty room.

With no other visitors in the gallery, it seemed strange and lonely. There was an aura about the place that made David feel like they were the last people on earth. The paintings hanging on the walls seemed to be waiting for someone to approach them, someone to admire them. If only he had had the ability to see more clearly, had that *second sight*, he would have seen that the room was not uninhabited.

There were spirits in that glorious hall, strolling around, eyeing the paintings.

A former director of the museum who died thirty years ago, a devoted man who loved the museum with all his heart. A lonely old woman who used to visit the great hall every week, her trips there the only joy she had left in life. A little boy who wanted to be a painter when he grew up, but didn't even grow old enough to experience his first kiss.

If David had the power to see what was hidden, he would have seen Claude Monet standing near him, his chin resting on his fist as he studied one of his own paintings.

David guided his mother's wheelchair over to a landscape painting. He stopped to let her study the picture.

"Oh, David," she said. "It's one of your paintings. In here. Surrounded by all these great masters."

David waited while she studied his painting. And then he backed up the wheelchair and pushed it in front of a painting hanging next to his.

Zelda stared in awe. Then a radiant smile lit up her face. "Emile Gruppe."

"Yes," David said. "Long live the memory of the genius who taught you how to paint."

Zelda's gaze returned to David's painting. Tears sparkled in her eyes. She reached up and offered him her trembling hand.

He lovingly accepted it. "And long live my mother. My first friend. My best friend. My forever friend."

David leaned down and kissed his mother's cheek.

HOW CAN YOU HELP END NEGLECT AND ABUSE IN NURSING HOMES?

1. Form a strong, persistent support group.
2. Demand that laws protecting the corporations who own nursing homes be rewritten with a focus on providing our elderly citizens with the care and respect they deserve.
3. Demand a law that states there shall be one nurse for every ten residents.
4. Demand a law that states there shall be one aide for every five residents.
5. Demand a law that states all aides must not only be state-certified, but must have completed required courses at community colleges in order to raise them up to a more professional standard.
6. Demand a minimum hourly wage of eighteen dollars for nurses' aides.
7. TAKE A STAND. Spread the word. Tell everyone you know about the urgent need for nursing home reform and encourage them to become involved.
8. TELL EVERYONE YOU MEET how understaffed nursing homes are. And how nurses' aides are paid poverty wages for a job that requires them to do heavy-lifting and to clean up vomit and feces on a daily basis. The aides do all the work while the corporate owners and executives sit back in their leather chairs, watching their goldmines deliver more and more of what means the most to them in life: BIG PROFITS.

REVIEW REQUEST

Please consider leaving a review on Amazon for *The Neglected Ones*. This will help both the book and your views on this subject reach a worldwide audience.

ACKNOWLEDGMENTS

My special thanks to Caitlin Hanna, Cara Hanna, Kathleen Hanna, and Peter Schmotzer for their assistance with this novel.